Muses That Align Us

Palisade Trilogy 2

Amber L. Werner

Contents

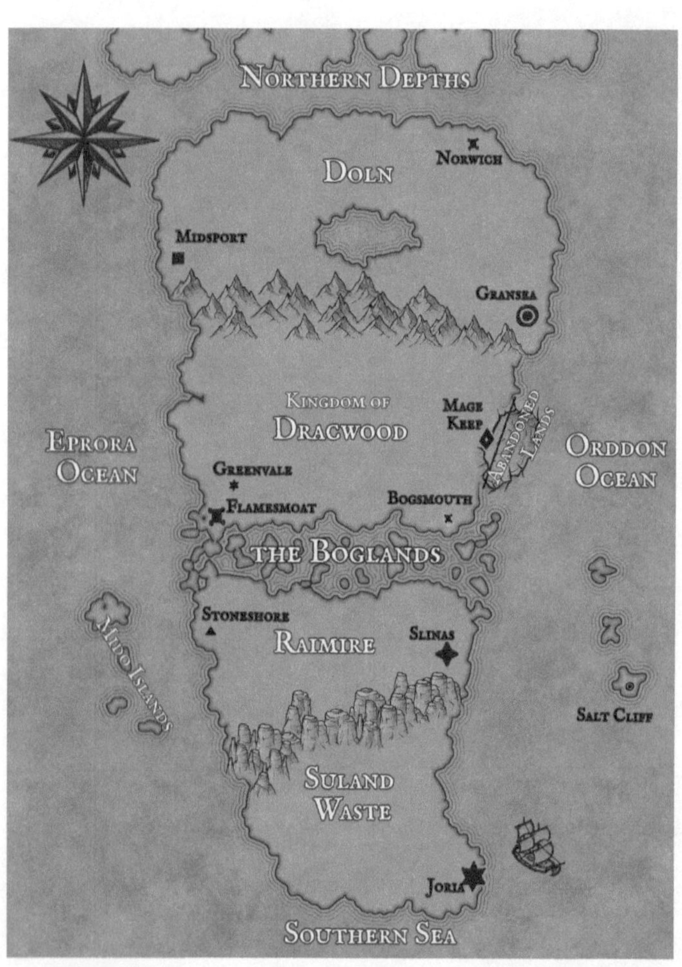

NORTHERN DEPTHS
DOLN
NORWICH
MIDSPORT
GRANSEA
KINGDOM OF
DRACWOOD
MAGE KEEP
ABANDONED LANDS
EPRORA OCEAN
ORDDON OCEAN
GREENVALE
FLAMESMOAT
BOGSMOUTH
THE BOGLANDS
STONESHORE
RAIMIRE
SLINAS
NIMO ISLANDS
SALT CLIFF
SULAND WASTE
JORIA
SOUTHERN SEA

Prologue

Ereni stared at a writhing carpet of fur and gnashing teeth from behind a wall of flame. The scourge had come to Flamesmoat.

It took a few weeks for the creatures to arrive. First in numbers so small their forces dispatched them wherever they terrorized the pockets of the countryside that had escaped the unchecked wildfires. After only a few days, they were forced to retreat.

Hundreds of the vile rodents came. Then thousands. And they kept coming. Every hour that passed brought more approaching on the horizon until they swarmed the land like carnivorous locusts feasting on everything that moved.

So far, the wall of flames erected around the capital, and the Riddle River cutting through the middle, had thwarted their advance. Fire and water were all that stopped the scourge from destroying a city of tens of thousands. The mages manning the fire moat held the lives of so many in their hands, working in shifts to ensure the flames stayed lit. But one instant of broken concentration might be enough to send all their defenses crumbling.

It wouldn't hold the scourge back forever. The constant scratching reverberating beneath the roar of flames guaranteed it. The scourge were digging.

They'd posted earth mages in the ancient tunnels ringing the city, desperately seeking to shore up the underground passages, but it was only a matter of time before the relentless beasts found some hole in their defenses. Some small spot to tunnel in and catch them unawares.

"Ereni. You called for us?"

Two young mages approached. Her seer sight picked up a vivid blue halo surrounding them both.

She turned to address them, the heat from the moat warming her back while the bite of an autumn breeze nipped her face. She smiled warmly and beckoned them closer. "Edrik, Oriana, I have an important mission for the two of you, if you're up for it."

Oriana nodded, her bright green eyes eager. "Of course. What do you need?" She curled a lock of brown hair behind her ear and thrust her tanned hands near the flames, warming them.

Edrik joined her, reaching out his hands, the chill air reddening his pale skin. "I'm in, too." His blue eyes reflected red from the flames dancing before them.

"I was hoping you'd say that. There's a ship on the docks in Southmoat waiting for you. We tracked down a captain willing to sail down the southern coast. I need the two of you to journey to Raimire to seek aid."

Edrik snatched his hands back and stuffed them in the pockets of his heavy brown cloak. "I thought that route was impassable. They say it's littered with jagged reefs, and even if you can dodge them, you have to do it all while fighting the strong northern current."

"That's why I'm asking you two to go. You're the strongest water and wind mages we have. I have faith that you can guide the ship there safely."

It was partially true. She had Oriana beat for wind talent, but only just. But there was no way she could leave the front lines. Not with the scourge beating down their doors.

It seemed the tiny lie had the expected effect. Oriana tipped up her chin and flashed a satisfied smile. "When do we leave?" She pulled her dark cloak closed tightly as the wind picked up, sending her long locks blowing in her face.

Ereni flicked the tail of her brown ponytail back, her blue eyes watering in the wind. "In the morning, with the tide. That gives you the rest of the afternoon and evening to pack and say your goodbyes."

Oriana nodded once and strode away, disappearing into North-moat. That left Edrik. She placed an arm on his shoulder, peering into his face. His brow wrinkled, his mouth drawn into a moue.

"I can find another, if you would rather stay. It's no trouble," Ereni said.

He schooled his features. The pout disappeared, exchanged for a sheepish grin. "No, I meant what I said. I'm in... it's just... I've never been sailing before. You would think a water mage would be the last person to be afraid, but the thought of being stranded out in the water has always given me the creeps. Silly, isn't it?"

"Not at all, Edrik. Fear is a strange thing. It gets the better of us all, sometimes. But I know you can do this." She squeezed his shoulder before dropping her hand and smiling encouragingly.

"Thanks, Ereni. You're right. I've got this." He set his shoulders back and turned to leave. "We'll secure the Raimish aid. You can count on it," he called as he strode off into the city.

She sighed. She could use a touch of that bold confidence right now.

Ereni frowned, taking a last look at the blanket of vermin spread out before her, then left the flaming moat. She roamed through the streets of Northmoat, dodging the tents and ramshackle lean-tos crowding the cobblestone streets. The city was stuffed to the rafters. Folk from all over the country had fled their homes, seeking the protection of Flamesmoat.

Though they'd begun to send boatloads of refugees up north to Minsport, progress was slow. Many city folk refused to leave, due in part to age-old prejudice against the Doln and also from the misguided belief that some solution would soon be found to save the city from their plight. Ereni was not so quick to assume the city would not fall. Not any longer.

She walked without choosing a destination, picking through and examining the tangled mess of plans in her mind while her boots ate up the road. As the sun sank down on the eastern horizon, she found herself standing in the first spot she'd insisted on seeing when they arrived in Flamesmoat weeks ago. The crumbling old cemetery bordering the Church of the Dragon.

The church grounds were just as littered with refugees as the city streets, but one spot of the ancient cemetery was given a wide berth by all. It was here she paused and gazed down into the gaping hole that had recently housed a dragon.

It brought back the same wave of hope that had washed over her when she first stared into the dark recesses that sheltered the majestic creature. Surely, if dragons had returned, they had a chance. They could save the world from the scourge.

Her hands clenched into fists at her sides. Humanity would survive. She would make sure of it.

The crunch of footsteps on grass rose behind her. Ereni turned, relaxing her hands and slipping them into the pockets of her brown cloak. "Hello, sire."

Prince Gideon shuffled forward, wearing a burgundy cloak and fur hat. "I see I'm not the only one who's drawn here. I still can't believe it. My girl… dragon bonded." Pride was clear in his tone, then he sighed, his shoulders slumping. "Any news of Kayda, or Tarquin?"

Ereni shook her head. "I'm afraid not, sire."

The prince hadn't given up hope for his children, no matter how many times he was reminded of the certain doom they'd faced in the Abandoned Lands. Neither of them had been seen since that day. They were all left to wonder whether they'd perished in the flames or at the scourges' hands. Every day that passed without the return of black wings in the sky made death seem more likely.

"How is the king?" she asked.

"The same," Gideon replied with a resigned shrug.

They lingered in a tense silence. Ereni could think of nothing to say, that hadn't been said a dozen times already, to comfort the man. He'd been forced to step up in a time of unprecedented danger and strife. She could sense the weight of rule chafed him.

A dark-skinned woman approached, a gray castle servant uniform peeking out beneath her unbuttoned black cloak. She hustled between tents, surprisingly spry for her old age. A dim blue glow surrounded her.

Izora's sharp brown eyes rested on Ereni briefly, but she pointedly ignored her, stopping before the prince. "Your Highness, there's been news. It's the princess. She's alive."

Gideon spun to face her, his jaw dropping. "She is? She is! I knew it." He clutched Izora's shoulders and stared down into her face. "Out with it, woman. Tell me everything."

"Seems there's a trader in Southmoat that has a fondness for doves. He's trained them to fly back and forth between here and Joria, to a cousin's house. They've been exchanging news regularly for years. The cousin sent word of a shipping vessel hugging the southern coast, on a straight track for Joria Port. A boat carrying a black dragon."

The prince listened closely, a smile slowly spreading across his face. "That's excellent. Excellent." He grabbed her arm and towed her away from the pit. "Come on, let's return to the keep. We must send for this trader. I want the news straight from the source."

Ereni smiled, watching their backs retreating in the setting sun's light. She'd come here seeking hope, and she'd found it.

She sucked in a deep breath and turned, resting her hands on her stomach from inside her cloak pockets as she headed back to the moat. It was time to do her part to hold back the invaders. Help would come. *He* would come. She had faith.

The day was bright and hot. The jungle lit with dazzling flashes of color from the flowers and creatures sprinkled amid the dewy green foliage. A symphony of bird song joined the gentle buzz of insects.

Mika stepped lightly on the overgrown footpath, his curiosity piqued by his companion's hasty demand this morning.

"How much farther?" he asked the young girl who led the way.

Ravenna had barged into his hut just after sunrise and begged him to follow, promising a mysterious creature waited.

She glanced back, not slowing in the least, her long brown braid swinging against her slim shoulders and swishing gently against her luct tunic. "It's just ahead on the coast. It's huge."

"And you really don't know what it is?" He peered at her closely.

She spared him another look, her brown eyes drifting over him appreciatively. "That's why I brought you. You can teach me." Her mouth twisted into a playful smirk.

Mika smirked back but reached out and ruffled the top of her head. "Keep your eyes on the path, and I'll teach you plenty."

She scowled at the dismissive gesture, swatting his hand away and smoothing her hair.

Mika pressed a fist against his lips, hiding his smile. He might be in the prime of his life, with a reputation as a generous lover, but he drew the line at bedding girls that still played with dolls in their spare time.

As they approached the coast, a rotten stench filled the air. He wrinkled his nose, lifting his luct sleeve to block his nostrils briefly before abandoning the action. The sheer green fabric was a blessing for keeping cool in the humid jungle and repelling the biting insects that thrived there, but it did nothing to stave off the foul odor. "What's that smell?"

Ravenna raised a brow. "Didn't I tell you? It's dead."

Mika stopped and rubbed his temple. "You dragged me out of my hut to see a dead animal?" He turned, taking a step back toward home. "I don't have time for this."

Ravenna darted around him, stopping him with her palms flat on his chest. "Please, Mika. We're almost there. You're gonna want to see this—trust me."

He should abandon this foolish errand. A dead animal. Ravenna ought to know he had live people back in the village waiting for his skilled touch.

His lips parted to tell her he was leaving, but the certainty in her eyes made him bite his tongue. He grasped her wrists and gently removed her hands from his chest. "All right, since we're almost there. Quickly."

Ravenna smiled, dashing around to lead the way. Soon, the crash of waves drowned out the chirping birds. That awful stench thickened so much he resorted to breathing through his mouth.

The trail ended at the top of a cliff. Below, the rocky shore met the pounding surf. That was where the carcass rested, brought in on the tide, no doubt.

Mika's eyes widened as he stared down at the massive beast. The bloated body was covered with gulls and crustaceans that picked apart its rotting flesh.

What was it? A whale? It was impossible to tell from up here. He had to get closer.

"I told ya, didn't I?" Ravenna said. "Just look at the size of that thing. It's bigger than my whole hut!"

"Is there a way down to the beach?" Mika tilted his head and scanned the cliffside.

"Sure, if you don't mind a climb." Ravenna walked as she spoke, her steps sure even as she skirted the cliffside's edge. "Some boys carved foot holes last summer that haven't washed away yet. Right... here." She sank down on the edge and swung her legs out below her.

Mika watched her descend until her boots thudded on the pebbly beach. Then he followed.

His heart picked up speed as he navigated the cliffside, reawakening the thrill he'd forgotten since the last time he'd made this climb as a youth. The wind whipped at his dark brown hair. He tasted salt on his tongue as he clung to the footholds, steadily making his way down. It only took a few moments until he landed on the beach, sending tiny rocks skittering across the wet shore.

They approached the carcass. He still couldn't say for sure what it was with all the scavengers feasting on it. Leaning down, he scooped up a handful of pebbles and shell fragments, the smooth stones moistening his skin. Then he flung the stones toward the dead beast and sent the gulls scattering, cawing in anger.

The creature's back was revealed. His breath caught in his throat. That was no whale.

"Ugh, it sure stinks. It must've been dead for a long time, huh?" Ravenna circled the creature and wrinkled her nose.

"Actually, it can't have been dead for long. Otherwise, the scavengers would've picked the bones clean."

"Do you know what it is?"

"I'm not sure. It's unlike any sea creature I've ever seen." He edged around the carcass, staring at it curiously, even as the boldest birds returned to their meal. "It's hard to tell with all the bloat and the missing pieces." The body was covered in green scales in the few spots where the top layer was still intact.

He circled around the top of the beast. The head was missing. No doubt lying on the ocean floor somewhere. As he rounded the creature, he spied another group of gulls tearing at the meat on the front of the body. He knelt down and grabbed another fistful of pebbles, then sent the birds scattering.

He squinted, moving closer to the beast's massive, strangely shaped flipper. Then he reached down and plucked free a bone that lay on the rocks.

How queer... It was hollow. Only birds had hollow bones. Birds and—

Rot and decay. He rocked back on his heels, staring at the beast with wide eyes. Could that flipper be a wing? Was he looking at the freshly killed carcass of a dragon?

"Mika, look." Ravenna stared at the waves, one hand shielding her brow and the other pointing into the distance.

He followed her gaze, gulping. Three more carcasses floated in on the surf. The trail of bodies led to the uninhabited Mido Islands, the largest of which was faintly visible on the horizon.

Were there dragons on that island out in the ocean? Had they survived there all this time, while the world thought them dead? What was killing them? His stomach filled with dread. He wasn't going to stick around to find out.

"C'mon, Ravenna. Let's head back."

"Wait. What is it? Aren't you gonna tell me?"

"It's just a whale. Diseased from the looks of things. You better keep off this beach for the next couple of weeks. Don't want you getting sick. Do me a favor, spread the word around to the rest of the kids, too."

She bristled and puffed out her chest. "I'm not a kid anymore, Mika."

He forced a smile. "Sorry. Just tell them, will ya?"

"Fine. I will." She headed back to the cliffside.

Mika followed, stuffing the bone in his satchel. He had a bad feeling those bodies would be the first of many.

Chapter 1

B itter.

The word epitomized his life. The bitter cold of the Turney Mountains was his constant companion. From sunup to sundown, it never ceased chilling him to the bone. Bitterness burned deep in his chest when he remembered all the years stolen from him. It stared back at him in every puddle and sheet of ice. And worst of all, when he thought of Ereni, her betrayal, the bitterness grabbed hold and wouldn't let go.

An elbow jabbed Conall in the side, hard enough to be felt beneath layers of fur. He glared down into the eager face of a boy at that awkward age where he was no longer a child but not yet a teen. His pale, freckled cheeks and nose flushed red in the chilly air.

"Shouldn't you be out there?" His bright green eyes sparkled, head tilted sideways.

Conall looked away, turning his glare on the mages training in a circle on the mountain plateau in the dusky light. "I'm no mage."

"That's not what I heard."

He ground his jaw, hazel eyes narrowing. "Don't believe everything you hear, boy."

"I'm Quent." He stuck out a gloved hand and tilted forward, aiming a smile up at him. "You're Conall, right? I heard all about how you brought down the Palisade. They say you can summon all the elements."

Conall glanced down at Quent's hand but made no move to shake it. "They talk too much. Like you."

Quent dropped his hand and backed up, staying at his side.

Conall sighed. Kid wouldn't take a hint. Not that he could blame him. The company in these mountains was decidedly lacking.

How had this become his life? Weeks of traveling at a snail's pace, plagued with grumpy old mages used to a warm keep. And children. So many boisterous youths and stinky babes.

He frowned. Even his bonded wolf, Shadow, had made himself scarce. He spent his time hunting for the group. Stalking the wild mountain goats that managed to thrive on this barren mountainside. Not that Conall could fault Shadow for that. He wasn't exactly the liveliest companion these days.

"Excellent," Delyth, the gray-haired mages' leader exclaimed, as she studied an old man forming a sword of ice. "Though, I'd wager you'd use less energy and fell more enemies if you made a dozen daggers instead." Her eyes connected with Conall's from across the plateau, and she nodded her head inward, toward the circle.

Conall held her gaze and remained perfectly still against the cliff wall. The Sade Prim was relentless in her attempts to sway him to train. But his answer was always the same. He was no mage.

One of the few young adults in the camp burst out of a large tent. She hadn't taken time to throw on any furs or gloves. Her hands shook, her voice loud and shrill. "Dena!" she screamed. "Eddena, this is no time to play hide and find."

Delyth approached the young woman, tugging the hood of her gray fur cloak as the wind sought to force it off her head. "What's wrong? Can we help?"

"Sade Prim, it's Eddena." The woman's breath clouded the air with each panicked breath she drew. "She was sleeping in the children's tent. I just closed my eyes for an instant, and now she's gone."

"It's all right, we'll find her." Delyth patted her shoulder.

The mages had already begun searching. "Over here," called a voice behind the large tent shared by the children whose parents weren't at Mage Keep when the Palisade fell. "I see tracks her size leading this way."

Within moments, a search party formed and headed in that direction while the remaining mages barged inside every tent, leaving Conall alone on the plateau. Well, almost alone.

"Dena's always wandering off." Quent shook his head and stuffed his gloved hands into his pockets. "I'm actually surprised this is the first time she's disappeared on this trip."

Conall scowled. "Dangerous place to be a child all alone." He paced forward to the plateau's edge and gazed down the steep slopes that sprawled below. Jagged gray rocks dotted a sea of white. One wrong step around here could be a death sentence.

"Brother," he reached out with his thoughts. *"There's a child missing from our camp. You don't see her by any chance?"*

"No, little brother," Shadow replied. *"Just goats over here. Do you need me to head back?"*

"No, keep hunting. I'm sure they'll find her soon, and everyone will still need to eat."

He stole one last look at the lower slopes, then turned back. *Seems Quent finally decided to look for more entertaining company.* The boy was gone from sight. Conall was about to head back to his own tent, to make sure the mages had wrecked none of his things in their search, when he spotted movement in the corner of his eye.

Blazes. There was the girl, Eddena. She couldn't have been more than five, and she was blissfully wandering off in the opposite direction of everyone searching, above and to the right of where he stood. He pivoted, trudging through the snow toward her.

He got about halfway to her when a second figure emerged from behind a snowbank, arms spread out to grab her. Quent.

Conall stopped in his tracks. *Good, someone else could be the hero for a change.*

The boy caught up to her and crept up from behind. Eddena seemed oblivious to his presence until he crouched down and scooped her up in his arms.

She noticed then. She shrieked, the screech deafening and sharp. She struggled within Quent's arms, causing him to stagger atop the snow. Conall grimaced, resisting the urge to cover his ears as the ear-piercing noise echoed all around.

Whoomph. A new noise sounded, a heartbeat before Quent and Dena started sliding.

Conall's stomach plummeted to his feet. *Avalanche.*

He flew into motion. He cleared one leaping step as Quent's eyes widened with fear.

The second step saw the girl give up her struggle, clutching tight to Quent as they torpedoed down the slope.

A third step. They were almost upon him, picking up speed so quickly.

He took a final leap and dove headfirst toward them as the boy fell, unable to keep his balance on the shifting snow.

A wall of cold slammed into him, forcing his breath out in a rush. He clamped his jaw shut before he got a mouthful of snow for his trouble. Groping forward, blinded by white, he clasped onto something. He prayed the object he clutched was one of the children and not some random tree branch. He held fast for an eternity while the snow tumbled him away.

Finally, it stopped.

He opened his eyes and shuddered. He was well and truly buried, surrounded on all sides, squashed so tightly it was hard to breathe. Squirming, he tried to move, only to realize his entire body was locked in place by the blasted snow.

Wait. Not his whole body. The hand still clutching—something—could move.

Was some part of him lucky enough to end up above the snow? There was only one way to find out.

He dropped hold of whatever it was and shoved his fist side to side, expanding the hole. An instant later, he jolted when something rubbed his wrist. He craned his neck up as the hole widened and spotted a pair of gloved hands joining in, digging from the other side. Conall breathed out a sigh. Those were the same gloves he'd refused to shake earlier.

He kept working, expecting at any moment to burst into the fresh air on top of the snowbank. When he finally pulled himself free, he collapsed into a heap, not atop the snow, but in a small spherical cave.

He stared so long and hard he forgot to blink, his jaw slack. The cave was perfectly circular—except for the spot where he'd burst through—and made entirely of snow. It was darkened inside but somehow light enough to see. Perhaps the sun still shined on them from above. "How in the world..."

"I don't know," Quent replied. "We just ended up in here somehow."

There was only one explanation that made sense. "What type of magic runs in your family, Quent?"

The boy's mouth fell open, his voice rising in pitch. "Air."

Eddena had been quiet until now, but she chose that moment to speak. "I want my daddy."

Her wobbly voice tore at Conall's heart. She curled up on the cave floor and clutched her knees to her chest, shivering so violently her brown hair vibrated, flicking little motes of snow into the air. The poor thing was dressed only in a sweater, trousers, and black boots.

"There, there, little one." He had to warm her. The cold was already seeping into his skin below all his layers of fur. She wouldn't last long in that garb.

He scooted closer to her, leaning down and forcing what he hoped was a reassuring smile onto his face. "Come snuggle inside my fur, Dena. I'll keep you safe. I promise." He unbuttoned his fur as he spoke, then opened it wide in invitation.

There was that bitter cold again, rushing in to greet him. Eddena stared up at him with tear-filled eyes. At first, he feared she would refuse, but then she crawled forward and climbed onto his lap, wrapping her little arms around his back. He shuddered as her bare fingers tangled in his shirt, tiny icicles spearing his skin through his tunic. Then he re-buttoned his fur, shrouding the girl in warmth.

"What now?" Quent smacked his gloved hands together, knocking the snow off them. "Do we dig?"

Conall shook his head. "It's too risky. We could dig the wrong way up into a huge snowbank, or cause the cave to collapse."

Quent gulped, his gaze darting around the small sphere.

"Don't worry." Conall squeezed the boy's shoulder. "Shadow will find us. Just give me a moment. I'll call for him."

Brother, I need your help. There was an avalanche. I'm buried in the snow, somewhere on the slopes below camp, to the east. He dropped his hand from Quent's shoulder.

Shadow answered almost instantly. *Are you all right, little brother?*

Yes, for now. I'm in a pocket of air, with two children. You need to find us.

I'm on my way.

Conall sent a small smile to Quent. "He's coming. When we hear him digging, we'll know which direction to dig."

Quent stared down at his gloves. "Are you sure he'll be able to find us?"

"Of course, he will. Wolves have the keenest sense of smell. Besides, Shadow's never let me down. He'll find us."

Time passed slowly. The darkness in their buried cave grew more complete as they sat in silence, waiting. A vibration pulsed along the cave wall. Was that their rescue? No... just Quent shivering so strongly the snow wall shook with the force of it. Conall shuffled beside him and wrapped an arm around him, pulling him close.

He cursed inwardly. If only he hadn't been so stubborn, maybe he would be skilled enough by now to melt the snow around them and free them from this bitter prison. As it was, he'd been less than useless. If not for the boy's bubble of air, they'd all be dead by now.

If he made it out of this frozen tomb—no, *when* he made it out—he wouldn't make the same mistake twice. He would swallow his pride and learn how to summon. Somehow, he would bury the bitterness in his heart and find a way to live with what had happened to him.

He was through letting the bitter rule his life. It was time to learn what he must to protect himself and the people around him.

"I've made it back to camp. I can see the path where the snow carried you. Hang on, little brother." Shadow's voice warmed his heart, even as the cold seeped deeper into his bones.

"We're still here, brother. Hurry."

"He's c-coming," Conall whispered through chattering teeth.

Beneath his fur, Eddena remained still. Was that a good sign, or bad? He closed his eyes and prayed she'd warmed enough from his body heat that she'd fallen asleep. *Please, let her only be sleeping...*

For some time, the cave had been getting dimmer, but as he sat there waiting, blackness overwhelmed the cave, leaving only the barest shadow of light. Did that mean night had fallen outside? As cold as it was, without the sun, it would only become colder.

On top of the temperature, the air became increasingly stale. His head throbbed dully, his breath coming faster than it should, like he was running and not sitting motionless. How long could they survive without fresh air? Would Shadow find them in time?

"If I don't make it out of here, will you do something for me?" Quent's voice was calm, steady. His body no longer shivering.

That couldn't be good. Conall's body shuddered so violently he could hardly force out any words. "You're g-gonna make it out of here, Q-Quent. Shadow will f-find us."

"Please, just listen. I need you to find my mother, wherever she is. Tell her I'm sorry." Quent's chin wobbled on his shoulder. "Tell her I love her." He pulled free from Conall's arm, his breathing speeding up. "Is it hot in here, all of a sudden?"

Conall sat dumbfounded, struggling to see what the boy was doing. Then something landed in his lap. He lifted it close to his face. Was that a glove? The *swoosh* of fabric on the ice told him the boy had shucked off its twin. Then came the pop of a button as he worked at removing his fur.

"N-no—are you m-mad? Leave it on." Conall lurched forward and grabbed the boy's fur, wrenching it closed.

Then he heard the *scritch-scratch* of an animal furiously digging in the snow. He laughed, grabbing the still struggling Quent and clutching him tight. "Listen. He's h-here. Shadow's f-found us!"

He sat still, or as still as he could while shivering uncontrollably, trying to determine the direction the sound was coming from. Before he could figure out where to dig, the snow around them simply dissolved.

He blinked, shielding his face from the sudden appearance of torches. Ahead of him stood Shadow, next to the same old man who he'd watched craft a sword of ice that evening. He held his arms out wide, eyes closed in concentration. Then he opened his eyes, and smiled.

Delyth strolled forward and clasped the mage's shoulder, holding a torch up in the moonlight. Her shrewd gaze flicked between him and Quent. When she spoke, her voice was shaky. "Eddena—is she with you?"

Conall nodded, even as Shadow raced forward and ducked beneath his arm, lending him strength and warmth. "She's h-here, b-beneath my furs. She's n-not moving."

Delyth exhaled, immediately composing herself and barking out orders. "Quick, now. Bring them to the closest tent. We'll need healers, blankets, warm clothes. Let's move."

How he arrived there was all a blur, but before he realized it, he was somewhere warm, and a mage was rubbing something on his bare chest.

He gasped and jolted up. For the first time in so long, the cold—that awful, bitter cold—was finally gone. Tears filled his eyes. He spun to the left and found Delyth watching him. "Quent, Eddena... are they all right?"

She nodded and pointed to a table to his right. Quent sat wrapped in a blanket, looking dazed but whole and unharmed.

He craned his neck around, searching for Eddena. Suddenly, a warm weight plopped onto his lap. Staring down into the little girl's smiling face—who he'd promised to keep safe—he grinned crookedly and hugged her close. And here he'd thought it was someone else's turn to be the hero.

He turned back to Delyth and met her eyes. He had a feeling from the way she stared back at him she already knew what he was about to say, but he said it anyway. "I'm ready."

Chapter 2

The sun beat down on Kayda's back as she lowered the spyglass on the bow of the *Sea Silk*. Even the cool ocean breeze so late in the fall wasn't enough to bring relief from the sweltering heat this far south.

Her boots thudded on the wooden deck, her scorched blue dress long ago exchanged for a pair of cotton trousers and a bright yellow button-down tunic pilfered from the former captain's room. She made her way to the bridge, a bead of sweat rolling down her spine beneath the loose-fitting silk.

"Is that what I think it is ahead of us?" she asked the tall, shirtless man at the helm.

"Aye, Princess." Jayan was clothed only in a pair of tan shorts, his dark brown skin glistening. "We'll be ready to dock before day's end."

She nodded and shifted to survey the *Sea Silk*. The wooden vessel was huge, equal in length to half a city block in Flamesmoat. Overhead, massive sails billowed in the wind.

Her bondmate, Druturion, lounged on the midship deck, seeming unbothered by the heat. In fact, he reminded her of the tiny lizards she used to spot basking in the sun in the Royal Grounds during the summer.

A handful of people milled on deck. Some bustled about, handling the many tasks that came with sailing a ship so large. Yet others stood staring at the rolling waves with uneasy expressions or fanning themselves in whatever shade they could find.

It had been a stroke of luck to find so many souls aboard this vessel. When she and Druturion commandeered it after the battle in the Abandoned Lands, she hadn't realized the work needed to bring the huge trading craft safely back to port.

When they'd first landed, she'd spent a few confused moments trying to make sense of the many ropes, sails, and dozens of other unfamiliar things. She quickly understood she had no chance of sailing the ship back to Joria on her own. If it hadn't been for the sounds she'd heard below deck, and her subsequent discovery of the slaves in the hold, the *Sea Silk* would still be anchored offshore the Kingdom of Dracwood.

Her hand curled into a fist. It was no wonder they all wanted to be above deck. She'd found them chained to the walls, half-starved, and begging to be freed. A fact made even more cruel when the ship had a galley packed full of salted meat, beans, and enough flour to feed an army. And now she was dragging them all back, within grasp of their captors.

"Dru, we're almost there. Time to make yourself scarce."

His eyelids lifted lazily, those crimson eyes connecting with her own. *"Are you sure about this? It's not too late to change the plan."*

A flutter tickled her stomach, but she drew a deep breath and nodded. *"I'm sure."*

"All right, I'll see you soon." He rose and unfurled his shimmering black wings. Then he backed up to the far railing, causing a few panicked people to scramble out of the way. He took two running steps and leapt into the air.

Kayda's breath caught as she watched him soar away. Her bondmate was truly magnificent. His svelte form soared through the clouds, full of power and beauty. Black scales glittered with flecks of purple, blue, and green.

Sometimes it still felt like a dream. Was she truly bonded to a dragon?

"Where's he going?" asked a lanky man, his voice thick with the desperation of someone certain he was watching his last chance of salvation being torn from his grasp. He stared at Kayda with wild eyes. "You can't mean to take us back there alone!"

Jayan spoke up before she could formulate a response. "Eh, that's *princess* to you, dust eater."

Kayda shot Jayan a glare and strode forward to the nervous man. She placed a hand on his shoulder and pitched her voice loud enough that all could hear above the wind and surf. "Don't worry. Druturion will return. We have a plan to assure everyone's freedom when we pull into port. I've not forgotten the promise I made to you all. You will not feel the bite of chains on your skin again. Not if I have anything to say about it."

A few people clapped or cheered. But most stared at her warily or avoided looking at her all together as they shuffled their feet and shook their heads.

At least the lanky man seemed to relax. Some of the tension in his shoulder lifted as Kayda gave him a squeeze and released him.

"Bless you, Princess." He backed away reverently.

Kayda smiled and turned back to Jayan, smoothing her long auburn hair. "You don't have to speak up for me. I can handle myself."

He raked a hand through his short, curly black hair, dark brown eyes twinkling. "Sorry, Princess. You just remind me so much of my sister, Nova. If I saw someone disrespecting her, I'd do much the same."

"You're forgiven." She grinned, then she narrowed her eyes. "Just don't pull the same trick when we arrive at port. I want the port master to know I don't need anyone fighting my battles for me."

"Aye, Princess," he said with a wink.

Kayda rolled her eyes and turned away. Jayan was a strange man, but he'd been instrumental in their voyage. Unlike the others, she'd found him chained up in the captain's room. From the way he knew every nook and cranny on this ship, she suspected he was much more than the captain's personal slave. He was the true captain of this vessel.

She strolled to the starboard rail and leaned against it, watching the city of Joria grow large as they approached. The city was immense. Far larger than Flamesmoat, with buildings sprawled up and down the coast, spreading out from the city center.

Huge factories rested on the Peat River's banks, home to the silk mills and dye-houses the region was famous for. In the distance, a handful of beautiful palatial mansions dotted the shore on the Peat's far side. The gorgeous buildings were a stark contrast to the crowded city center, which was overrun with tiny shacks and storefronts.

Soon, they altered course, heading for the massive wharfs lining the Port of Joria. Kayda's stomach churned as they sailed closer. The crowded docks were alive with activity. Dozens of boats were moored already. Sailors and slaves packed the walkways, carrying goods, making ready to depart or unload.

It was into this organized chaos they landed. Jayan expertly glided their large ship into port with the ease of a natural sailor.

A short, pudgy fellow, dressed in a suit of fine blue silk, barreled down the wharf, his tanned face reddening with each step. Kayda made her way down the gangplank, on a course to intercept him.

"The *Sea Silk*, back in port? No, no, no. You're not supposed to be here." The man pulled up short and scanned her up and down with a frown. "Who, pray tell, are you? Where is Captain Kent?"

"Dead, I'm afraid," she answered, hopping off the gangplank and onto the wharf. "Are you the port master? I claim finder's rights to this vessel."

"Finder's rights," he exclaimed, shaking his head vehemently, his jowls wobbling with the motion. "Are you mad? Don't you know who this ship belongs to?"

"Yes." She grinned. "This ship belongs to me. I found it unmanned off the Abandoned Lands' coast, all the crew dead. I sailed it back. And now I claim the ship and all the cargo, as is my right." She paused, doing her best to hold back laughter as the man's face turned redder still, until he looked ready to explode. Then she leaned in close, ignoring the crowd of curious onlookers gathered around to watch. "Now, point me in the port master's direction, please."

"I am the port master," he said through gritted teeth.

"Well, why didn't you say so?" She strolled forward, her hands clasped behind her back. "We'll be changing the name. Mark it down in your ledger. This boat is now *Nova's Champion*." She spun sideways and sent Jayan a wink of her own, where he stood watching from the side rail.

Then a handsome dark-skinned man, clothed in an even finer suit than the port master's, his a deep burgundy, came upon the scene.

Though he carried himself with the bearing of a man twice his age, it was clear he was barely older than she, perhaps in his early twenties.

He strode forward, and as the folk crowded around spotted him, they parted hastily. He marched past them all with his nose in the air, as if they were beneath his notice. Within moments, he stopped before her, eyeing her just as vigorously as the port master had.

"I see the *Sea Silk* has returned ahead of schedule. And who do we have to thank for her safe return?" He raised a brow.

Who should we thank, he'd asked? So, this pompous man must be the owner. Time to play her cards.

"I'm afraid you're mistaken. As I just finished informing the port master, this vessel is now *Nova's Champion*, and she's mine, along with all her cargo, by finder's rights." She turned aside dismissively and raised a hand to her face, pretending great interest in her nails.

"I see you don't quite understand how finder's rights work, girl. You have to make every effort to find the found property's owner before claiming it as your own." He smirked and spread his arms. "It appears you're in luck. You found me." He strode forward, headed for the gangplank.

"So, you admit to treason, then?"

He stopped in his tracks and swiveled slowly to face her. "Excuse me? I said nothing of treason."

"But you admit to owning this vessel. The same vessel that sent a landing party into the Abandoned Lands, breaking the Palisade Treaty." She leaned back on her heels as a chorus of gasps spilled from the onlookers. "That sounds an awful lot like treason to me."

"That's where you're wrong, girl." He stepped closer, leaning close to her face, a lock of his perfectly coiffed curly brown hair falling forward on his forehead. "That treaty has expired."

"I'm afraid you're the one who's wrong. I've read that treaty. It's void only after 500 years have passed since the death of each member present at the signing."

The man scoffed, his chin lifting. "That happened over a decade ago. Believe me, we checked."

She let a smile spread slowly across her face. *"Dru, that's your cue."*

She took a step closer, standing toe-to-toe with the man, looking directly into his dark brown eyes. "Are you sure about that?"

At that moment, the crowd spotted Druturion flying through the sky. Chaos erupted as dozens of people screamed and scuttled away, bumping into each other in their haste. Some of the terrified onlookers jumped into the ocean rather than face the fearsome dragon, their splashes echoing and water erupting in the air. Dru hovered briefly, then thudded down on the wharf, causing the entire structure to shift with his weight.

As the wharf came to rest, the man and the port master stared at Dru, their mouths hanging open.

Kayda strolled forward, reaching out to stroke his massive head. "This is Druturion the Black, in the flesh. If you check the treaty again, you'll find his name listed among the signatories."

The man turned his wide eyes to her again, his brows furrowing. "Who are you?"

"I'm Kayda."

She watched recognition strike the man. Both his brows shot up and he took a step back. "Would that be *Princess* Kayda of Dracwood?"

She grinned. "It would."

Then the man surprised her. He slapped the port master's back, nearly sending the poor fellow tumbling off the dock into the ocean. He grinned even wider than she had, showcasing a set of perfect, white teeth. "*Nova's Champion* is a fine name. I'll have the papers drawn up. The ship and all the cargo are yours."

A cheer erupted from the ship's deck as the former slaves heard the news.

Kayda was not so quick to celebrate. "That's it? It's all mine?" She lifted a brow and cocked her head sideways.

"Of course, of course. We are family, after all." The man laughed and strode forward, pulling her into an embrace. "It's nice to finally meet you, cousin."

Kayda gulped, holding herself stiffly in his arms. This arrogant stranger was her kin? A man who traded in slaves and had no problem flouting the customs of her kingdom by striking a deal with the prince behind the king's back?

He released her and gazed down at her with that wide grin. "I'm Wyll. Come, let me introduce you to the wonders of Joria. And after, we'll head home, and you can meet the rest of the family."

She backed up, considering his offer. "*Dru, what should I do?*" She didn't need to explain. She'd learned aboard the ship that Druturion had spent enough time with humans he could understand humans' speech, but he could only speak to those he bonded with.

"*Go, meet your family. I'll stay here on the ship. No sense in scaring half the city into the ocean. If you need me, just say the word, and I'll find you.*"

Her heart racing, she stepped forward. This was what she'd come here for, after all. She looked to Wyll—her cousin—and smiled. "After you."

Chapter 3

They sailed through a maze. Twisted mangroves loomed on all sides of the canoe, their gnarled roots plunging into the salty waters. The stench of decay lingered in the air. Croaking, chittering reptiles and the splash of hidden creatures echoed in her ears.

Just one more day. One more day until they reached Raimire, and this place would become a memory. Lark shuddered and stroked Sunny's yellow fur. It couldn't come fast enough. This place gave her the creeps.

"Cheer up, blue bird. We're almost there," said a voice in her mind.

Lark rolled her eyes and swatted a bug off the back of her hand. *"Please, no. Not this again."* The weeks spent traversing the Boglands' tangled waters had been a chore in more ways than one. *"Can you quit it with the nicknames already? Each one is worse than the last."*

Her bondmate, Muse, sat preening on her perch in the center of the canoe. The strangeness of speaking with a falcon in her thoughts had morphed into familiarity during their travels. But sometimes Lark wished she wasn't quite so familiar.

"Don't be so morose. Your face, your thoughts, they're so dark." Muse paused scratching her feathers and lifted her beak from her chest. *"Ha, dark Lark. That's a good one."*

Lark groaned. *"No, it's not."*

"Everything all right?" Aren tipped back his wide-brimmed hat, his blue eyes peering at her curiously.

Her stomach fluttered. She sent her handsome companion a crooked smile. He sat behind her in the crowded canoe, wearing plain brown traveling clothes and a leather gauntlet on his right arm.

"It's nothing. Just Muse thinking she's funny when she's clearly not." She punctuated the statement with a glare at her bondmate, but Muse only went back to preening, fluffing the gold and white checkered feathers on her chest.

Aren smiled. "It must be amazing, your bond. I have to admit I'm envious. I would give anything to know what Whisper is thinking." He lifted his gloved arm and whistled. Whisper, Aren's trained hawk, cocked his head at the sound, then dutifully flew from his perch at the front of the canoe and landed gracefully on his outstretched arm.

"What's he saying?" Muse turned, watching Aren toss a small morsel to Whisper.

"He wishes he could understand Whisper the way I understand you."
A strange sound filled her mind. Was that a scoff?

"Ha, he's lucky he can't. He would be bored to tears by that one, trust me." Muse shifted on her perch, her talons digging into the wood.

"She's probably restless. It's about time for their afternoon hunt." Aren whistled twice. The sharp blares sent Whisper soaring. Muse reacted just as quickly. Both birds blasted into the sky, climbing so high they were obscured by mangrove branches almost instantly.

"Great." Tiora smoothed her golden-brown dress from her seat next to Lark. "Sounds like we're having sparling for dinner. Again."

The small brown and white spotted aquatic birds made their home in the Boglands. Muse called them easy pickings.

"At least it's better than fish," Fillan said, sporting mud-covered overalls in the back of the canoe. He jabbed a long pole into the murky water. "I'm usually so sick of fish on this run that by the time I make it back to Bogsmo—" His shoulders slumped, and he clamped his mouth closed, either unwilling or unable to complete the sentence.

Lark's stomach churned. It was still hard to recall the carnage they'd witnessed as they fled for their lives. When she closed her eyes at night, she could still hear the screams from the poor townspeople who'd been eaten alive. It must be even worse for Fillan. His whole life was changed forever when the scourge destroyed his hometown.

At least he still had his father, Dal. He steered the smaller canoe behind them. The pair agreed to ferry their group of performers through the Boglands before disaster struck. As far as they could tell, they'd been the only ones to make it out of Bogsmouth alive.

Lark tugged her dark-blue dress, the cotton sticky in the humidity. Muse had saved them all. Without her warning, they wouldn't be here. She wouldn't have the chance to find a teacher, someone who could show her how to control her powers.

Just one more day.

A blur of movement set her heart racing. Muse dove through the air, dropping on an unsuspecting sparling in a flash. The poor thing didn't see it coming; it was over in an instant. Muse lifted the sparling in the air, triumphant. Then she dropped the dead bird with a splash.

"Oops. That was a fat one." Muse chuckled. *"Grab that one, will ya? I'll catch another."* She lifted back into the sky, and was soon gone from sight.

Lark grinned. Then a second splash sounded, this one close enough to spray her skin with warm water. Her stomach dropped to her feet.

"Sunny. Get back here!" She stood in the wobbly canoe, hands on her hips.

The old mutt didn't listen. She was already halfway to the spot where the sparling bobbed on the water's surface. She swam until she reached the bird, then scooped it up in her jaws and turned, swimming back to the boat.

That was when Lark saw it. A shadowy form beneath the water stalking Sunny. Lark's eyes popped wide, her heart thudding madly. She couldn't tell what the creature was, but it was big and fast—really fast. Sunny wasn't going to make it.

"Fillan," she screamed, pointing to the shadow racing beneath the water.

"I see it." Fillan shoved the stick into the bog with renewed vigor. "Sit down, we'll get her."

Lark wobbled as the canoe lurched, coming dangerously close to falling in. Tiora grabbed her legs, steadying her.

She sank down to the wooden boat's floor, reaching out the side, preparing to scoop up Sunny as soon as they pulled alongside her. Aren held tight to her hips, ready to pull her in should she need help.

"C'mon, girl," she pleaded.

Sunny was just out of reach, her tail weaving back and forth through the water blissfully, when the creature surfaced.

Lark's jaw dropped. The beast was massive, at least five times as big as Sunny. It was a monstrous reptile with brown scales and a long, thin snout that opened to reveal a set of jagged teeth. Teeth aimed straight at her dog.

Not on her watch.

She shot forward, heaving her torso free of the boat, trusting Aren to keep her out of the water. Pain stabbed her stomach as the canoe's side rammed into her, but she ignored it, straining forward. She wrapped her arms around Sunny's neck, her fingers closing on the wet fur on her back. She grabbed Sunny and hauled her forward as the beast's jaw snapped closed on the spot she'd been at an instant before.

They weren't safe yet. "Pull us in," she yelled, as its jaw snapped open again. Her heart thundered. The creature drew so close she could smell its rank breath.

It was so fast. In a heartbeat it was even closer, the bottom of its jaw diving below the water, directly beneath them. The shadow of its jagged maw hovered above her head. They were too late! She screamed.

Thunk. She landed back in the boat, atop Aren. Squirming fur drenched them both instantly. The boat careened sideways, coming dangerously close to dumping them all in the bog until Fillan stabbed his pole down to steady them.

Sunny dropped the sparling. It smacked Lark in the face before rolling to the side. Great.

Then Sunny proceeded to cover her face with slobbery kisses. She should've been gagging—Sunny did just spit out a dead bird after all—but she was too happy to care. She grabbed her neck, clutching her tightly. "Never do that again."

As she hugged her close, Sunny saw an opportunity to reach Aren where he lay beneath them and exploited it.

"Blech." He twisted his face sideways but couldn't avoid her slobbering tongue.

"Guys..." Tiora's panicked voice halted the laughter bubbling inside Lark's chest. "It's turning around."

Lark's breath caught. The beast sped through the water, heading straight for them. It was easily as big as the canoe. If it rammed them, they didn't stand a chance. But her hands were full of squirming dog, and she was not about to release Sunny when she was in the mood to swim. She gulped. What were they going to do?

"Ti, the sparling. Throw the sparling!" Aren yelled.

Tiora's eyes widened, but she was already in motion. She snatched the bird off the canoe floor and tossed it directly on the beast's snout. The sparling landed with a *thunk*, then splashed into the water beside the beast. The shock of the hit must have startled it. It halted its advance, dunking its head beneath the water, surfacing a moment later and seizing the bobbing carcass with a sickening *crunch*.

Lark sighed as the creature turned, slipped under the water, and swam away slowly, satisfied with the free meal. She climbed free of Aren, sending him a sheepish grin, and deposited Sunny on the canoe's floor as Muse and Whisper reappeared. They both landed on their perches and dropped a pair of sparlings on the wooden boards.

"Ha, what did I miss?" Muse's head jerked back and forth merrily.

"Don't ask," Lark replied, wringing out her sopping, brown curls.

"I didn't realize we'd get a show before dinner tonight," called a voice behind them.

Lark spun around, sending a wry smile to Dausius in the second canoe.

"Everyone all right?" he asked, his beaded hair clinking as he shifted his gaze over them.

The second boat pulled up alongside their canoe. The twins, Mazen and Meital, smirked from the back as they caught sight of the others' sodden clothes.

"We're good," Aren said. "What was that thing?"

"Bogbeast," Dal answered from the rear of the smaller canoe, tugging the front of his mud-splattered overalls. "There'll be plenty more this close to the mainland. No more dips in the bog if you want to make it to Raimire in one piece, ya hear?"

Sunny picked that moment to shake the water from her fur, splattering everyone with droplets.

Lark laughed and tussled her wet, yellow fur. "I hope you heard that, girl. No more swimming."

Sunny stared back, her tongue dangling happily and tail wagging. Lark sighed. Too bad she could only speak to one animal.

Aren reached down and grabbed a sparling. "Here, Daus, catch." The bird sailed through the air. Dausius caught it with his lanky brown arms.

"Great, more sparling." Mazen's multicolored shirt glimmered in the sun as he leaned forward, frowning.

Meital slapped his back, her matching shirt shining just as brightly. "One more day, and we'll be home stealing fruit from tree monkeys like when we were kids." She shot him a cheeky grin.

Lark smiled, too. She was looking forward to reaching the mainland. And not just to leave this creepy place behind her. It had always been one of her dreams to travel. Next to becoming a mage, there was nothing that would bring her more pleasure. Now that she was traveling the world with the Wandering Bards, she was living the life of adventure she'd always dreamed of.

If only there wasn't a horde of vicious, blood-thirsty *ichneumon* ravaging her homeland to worry about, it would be practically perfect. A shiver raced down her spine. At least they would be safe in Raimire. There was no way those creatures could make it through the Boglands. She'd watched one drown to death before her eyes. The twisted water-logged maze they'd traversed would keep them safe long enough for her to find a teacher. And once she learned to control her earth talent, she would return and help set her country free.

Slap. Another bug, on her ankle this time. She grimaced and flicked the squashed bug off her palm, resisting the urge to scratch.

As she lifted her gaze from her leg, a small movement caught her eye in a gap between the tree cover. She spun sideways, peering at the mangroves curiously. They grew so thick that once they sailed past the small hole it was impossible to see anything but wood and vegetation.

"Something wrong?" Aren joined in her examination of their surroundings, tilting his hat back.

"I thought I saw something beyond those trees just now," she replied.

"Probably just a bogbeast or some other animal," Fillan said. "They won't bother us so long as we stay in the canoe."

She gasped. There it was again. A flash of bright color, there and gone in an instant. What was it?

She squeezed Aren's knee. "Did you see that?"

He shook his head. His gaze flicked to her and then back, squinting into the trees. "No."

"Whatever it was, it was bright pink. Are there any creatures or flowers that color in the bog?" she asked.

Fillan leaned down and scrutinized the crooked trees. "None that I've ever seen."

A pit formed in her stomach. She spun forward, realizing the path they were on would soon curve around, landing them directly in front of—whatever it was.

"Muse, there's something ahead of us on our path through the bog. Can you fly ahead and scout for us?" Lark's brow furrowed as she met her bondmate's gaze.

"All right, boss. Hm, that's too plain, I think. Cross boss? Ha, that's better. Just look at your face."

She scowled. *"Very funny. Just go see what's out there."*

Muse lifted into the air and hovered over the treetops. *"Lark... we have a problem."* She circled, flying above the next turn.

"What is it?"

"There's a bunch of boats blocking the way ahead. Lots of strangely dressed people on board. And weapons."

Lark stiffened. "We're about to have company," she announced. "Muse says there's a group of people in boats blocking the way up ahead."

They all stared at Muse circling the sky, frozen, their mouths hanging open, eyes wide.

"That doesn't make any sense." Dal pinched the bridge of his nose. "I've been this way hundreds of times. It's never been blocked once. You sure she's seeing it straight?"

The question had just escaped his lips when an arrow soared through the sky, heading directly for Muse.

Lark's heart skipped a beat. *"Look out!"*

"I see it." Muse sank like a stone in the bog, dodging the arrow then weaving between tree branches until she landed deftly back on her perch in the center of their canoe.

"Well, I guess that answers my question." Dal rubbed the back of his neck.

Lark gulped, her gaze flitting between the faces of her friends. What were they going to do?

Chapter 4

"What do we do?" Lark asked. "Can we turn back? Find another route?"

Dal shook his head. "This is the only path to the mainland. Unless we want to head back the way we came, or out to sea."

She swallowed, her heart sinking. The way back only led to death, fire, and ash. And she didn't need to be a sailor to understand these canoes were built for sailing the Boglands' shallow waters, not the open ocean.

"We can't just sail straight for them—they tried to shoot Muse out of the sky." Mazen's hand curled into a fist. "What if we're next?"

"Don't fret, my boy." Dausius squeezed Mazen's shoulder. "We just need to show them we're not a threat."

Lark raised a brow as they drifted closer to the turn. Although Dal and Fillan were not actively polling, the current was determined to see them forward, toward the blockade. "How exactly do we do that, Daus?"

"Easy." Dausius' grin widened. "By doing what we do best. Aren, your lute, please. Lark, hit them with our opener. Loud as you can until we make the turn, then cut to silence so I can make introductions."

"What's happening?" Muse shifted on her perch. *"We turning around?"*

Lark shifted on the bench as Aren strummed the lively tune's opening chords. *"Not exactly. We're going to show them we're no threat with a song."*

"Bold plan. I like it," Muse said.

Lark exhaled, shoving aside her nervousness. Then she opened her mouth and sang like her life depended on it. Her voice sprang free, bouncing off the water, joining the lute in perfect harmony.

She had to admit the song choice was inspired. It was energetic and catchy. The type of tune that always had everybody itching to dance. Dausius clapped and stomped in time with the beat. The music bubbled up in the air, infecting everyone with a smile. For one blissful moment, Lark forgot all about the danger ahead and the destruction behind them. Then they turned.

The boats appeared before them, exactly where Muse said they'd be, breaking the trance. The lyrics caught in her throat. Silence enveloped them as Aren halted his strumming and Dausius stopped clapping.

They all stared with trepidation at the strangers, half of them glaring back at them behind nocked arrows. There was a mix of men and women, their skin varied hues of tans, olives, and browns, on shocking display beneath the sheer green fabric they used to fashion their clothes.

They were practically naked. Lark's cheeks burned, and she tore her gaze away from all that flesh, examining the boats instead. The canoes these people sailed looked much the same as their own, only slightly larger, with polers on the forward and aft ends. They were positioned diagonally, all in a row, leaving no room for Lark's or Dausius' craft to slip past on the narrow waterway.

Dausius broke the silence, his voice merry and full of welcome. "Hello, friends! What a delightful surprise. We weren't expecting an audience until tomorrow." He stood, managing a graceful bow despite the wobbly canoe. "We are the Wandering Bards. It's a pleasure to meet you all."

A tense moment of silence followed until the clunk of boots on wood echoed across the water. Prowling forward to the aft poler, in the boat in the center of the bog, strode a tall, statuesque woman with a square jaw and her short brown hair braided tightly to her scalp. Around her neck hung a necklace adorned with a small, bright pink stone.

Lark stifled a gasp. Was that tiny stone the pink flash of color she'd seen? It didn't seem possible. How had she glimpsed something so small from so far away?

All eyes swung to the woman as she stopped beside the poler. She raised her hand as if to wave, but she did not smile, only slapped her hand on her thigh.

Lark's heart leapt into her throat. Was she signaling for an attack? But the next instant, she blew out a sigh. The archers dropped their bows, and the tension in the air subsided.

"Greetings, wanderers," the woman called out across the water, her voice strong and thick with command. She nodded to the polers in her boat, and they stabbed down at the bog, pushing the center canoe closer. "You come from Dracwood?"

Dausius cleared his throat. "Yes, we've spent the last season traveling and performing across Dracwood. Now we've returned to delight the villages of Raimire."

Swiftly, the canoe approached until they pulled in front of them. Lark's cheeks heated further. How could they walk around like that, with their whole bodies on display? She was no stranger to the human body, and had seen more than most with her work as a healer, but that was always behind closed doors, in private. She couldn't imagine wearing something so revealing out in broad daylight.

As she worked up the courage to look more closely, she noted they wore tiny opaque shorts underneath the gauzy green fabric, but they were so short and tightly fitted they left little to the imagination.

None of the folk in the boats seemed to register any discomfort with their attire. The aft poler even sent a smirk in her direction when he spotted her blush and shoved his chest out with pride. Lark tore her gaze away, glancing down at her lap and wrapping her arms around her chest.

The tall woman spoke again, her tone and bearing marking her as the group's leader. "Have you news from the north? We've seen smoke on the horizon. Great clouds of haze drifting through the sky." She pitched her voice softly and leaned toward them with gleaming brown eyes.

Dausius nodded, opening his mouth to explain, but the leader jumped in before he said a word.

"I can see that you do. The Matas sent us to bring any travelers with news to the village conclave. Come, we'll escort you."

Lark's belly fluttered. Village conclave? Matas? The words meant nothing to her but smacked of importance.

As the stranger's boat slipped forward through the hole left in the bog's center where they'd recently been stationed, and Dal and Fillan moved to follow, she realized she wouldn't have long to wonder.

Soon, they passed the line of boats, which spread out after they sailed by, blocking the bog once more. When Lark judged them far enough behind to be out of earshot, she leaned forward and poked Tiora's side. "You might've warned me the people here walk around half-naked."

Tiora had the audacity to giggle, dragging a hand through her short brown curls. "I believe I once told you modesty was not something they worry about here."

"They call that stuff luct fabric. It's made from some jungle plant. I think it helps keep the insects from biting." Fillan tilted his head and grimaced as he examined the folk in the boat ahead of them. "Ya still won't catch me wearing it, though," he added with a chuckle.

Lark shook her head, gazing at the boat of Raimish folk leading the way. She wasn't planning to don any of that fabric, either.

The lead boat took a sharp turn, steering toward a section of the bog that looked impassable. But the aft poler lifted his pole and nudged aside a section of branches, revealing a small channel, just wide enough for a single canoe to squeeze through.

"I've never been this way before." Fillan stared at the passage with bulging eyes. They sailed through, one after the other, the polemen crouching to avoid the low-hanging branches of mangroves until the waterway opened up again. "This is amazing. I bet this path will cut half a day's travel, at least."

It was soon apparent Fillan's guess was correct. Off in the distance, the first glimpses of the jungle rose beyond the mangroves.

Lark sighed and stroked Sunny's back. She couldn't wait to set foot on solid land. Except for the little marshy islands they'd stopped on through the bog to stretch their legs, it had been weeks since they'd left these canoes. She would be happy not to sail again for a good long time.

The jungle brimmed with life and color. It was a welcome change from the dreary swamp of the bog. Brightly colored flowers and birds teemed in the lush green canopy.

As they drew closer, the water echoed with sounds of wildlife. They sailed past a troop of small, orange tree monkeys. Some of the group trailed their boat and chittered excitedly as they leapt from tree to tree. Lark and Tiora giggled at their antics.

"Hm, I wonder what those taste like," Muse said.

Lark spared her bondmate a glance, raising a brow. *"Surely, they're too cute to eat."*

Muse bristled, her feathers shaking. *"Too cute to eat? Ha. Nothing is too cute to eat."*

The waterway curved around a bend, revealing sturdy wooden docks along the shore of a massive bay. A handful of people strolled along the banks, seeming to regard their appearance with little interest. Even the children wore the same flimsy green fabric. A few played on the shore, splashing rocks into the water and laughing.

The bay was dotted with half a dozen canoes. The people on board relaxed, occasionally flicking out and reeling in the lines of their fishing poles. Even more empty canoes neatly lined the docks, looking well cared for despite a few dents and dings.

Fillan followed the Raimish boat to an empty dock on the bay's far side and hopped off to tie them fast as they slowed.

Aren clambered out next. Fillan reached down, lending a hand to Tiora. That left Aren to help Lark. She slipped on her leather gauntlet before standing, then accepted Aren's hand and bounded up onto the dock, clicking her tongue at Sunny to follow.

"C'mon, Muse, you're with me." She held her arm out stiffly.

Aren whistled for Whisper at the same instant, and both birds flew forward, abandoning their wooden perches on the canoe. Then all of them plodded forward on the wobbly docks, joining the rest of their group on the shore. Lark breathed a sigh of relief when her boots sank into the spongy soil.

The tall woman was the last to climb out of the Raimish canoe. She strode toward their group, nodding backward to the water. "My people will carry your things into the village. Come, the Matas will want to speak with you right away." She started down a path leading into the jungle, beckoning them to follow. "My name's Gia. What are your names?"

Dausius fell in beside her, introducing them each by name. Lark nodded and smiled as he named her, then pulled Tiora toward the back of the group, while keeping pace with the others through the winding footpath. "Do you know where they're taking us? What's a village conclave? Who are these Matas?" she asked quietly.

Meital must have overheard her question from where she hiked behind them. "The Matas are the leaders of Raimire." She leaned forward, her voice soft and laced with pride. "Most of the time, the Matas stay in their own villages. A conclave is called when something big happens. Then a wise woman from each village is chosen to represent their people at the conclave."

Lark's eyes widened. "The Matas are all women?"

"Yes. Women have always led in Raimire. The men are always too busy hunting and getting into trouble, so women take care of things in the villages."

Things certainly were different here. Lark breathed in deep, bright notes of flowers and fruit mingling with the fresh scent of moist earth. Chittering, buzzing, and chirping echoed from all sides. She smiled as she picked out new birdsongs among all the sound. The jungle was so much louder, so much more alive than the forests back home.

But would the people who lived here welcome them after they shared the events they'd witnessed? The question sent a shiver down her spine as the path curved again. A village of bright green huts appeared before them, crowded closely together in a cleared valley within the jungle.

"I was expecting it to be bigger. There's hardly enough space for a hundred people here," Tiora said.

"There are likely more clearings like this nearby. A half dozen or more," Meital explained. "The jungle is allowed space to thrive in between. You won't find vast swaths of forest cleared here, like in Dracwood. No one here farms or raises livestock. There's no need. The jungle provides more than enough to feed everyone."

"As long as you can find it without getting yourself killed," Mazen chimed in with a grin.

Lark gulped, following Gia as she wove between buildings. "Is it really that dangerous?"

"Sure. There's poisonous plants, venomous snakes, and all manner of creatures happy to eat you for breakfast." Mazen's brown eyes sparkled, and his smile widened. "It's no wonder the women rule when half the men meet their end in the jungle."

Meital gave her brother a gentle push. "Stop teasing, Maz." She turned back to them, flicking her long, brown braid behind her shoulder. "It's true there are dangers in the jungle. But as long as you know what to watch for, you'll be fine. Don't worry, me and Maz will look out for you."

They stopped before a hut twice the size of all the rest. Gia pulled back the covering over the door—a slightly thicker sheet of the same sheer material the people here wore—and ushered them inside. They piled into a small room, which was empty except for shallow wooden benches lining the walls.

"Have a seat." Gia walked past them, headed for a set of wooden doors leading deeper into the building. "I'll be right back."

Everyone found a seat on one of the benches, except for Sunny, who circled the dirt floor by Lark's feet before lying down. Lark leaned forward, letting Muse hop down off her arm. Then she sat beside her on the hard bench, tugging the moist cloth of her dress.

She'd hoped Raimire would be less humid than the Boglands, but it was just as bad, if not worse. Perhaps that was why the people here were happy to stroll around all day in such flimsy clothes.

Gia returned, carrying a large ceramic bottle and a stack of wooden cups. She closed the door behind her with her foot before placing the cups and bottle on a bench beside the door. "The Matas will see you now. But they only wish to speak to two of you. They asked me to bring the elders among you."

Dausius and Dal rose and joined Gia by the door. "The rest of you, help yourselves to some refreshment while you wait. We'll be back in a moment." With that, Gia reopened the door, and all three disappeared within.

Mazen hopped to his feet and grabbed the bottle. "Figures. I've never met a Mata who didn't treat anyone under forty like a child." He lifted it to his nose and twisted off the lid, giving the contents a sniff. A mischievous smile lit his face. "At least they left us the good stuff."

After setting the bottle back down, he lined the wooden cups up on the bench and poured a measure within each before handing them out to everyone.

"What is it?" Lark cradled the wooden cup Mazen offered and gazed down at the burgundy liquid he'd filled to the brim.

"Fruit wine." He took a long swig from his cup with a grin and sighed. "Nothing like a taste of home, eh, sis?"

Meital smiled then drank deeply from her own cup. "Mm-hm."

Lark's stomach turned, and she glanced at Tiora. She was staring into her cup as well, her brows drawn and a tiny frown on her lips. Would either of them ever be able to stomach the idea of drinking after all they went through with Rasmus and Pax?

She sucked in a deep breath through her nose and sat up straight. *No. It stops now.* She was done letting the memory of those evil men rule her life.

Lark lifted the cup and took a sip. The sweet liquid danced on her tongue. She grinned and took another. It wasn't long before she drained it.

She sat there on the bench, a pleasant warmth spreading through her veins, listening with half an ear to the chatter of her friends in this little hut, halfway around the world from everything she'd ever known. Maybe it was the wine, but suddenly it didn't seem so strange to think everything would all work out in the end.

She sent Muse a wobbly grin. The bird cocked her head sideways, studying her. "What?" Lark asked aloud, then hiccupped, covering her mouth and giggling.

Yeah... It was definitely the wine.

"I ought to have a joke for this," Muse said. *"Give me a moment. I'll think of something."*

She laughed even harder at that, earning a chorus of raised brows and side-eyed glances from the rest of the group. Waving a hand, she snapped her mouth shut, holding her breath to still the hiccups just as Sunny padded over and rested her head on her lap.

Suddenly, all of her mirth disappeared. She cradled the mutt's head in her hands. Her chin wobbled.

Sunny was only here with her because Conall wasn't. Her brother, her mother... They were dead, and she'd never see them again. The grief she'd been tamping down for so long sprang to the surface, and she let out a weary sob.

Aren slid closer, grabbing her empty cup and settling it on the floor so he could wrap an arm around her shoulders. "It's all right," he whispered.

"I got it," Muse exclaimed. *"Laugh, cry,* wine—*don't keep your feelings* bottled *up."*

Lark shook her head where it rested on Aren's shoulder, a tiny smile curving her lips. The absurdity of the situation hit her full force. She was in a hut in the jungle, crying on a Dolnman's shoulder while a falcon cracked awful jokes only she could hear. Life had certainly thrown a few surprises her way... No wonder she was a mess.

The door opened. Dausius and Dal returned, followed by Gia. Lark sat up straight, drying her eyes on her sleeve.

"Good news," Dausius said. "We're free to perform throughout Raimire. The Matas have just advised us to keep quiet about the recent events in Dracwood as we travel."

"Keep quiet?" Fillan jumped to his feet. "Do they mean to act like nothing ever happened? We have to do something!"

"We are doing something," a weathered voice declared, as a brightly colored walking stick slammed down on the ground.

An old woman stepped out of the interior doorway. She was all skin and bones, her gray hair tied up in a knot, eyes almost the exact same charcoal shade. "Hm, this must be the son you mentioned, Dal." She eyed Fillan up and down, frowning. "Don't be so quick to judge, boy. Your father volunteered the both of you to join the people we're sending to keep watch over the Boglands for any sign of the foul vermin. We don't need the rest of you lot causing a panic in the villages."

"This is Mata Moyra," Dausius explained. "She and Gia have graciously agreed to accompany us to the western coast, where we'll find a healer who may be able to help Lark. Thank you again, my ladies," he added with a bow. "We are most appreciative of your assistance."

Moyra nodded and made her way swiftly to the outer door, slamming the stick with every step, though she seemed nimble enough she had little need for it. "Yes, yes. See that you are ready bright and early on the morrow," she called over her shoulder as she exited.

A healer. The pieces were finally falling into place. Maybe her earlier intuition had been right. Everything would work out... It had to.

She smiled. Tomorrow couldn't come soon enough.

Chapter 5

So, this was what it felt like to blend in.

For the first time in her life, Kayda was surrounded by people who looked much the same as herself. Jorians crowded the city streets, most dark-skinned or various hues of brown, much like her own light brown freckled skin. Their clothes and hair were dyed all shades of the rainbow, a dazzling kaleidoscope of brilliant variety. Her auburn hair, so rare in Dracwood, was common here, though whether dyed or natural she couldn't be sure.

Sand crunched under Kayda's boots. Wyll steered her through the city, past countless shops and cramped-looking houses built of yellow brick and clay tiles. Everywhere they turned, people made way for him. Not even the boldest shopkeeps yelled out for him to sample their wares. Was it fear keeping them silent, or respect?

"You would think him a prince," Kayda mumbled under her breath.

"Pardon?" Wyll dipped his head from where he strolled beside her, quirking a manicured brow.

"Nothing. Just wondering why the people here are so keen to avoid you." She lifted a brow of her own. "Should I be worried?"

He barked out a laugh. His voice was so loud and deep a child ahead of them jumped at the sound and clutched his mother's leg before the woman ushered him inside a nearby store. Wyll frowned, watching them disappear into the darkened interior. Then he shrugged, his frown disappearing so quickly she could've almost missed it.

"Trade is king here in Joria. And my family—our family"—he added with a smile—"we're responsible for nearly half of it. No one wants to anger the people who put bread on their table."

It was fear, then. Strange. She hadn't known Wyll long, but for some reason, she had a hard time picturing him angry. During their interaction on the docks, she'd said much that might drive a man into a rage, but he had remained cool and calm. Was it Wyll these people feared, or someone in the family she'd yet to meet?

She was still struggling to get a read on the man. There was still the problem of the destruction in Dracwood and her promise to find aid for her people. Would she be able to find allies with her family? Would she even want to be allied with them once she knew them more closely?

She tried to erase the thought from her mind. There was much to see. Kayda had never traveled outside of Dracwood. It sparked an odd thrill in her chest.

Her own mother might have explored these same streets. She could picture her as a young girl, baking in the heat. Smelling the roasting meat and nuts from street vendors. Marveling at the decadent lengths of silk displayed in the store windows. Kayda had read all about Joria and listened to her nurse Izora's stories over the years, but there was nothing quite like seeing it all with her own eyes.

A flash of metallic shimmer caught her eye. She stopped before a shop window and gaped at the gorgeous dress on display. The fabric reminded her vaguely of her ceremonial gown, but it was a dazzling shade of gold instead of red and cut in a much slimmer silhouette.

"You have a good eye, Princess." Wyll joined her at the glass. "That's one of our newest dyes, cultivated from a flower recently discovered in the depths of the Raimire jungle. Aurelia predicts the shade will be all the rage before long."

She glanced sideways, curving a brow in question. "Aurelia?"

"My great aunt. She's rarely wrong about these things."

"If she's your great aunt, that would make her my...?"

"Your grandmother. You'll meet her later, at Oasis Manse."

Kayda straightened and rolled her shoulders back, trying not to let the shock that rocked her with those words show on her face. She stole a last look at the lovely dress and turned to follow Wyll again.

She had a grandmother... Why was this the first she'd learned of it? How much more family did she have in this strange land? Why hadn't they ever tried to contact her? It was a long journey, for sure, but these people were obviously wealthy. In the shipping business, no less. And they couldn't even be bothered to send her a letter all these years?

She'd come here searching for her family, but the part of her that ached for a connection to the mother she'd never known bristled at the news. Deep down, she'd been expecting to find nothing, or at the least, having to look much harder. Discovering they'd been here all along, happily living their lives without feeling the deep longing—the loneliness—she'd lived with her whole life, stung more than she wanted to admit.

A breeze blew in with the promise of moisture ahead. The murmur of running water filled her ears. They must be approaching the large river she'd seen cutting through the city. Kayda gasped as they rounded a corner and her guess was proven true.

The river was massive, with at least a dozen bridges spanning the channel. Children splashed in the water or crawled along the banks, searching the long grass covering the riverbank on both sides.

All of that she noticed in passing, for something much more wondrous hovered in the air all along the river's length. Thousands of butterflies fluttered over the water, a shimmering curtain reflecting the sun in shades of silver, white, and copper.

"Jorian butterflies." Wyll strolled toward a large wooden footbridge to the north. "They live along the Peat River's banks. Without their cocoons, there wouldn't be any silk to trade."

"They're beautiful." Kayda held out her hand as a silver butterfly floated beside her, its gossamer wings sending warm air shivering over her skin.

"Yes... beautiful." Wyll smiled at her. Then he reached the footbridge and turned, beckoning her to follow. "Here it is. Oasis Manse."

Kayda's breath hitched, her mouth falling open. She'd been so charmed with the butterflies she hadn't yet looked across the water. The home they headed toward was equally captivating. It sat on a hill of lush grass overlooking the riverbank. One would think a girl who'd grown up in a castle wouldn't be so easily impressed, but the large mansion made her home seem garish and cold in comparison.

Oasis Manse was beautifully constructed, sporting circular spires and peaked roofs. Ivy and flowers crawled over the yellow brick. It must cost a fortune to maintain the all that greenery in this arid country.

Her boots thumped along the wooden footbridge. They crossed the river quickly and stepped onto the long, winding path to the house. Sweet jasmine and rose drifted through the air, courtesy of the immaculate gardens. There was a large stable in the distance, no doubt filled with the finest mounts.

No wonder Wyll didn't bat an eye at handing over an entire ship to her. If this was how they kept things outside of their house, what would the inside look like?

Kayda clenched her hands together. "Is there anything I should know before I meet your family?"

She glanced sideways. Wyll had no reason to confide in her. They'd only just met, after all—and she had swindled him out of a ship—but she hoped he might say something, anything, to set her mind at ease.

"Well, I've already told you about Auntie Aurelia. She'll be eager to meet you, no doubt. I have a brother, but he won't be at home. Just Auntie and Father." His face tightened at the mention of his father, but he quickly smoothed his features with a smile. "We don't have a huge family, I'm afraid, but we make up for it with big personalities." He laughed again at that, his smile spreading. "I think you shall fit in nicely."

Well, that was something. His words didn't fully banish the sinking feeling in her stomach, but it helped to know she wouldn't be bombarded with a dozen faces and names all at once. She took a deep breath as they approached the front entrance, and Wyll opened the door, ushering her inside.

The entranceway led to a room featuring a winding marble staircase with halls leading off into the wings on the top floor. Skylights let in the sun, brightening walls painted a glossy cream.

Wyll turned from the stairs, his boots tapping on the tiled floor, and opened a door to the left. Kayda followed, stepping inside a sitting room decorated in emerald and ivory. Sunlight filtered in through floor-to-ceiling windows along the far wall, the forest-green silk curtains pulled back to let in the afternoon sun.

They weren't alone. An old woman reclined on a white silk settee by the window, her sharp brown eyes lifting to inspect them as they entered. Her hair was pinned up in a tight bun and dyed the same lovely golden shade of the dress she'd spotted in the store window. The color brought out the warm tones of her brown skin as she bathed in sunlight.

"Auntie." Wyll crossed the room. "You're looking particularly ravishing today." He pulled her hand from her lap and placed a kiss on the back of her wrinkled skin, then sank down beside her.

"I look like death warmed over, and don't you forget it." Aurelia snatched her hand back and smoothed her bright orange silk dress. "What are you in here sweet-talking me for, boy? What's the trouble?" Her gaze lit on Kayda then, where she lingered inside the doorway. "Who's your friend? Come in and have a seat, child. I won't bite." She smiled warmly.

Kayda crept forward, studying the woman before her. So, this was her grandmother. She returned her smile as she took a seat on an emerald settee opposite the pair.

Despite Aurelia's abrupt tone with Wyll, Kayda could sense affection and warmth behind their interaction. If Aurelia could care so deeply for her nephew's son, then why not her own daughter's? Kayda opened her mouth to introduce herself, but the crack of a door slamming open made the words die on her lips.

"Wyll! Where are you, boy?" yelled the gruff voice of a man from the entranceway.

"In here, Father," Wyll replied, lounging back on the sofa.

Kayda craned her neck back to the sitting room's door in time to see a hefty man, the dark skin on his forehead glistening with sweat, burst into the room. His short, dark brown hair was disheveled, his bright green suit stained with perspiration. He stopped in the doorway, and crossed his arms, glowering at Wyll.

"What's this I hear about the *Sea Silk* being back in port? And you giving it away to some charlatan?" His deep voice boomed through the room.

Kayda fought the urge to shrink back on the settee. This must be the reason for the townsfolk's avoidant behavior toward Wyll. She frowned, picturing him laying into some poor shopkeep with that temper.

Wyll wasn't fazed by his father's anger. He remained relaxed, lounging as if he were listening to a gentle ballad and not an irritated accusation. "I suppose you missed the part where the *charlatan* brought a real-life dragon into port with her?"

Aurelia sat up straight, her eyes twinkling. "A dragon! Then the rumors are true?"

"I don't care if they flew in on a damned cloud of dust or a sea serpent." Wyll's father—her uncle—jabbed a finger at Wyll. "You've got a lot of nerve making decisions about my business without even consulting me."

Wyll leaned forward. "The *family business*, you mean. We agreed everyone in the family would have a part to play. Or are you forgetting about Saltcliff?"

He said the last word as casually as the rest, but it must have held some deeper meaning she couldn't decipher. Her uncle's shoulders slumped, and some of the tension in his face evaporated.

"Yes, yes. You're right on that count. The family business," he conceded.

"Well, now that we're agreed on that, let me introduce you to our long-lost relation." Wyll smirked. "May I present Princess Kayda of Dracwood." He stood and lifted his hand, palm outstretched toward her.

That statement earned her shocked stares from her grandmother and uncle. She rose to her feet, positioning herself so she could look at each of them with a glance. Aurelia blinked rapidly, her palm raised to cover her mouth.

Her uncle was a different story. He'd ignored her in his rage at Wyll, but now that his incredulous stare flashed on her, sweat moistened her skin. He swayed slightly where he stood and huffed out a series of shaky breaths, a fist pressed to his chest.

"Aurelia." He directed his stare on his aunt, his voice steady and cold, tinged with carefully leashed anger. "You told me I'd never have to deal with this. Take care of it, or I will." With that, he spun on his heel and fled the room, slamming the door behind him.

Kayda flinched as the door banged closed, rattling the candlesticks on the walls. What was that all about? She turned to Aurelia—her grandmother. Would her welcome be just as hospitable?

"Sit back down, child." Aurelia sighed. "I suspected this day would come before long. You, too, Wyll. It's time you both learned the truth."

Wyll seated himself across from Aurelia on the emerald settee. Kayda sat beside him, perching on the cushion's edge. Aurelia drew in a deep breath, reaching for a silver bell on a side table. "Perhaps we should call for refreshments. It's a long story—"

"We're not hungry, Auntie." Wyll snatched the bell from the table and silenced it in his fist. "Let's hear it."

Aurelia narrowed her eyes at Wyll, frowning. Then she folded her hands in her lap and shifted her sharp brown gaze to her as she spoke. "You are not our kin, Kayda. It was all a lie. I'm sorry."

Kayda leaned back, her thoughts swirling around like a storm. "What do you mean? My mother was Solenne of Joria, daughter of traders. Are you saying she wasn't your daughter?"

Aurelia's eyes softened. "Solenne was my daughter. But she wasn't your mother."

Wyll rubbed his chin with his knuckles. "Let me get this straight... Our family—we built a reputation over the years, partly on the fact that we share blood with royalty. That was all a lie?"

"Yes," Aurelia said.

"Well, if she's not my mother, then who is?" Kayda asked.

"I don't know, child."

Kayda sagged in the seat, her limbs feeling too heavy to move. The certainty behind the words twisted her stomach in knots. It was all too much. First the mystery of her father, and now her mother as well? She thought she'd finally found a link to her past, only to have it snatched away before it was fully in her grasp.

"Tell us everything, Auntie," Wyll demanded. But when the old woman shot him a steely glare, he added, "Please."

"Solenne was a delicate girl. Sweet, biddable. And talented." Aurelia glanced at the ceiling before looking back at them. "It was a fluke. We've never had talent in the family before, and Solenne wanted nothing to do with being a mage. But her father insisted she be sent to Mage Keep for training. Before she was sent away, we were surprised with another offer—her hand in marriage to Prince Gideon. She only said yes out of fear. Fear and a healthy dose of guilt from her father and uncle, insisting she do what's best for the family."

Aurelia sneered at the memory, her fists clenching around the silk of her dress. "So, when the offer came to save her from the marriage, I took it. And I don't regret it for a second after I learned what happened to that poor girl who replaced her. All those mysterious deaths happening to royal wives in Kings Keep. It would've been her dead instead."

The girl who took her place… that was her real mother, then. Whoever she was.

"What offer?" Wyll asked.

"A mage approached me the week before Solenne was set to sail off to Dracwood for her wedding day. They said they could make a trade. Solenne for a girl of their choosing. She would have to disappear, but would be free to live her life as she chose."

Kayda's heart sped up. The mages were behind this? Who had they switched for Solenne, and why?

"So, Solenne is out there somewhere? Living her life with none the wiser?" Wyll leaned back and crossed his arms.

"No." Aurelia sighed. "She died a few years back." A bittersweet smile crossed her lips. "But for a long time, yes, she lived. Carved out a place for herself as a singer in a traveling show, if you'd believe it. I snuck off to see her every chance I could get. That's how your father found out, Wyll. He agreed to keep it all a secret. Please, you two must keep it to yourselves as well." Her gaze darted between them, full of urgency.

"Yes, yes, of course." Wyll waved a hand. He turned to her. "What do you say, Kayda? I gather you have as much to lose if this information became known as we would."

She nodded. "Yes, I agree. On one condition. Please, Aurelia, can you tell me anything more about my mother or the mage who made this deal with you? Anything at all?"

"I never learned the mage's name. But she was dark-skinned like me, average height and build, with white hair. Jorian by her accent."

Her stomach lurched, confirming the suspicion floating in the back of her mind, which she was too scared to voice. That sounded just like Izora.

"What about my mother?" Kayda asked. "Did you ever meet her?"

"Just once. I only saw her in passing. Long enough to know she could be mistaken for Solenne if you didn't look too closely." She closed her eyes, her brow furrowing. "I'm afraid she looked much the same as any number of young women who hail from these parts. But there was one thing that set her apart."

"What?" Kayda leaned forward again.

The old woman's eyes shot open. "She had her hair plaited in dozens of tiny braids."

Wyll stared at her curiously. "Sounds like your mother was a Sul. They all wear their hair like that. Some tradition of theirs."

A Sul... Blazes. Of course, her mother belonged to the most reclusive group of people in the whole southern continent. At least she had a clue. It was a start.

Kayda drew in a deep breath and stood. "Thank you, Aurelia. Wyll. You've been very kind. It's a shame we aren't kin. I would've enjoyed getting to know you both better." She strode forward, straight for the door.

"Wait, Kayda." Aurelia's plea made her pause. "You don't have to leave so soon. Stay for dinner."

She considered the offer for a brief moment. There was still the problem of finding aid for Dracwood. But it was probably best to wait for Wyll's father's temper to cool before broaching the subject. There would be time for that later, after she solved the mystery of who her real mother was.

She sent the old woman a grin. "Thank you for the offer, but I have a desert trip to prepare for." Then she opened the door and was soon gone from Oasis Manse.

Chapter 6

"Concentrate," Delyth said.

Conall stared at the sack of flour perched atop a hard slab of rock across from him on the Turney Mountains' lower slopes. Dim dusk light surrounded them, the chill air biting his cheeks. He sucked in a deep breath and held it, willing the sack to topple over. The hair on the back of his neck prickled.

Thunk.

"Excellent, Quent." Delyth smiled warmly at the boy, her cheeks rosy.

Conall glared beside him, but his expression softened upon seeing the boy's face lit with joy over his success. He blew out the breath and returned his attention to his sack of flour, still stubbornly standing on the rock and not flat in the snow like Quent's.

Blazes. It wasn't enough that a boy who hadn't yet finished growing had shown him up; he was growing, too. Growing soft. He had to concentrate.

They'd been at this every day since the avalanche. Delyth took every opportunity to train her newest recruits whenever they stopped to rest. But though their journey into Doln had almost ended, he was still struggling. Even with the simplest and most abundant of the elements.

"Empty your mind," Delyth repeated the instructions he'd listened to so many times. "Feel the air flowing through you as you breathe. Shape it to your will."

Conall sucked in another breath, his gaze glued to the brown sack. He watched the blasted thing fall in his mind. He felt the wind rushing forward and heard that satisfying *thunk* echo through the air. All this he imagined while he held his breath until little dots formed in the corners of his eyes. He exhaled.

Nothing.

He clenched his jaw. "It's no use. I'm not meant to be a mage."

Delyth strode closer, the blue of her eyes piercing from within the hood of her gray fur. "It will come with time and practice." She didn't appear flustered in the least by his lack of progress. She turned and addressed them both. "That's all for tonight. It's getting late. Get some rest." Then she made her way across the small plateau, disappearing beneath the flap of her tent.

"Maybe you have a block," Quent said.

Conall raised a brow. "What's that?"

"Something stopping you from summoning, even when you ought to be able to." The boy strode over to the rock slab, retrieved his sack of flour where it rested in the snow, and hefted it up in scrawny arms with a huff. "You heard what Delyth said. We ought to be the strongest mages in centuries, since the Palisade didn't use our power." He glanced down, his gaze shifting rapidly. "Well, it took some of yours, but... you know what I mean."

Conall lifted his sack and grunted. Not from the weight—he'd hefted much more working daily on his family farm—but at the reminder of the Palisade's fall and what it had cost him. Not just years of his life but a measure of his power, too. He shrugged off the sick feeling of regret. He'd lingered enough on those emotions.

"That happen often? Someone gets blocked?" he asked.

Quent hobbled across the plateau, lugging the sack between his legs. "No, not exactly. But I heard my mom talking about it once. It happened to one of her friends years ago." He hefted the bag higher in his arms. "He found a way to work around it, eventually."

"How'd he manage that?" Conall stopped before the supply pile, lifted the tarp, and set the bag of flour beneath it.

Quent plopped his bag down beside his, then stood and stretched. "Sorry, I don't remember. It was a long time ago."

Conall sighed, dropping the tarp and heading for his tent.

Figures.

Quent shuffled forward, rubbing his back. "Well, I guess I'll see you tomorrow."

Conall lifted the flap to his tent. "C'mon in, Quent. Have a bite to eat."

They'd both skipped dinner to train. There'd be no one awake in the children's tent after the day's travel. He couldn't send the lad to bed on an empty stomach.

"Really?" Quent's green eyes lit up, and his posture straightened. "Thanks." He rushed forward, all signs of his earlier sluggishness disappearing with the invitation.

Shadow rested inside, atop a bedroll. He lifted his head lazily as they both crowded in, his tail wagging. *"Any progress?"*

"'Fraid not." He left the flap lifted while he pulled out his tinderbox, using it to light a stumpy candle within a glass and metal lantern the

mages had provided him, before sealing the tent against the wind. The small tent he and Shadow called home the last few weeks was too small for a fire, but with the flap closed against the worst of the wind and bundled together beneath piled furs, it was cozy enough they slept soundly most nights.

"So, what've ya got to eat?" Quent plopped down beside Shadow.

Conall fought the urge to scowl, seeing the boy sitting so closely with his bondmate. Most of the children still kept a wary eye on the large gray wolf, especially after watching him stalk and slaughter peaceful mountain goats.

Not Quent. Ever since the day Shadow saved their lives, he'd treated the wolf like a treasured friend, no matter how many times he came back to camp covered in blood, dragging a fresh kill behind him.

Conall grabbed his pack and pulled out his waterskin and enough dried meat for all of them. "Here." He handed the boy his share and tossed a portion to Shadow.

They all chewed in silence for a time.

"Can I ask you something?" Conall handed the boy the waterskin.

Quent swallowed his mouthful of meat. "Sure." He lifted the skin to his lips and took a long drink.

"You mentioned your mother tonight. I'm not sure if you remember, but you brought her up before. When we were trapped under all that snow, before Shadow found us."

Quent nodded and handed the skin back. "I remember," he said solemnly.

"Why'd you want me to tell her you're sorry?" Conall grabbed the skin, took a quick gulp, and waited for the boy's reply.

Quent's gaze dropped to the tent floor, and he absentmindedly shredded the last of his meat between his fingers. "They sent her on assignment a few days before the Palisade fell. When she left, she asked me to keep an eye on my sister."

Quent had a sister? The meat he'd just swallowed caught in Conall's throat. By now, he'd met everyone on the mountain. Whoever she was, she wasn't with them.

"Oriana is four years older than me, but she's always been the one more likely to end up in trouble. She should've been the one looking out for me... Funny how that works out." Quent looked up, a half-hearted smile curving his lips.

"She ran off with Ereni?"

Quent nodded again, shoving the shredded meat into his mouth. "I ought to be heading back," he mumbled. He moved to stand.

Conall shot out a hand to still him. "You can stay here tonight, with us. No sense in you blasting the rest of the kids with the cold breeze and waking all the babes."

"You sure?"

"Yeah, it's no problem. We've enough room for the three of us."

Shadow raised his head again as Quent settled down against his side. *"Are we collecting strays now?"*

"It's just for the night." Conall reclined on the opposite side of Shadow after snuffing out the lantern.

Shadow snorted.

So, maybe he was growing soft. But it was hard not to feel for the lad. His mother had been thoughtless to leave a boy so young with so much responsibility.

His own father's last words to him had been much the same before the fateful sea voyage that led to his death. "Watch over your mother and the new babe," he'd said. Now, all these years later, hearing news of his father's supposed return from the dead, the heedless request burned him anew.

How could he have asked that of him—a mere boy of six—knowing he was destined never to return? All these years Conall had struggled with guilt and inadequacy over that request. His father should've been the one taking care of his family. Not pushing the responsibility off on a child.

Why had he left? What could have made his father turn his back on his family, fake his own death, and start a new life?

The questions nagged at him as he lay there on the mountainside. Sleep was slow to find him that evening, but eventually, his body's weariness overrode the swirling thoughts in his mind.

Riders from Gransea found them early the next afternoon. They'd just stepped down on the first level land they'd seen since setting out on the mountain passes weeks ago when two burly men galloped astride them. They dressed in dark furs, their thick beards obscuring the bottom halves of their pale faces.

"Ho, Dracians. We're charged with escorting you to Chief Aundrea," said the taller man as he pulled his chestnut mount to a halt.

Delyth swept forward from the center of the group. "Thank you. That would be most helpful."

The riders silently moved into position, one at the group's head, and the other bringing up the rear. Conall drifted among the mages and children, trying not to feel like a stray lamb being herded toward the city.

The air was slightly warmer at the lower elevation but still held a chill, unlike what he was used to this time of the fall. A thin layer of snow lay on most of the ground and covered the evergreens with a dusting of white. The rider led their group down a wide trail cutting through the forested countryside. At first glance, the path and surrounding woods appeared deserted, but the sight of several footprints the size of his head in the snow was enough to keep him from falling behind.

Conall lengthened his stride, the snow crunching beneath his boots. Soon, he reached Delyth's side, where she trekked behind the tall Dolnman and his mount.

"So, who's Chief Aundrea?" he asked.

Delyth cocked her head sideways. "He's the leader of these people. Well, one of them."

"And you think he'll help us?"

"I expect so. Doln differs from Dracwood in many ways, but Chief Aundrea is a good man. Just be sure to keep your opinions to yourself, if they're not favorable."

"What do you mean by that?"

"The chief is not the sharpest knife, but he is the rustiest. If you give him cause to cut you, you'll regret it."

"He has a bit of a temper, I take it?"

"Yes. And you'd do well to steer clear of it while we're in Gransea. I expect we won't be there long. Only a few days to make sure our people have settled in, then the three of us..." She glanced at him and Shadow in turn, "Will head out to meet the Winter Witch."

Conall's stomach clenched at the reminder. He'd not forgotten the reason for his journey into this frosty foreign land. He had to know, once and for all, what had happened to his sister. The journey to meet the Winter Witch couldn't come fast enough.

The forest path curved around a bend and opened to reveal a large valley. A walled city sat at the bottom, nestled along the coast. In the distance, the ocean sparkled in the afternoon sun, dotted with ships spanning the coastline and harbored along the shore.

The rider led them through wide swaths of farmland encircling the city, fallow now, so late in the season, and on a course straight for the massive gate standing at the trail's end. They passed without issue through the entrance onto the cobblestone streets. Except for the curious glances of a few pale-faced Dolnmen and women, no one made a move to greet or speak to them.

Port cities were used to foreign visitors. Still, it seemed strange to be met with so little fanfare after all they'd been through to reach this land. Back home, in Greenvale, there were a handful of busybodies that couldn't stand to let a traveler pass by without badgering them for details about their lives.

It was odd so many on the crowded streets of this great city would watch such a large group of mages and children—obviously worse for the wear—pass by with no remark. Perhaps this lack of curiosity was one of the differences Delyth had been referring to?

Even the shopkeeps kept quiet, content to sit silently over their wares, not hawking their goods to any who passed. The buildings, at least, bore a resemblance to the cramped houses and shops of Flamesmoat. Only these were built out of the silver and white mountain stones instead of the red brick prevalent further south.

They traveled long enough the smallest children began to tire, tugging the adults and older kids' sleeves, whining for a break. Then the tall rider pulled to a stop before an immense stone wall somewhere in the city center. He hopped down from his horse and rapped on a wooden gate in an elaborate pattern. It was likely some coded response, for the door slid open immediately. The man strode in without a word, and their group followed.

Inside, they found a large courtyard surrounding a stately square keep built of silver and white stone. A handful of burly, bearded men, dressed in the same dark furs as the riders, encircled the yard. Their stares locked on a pair of men fighting with blunted swords in the center of a dirt ring. The two fighters had doffed their furs and fought in similar garb—brown wool trousers, plain shirts, and calf-length leather boots.

At first glance, the shorter and older of the pair appeared to be faring worse. His white shirt was stained with sweat and his long golden hair hung lank, an odd contrast next to his neatly trimmed beard.

The second man stood nearly a head taller and was at least two decades younger, gauging by his pale, unwrinkled face. Though his fiery red beard was more unkempt, his bald head barely glistened. His muscles rippled beneath his tan tunic as he lunged and parried. His incredible speed and massive reach caused the smaller man to dodge and spin like a frenzied dancer to avoid his blows.

Conall did his best not to gawk, but it was a hard feat to accomplish. He'd never seen such a mesmerizing display. The clash of their blows and grunts of exertion rang out, their feet kicking dirt into the air. The mages and children drew closer, everyone craning their necks to watch.

It went on for ages with neither man gaining ground, though sweat continued to pour off the blond man as he whirled to evade blow after blow.

Then a child screamed. One of theirs, no doubt, for it was a sound Conall had become so accustomed to during their mountain trek it barely registered. But that was not the case for the red-bearded man. He flinched at the scream, and that single moment of distraction was all the blond fighter needed. He darted in quicker than a hare, sweeping his foe's leg, crashing the larger man to the ground and pointing his blunt sword at his neck.

"I yield," said the man on the ground, dropping his blade and holding his hands up flat in surrender.

The blond fighter only laughed, an airy chuckle full of pleasure. He speared his sword in the dirt at his side and reached down to help his opponent to his feet. Then he nodded to the larger man with a smile as his gaze zeroed in on their group.

The smile dropped from his face, replaced with a flat stare. He strode purposefully past the circled men, directly for Delyth.

"Well, it's not every day the Sade Prim comes for a visit." He slid a hand through his sweat-soaked locks, slicking his long hair out of his blue eyes. "What do I owe the pleasure?"

"We've come seeking aid, Chief Aundrea," Delyth replied. "The Palisade has fallen."

Aundrea showed no surprise at the announcement, only nodded his head somberly. "So, the rumors out of Minsport are true then. Dark days are ahead for us all." He took a deep breath, then turned his attention to the rest of the group, his gaze sliding over everyone until he caught sight of Shadow. His lips quirked up in a smile. "Son of a slushstorm. Is that a wolf? There haven't been wolves this far north in centuries."

"I think the chief likes you," Conall said.

Aundrea dropped to one knee, holding out his hand and clicking his tongue, as if inviting a pup over for a sniff.

Shadow snorted from where he stood at Conall's side. He stared straight at the chief and sat flat on his haunches. *"No thanks. I can smell him from here."*

Delyth jumped in. "That's Shadow. And this is Conall of Greenvale, his bondmate."

Conall stepped forward, holding his hand out. "Nice to meet you."

Aundrea clutched his hand and shook, his grip crushing in its intensity. "Bonded to a wolf. I'd love to pick your brain, Conall of Greenvale." He let go first, the wrinkles around his eyes crinkling as he smiled.

Conall resisted the urge to rub his hand after the brutal shake, forcing a tight smile.

Aundrea directed his attention back to the crowd, opening his arms wide and raising his voice. "You all must've had a rough journey through the mountains. Where are my manners? Come into the keep. We'll have a hot meal prepared and find a spot for the little ones to rest."

The gathered men had already begun heading inside. Upon hearing their chief's announcement, a pair of them threw the doors open wide, using a couple of large gray stones as doorstops. Children and mages streamed forward eagerly, likely excited about the promise of an actual roof over their heads for a change.

Conall moved to follow, but Delyth stopped him with a hand on his arm. Within a few moments, nearly everyone filed inside.

Not quite everyone. There was an old man, his olive skin standing out starkly among all the pale-faced northerners. He leaned down in the dirt pit, struggling to pull free the blunted sword Aundrea had stabbed into the ground. The red-bearded fellow approached him with a gruff, "Hey," and a pit formed in Conall's stomach.

Everyone knew the Doln kept slaves, but this was the first evidence he'd seen of it. He inhaled sharply as the bearded fighter approached the man, ready to rush over should he harm the poor fellow. But the fighter only shooed the man aside with a wave and pulled the sword free on his own, leaving the old man to shuffle inside the keep.

Despite the calm interaction, Conall had half a mind to say something. Slavery just didn't sit right in his mind. No man should be forced to work for another. But he took one look at Delyth's face and remembered her warning. His gaze slid to the chief. Perhaps now was not the time to debate the evils of slavery.

The red-bearded fighter tossed the sword into a nearby box, then made his way to the keep and knocked the rocks free. He closed the doors and strode over to stand at his chief's side. That left the four of them, and Shadow, standing out in the courtyard.

"This is my son, Taul." Aundrea nodded to the red-bearded fellow and make introductions.

Delyth spoke up as soon as they exchanged pleasantries. "I'll get straight to it, Chief. The scourge have returned." She strolled back toward the stone wall, where their group had stacked their various supplies and baggage once they entered the courtyard. She stopped beside a blanket-shrouded oval.

He'd seen beneath that blanket once before. Back then it had shuddered and swayed, the creature within shrieking and snarling. Not today. It sat silent and still.

Delyth lifted the blanket, revealing the carcass of one of the scourge. It appeared her prediction that the ferocious rodent wouldn't survive the Turney Mountains' extreme cold was correct.

In death, the silver and brown-striped creature seemed much less of a threat. But Conall remembered its viciousness. The wild, fearless way it strained at the metal cage bars, snapping and scratching to be free. He shuddered at the reminder that thousands of those beasts were roaming unchecked across his homeland, feasting on anything that moved.

"They don't look so fearsome." Taul crouched beside the cage and peered within.

"If it were just one, then I might agree." Delyth dropped the brown blanket to the ground, letting the men look their fill. "But there are thousands more where that one came from. Hundreds of thousands before long."

Aundrea jostled the cage, flipping the creature on its side. "Look at the teeth and claws on that thing." He stood and addressed Delyth. "We've already begun to assist the refugees from Dracwood pouring through Minsport. Your people are welcome, too, of course. When the time comes that we must battle these foul vermin, we'll add our steel to the fray. I have only one condition."

Delyth sent a shrewd glance to the chief. "Which is what?"

"Some of the mages you've brought with you must stay, both here and in Minsport, to defend our lands against the inevitable invasion, should we fail."

"That's reasonable." Delyth nodded. "Done." She lifted the blanket and covered the cage once more. "I have a favor to ask, in exchange."

Aundrea laughed again, an incredulous bark this time. "Have I not offered enough in exchange already?"

She ignored the question and tossed her long gray braid over her shoulder, extending her arm toward him and Shadow. "We've need of a guide. We have to see the Winter Witch."

All the humor drained from his face at the request. "That... I can't do. In the spring, certainly. Now?" He shook his head. "It would be suicide."

Conall's chest tightened, and he schooled his features, forcing his face to remain still instead of sending a heated glare in Delyth's direction.

Suicide... Why was this the first mention he'd heard of the dangers of this journey? What would they face that even this incredible fighter balked at the thought of undertaking this trip?

"The guide need not travel all the way to her hut. We just need someone to take us as far north as Norwich." She clutched Aundrea's forearm and gazed up into his face. "Please, Chief. This is of the utmost importance."

Taul sauntered forward. "I'll take you."

Aundrea frowned, opening his mouth, only to close it a heartbeat later and nod, his jaw clenched tightly. "Well, you have your guide, Sade Prim," he said, a lightness to his tone that sounded forced. "I wish you fair weather and good luck for your journey. You're gonna need it."

Chapter 7

Lark's body swayed in the warm early morning breeze. A cacophony of noise that never ceased pervaded the air.

The jungle never rested, but the Wandering Bards did. Each of them cocooned within a hammock strung in between the trees, high in the dense canopy. It was the only way to sleep safely in the deep jungle. Nocturnal hunters stalked the forest floor in the dark. And out here, between villages, they were all alone, with no one to call on, should disaster strike.

The first night had been the worst. The thought of sleeping high above the ground, one wrong move away from plummeting into the dirt in the black of night, sent goosebumps all over her flesh. But after watching ancient Mata Moyra climb one of the spindly jungle trees and hoist herself into a hammock, Lark had felt compelled to follow. Truth be told, it was quite relaxing once she got the hang of it.

A yawn rose from her lips, followed by a smile as her gaze drifted to her attire. She'd had more than her share of getting used to new things over the last few weeks of travel.

All of their group now wore the sheer green luct fabric so popular in the jungle. She'd balked at trying it on when Moyra presented the outfits on the first morning of their trek. But she'd relented once offered a thin sleeveless top to wear along with the tiny shorts beneath the transparent fabric.

Fillan's explanation on their journey through the bog proved correct. Since donning the garb, the multitude of biting insects swarming the jungle had ignored her. That alone was enough reason to keep her wearing it, even if it hadn't been a thousand times more comfortable in the thick humidity than the dresses and skirts she'd packed from home.

"Morning, Muse." Lark spotted her bondmate perched next to her on the branches of a massive diquat tree.

"Morning." Muse shook her feathers and stretched her wings.

Lark stretched, too. Then, balancing carefully, she left Sunny where she lay by her feet and crawled across the hammock. She climbed to the jungle floor, plucking one of the diquat fruits on her way down.

Her boots sunk into the spongy soil as she picked her way silently through the trees to the banks of the stream they'd camped next to. She leaned down and rinsed the diquat in the warm water before taking a bite of the sweet pink fruit. Diquats were smaller than the apples of Dracwood, and their flesh softer, but they were just as delicious.

"I thought I told you not to wander off on your own?"

Moyra's booming voice startled her, and she almost lost her balance on the slick rock she perched on.

"I'm not alone, Mata." She stepped back from the stream's edge, nodding to Muse in the branches above her head. They had taken to doing everything in pairs. With so many dangers in the jungle, it made sense to have a second set of eyes on alert for any trouble. "I might say the same to you..." she added with a smile, taking another bite of her breakfast.

The old woman huffed and inched past her, slamming her walking stick in the dirt before filling her waterskin from the stream. "The jungle hasn't killed me yet. Today will be no exception. Come, let's wake the others. If I'm right, which I usually am, we'll reach Stoneshore this afternoon."

Lark swallowed. She chucked the pit of her fruit into the water and followed Moyra back through the trees. "Really? That's great news."

Stoneshore was the coastal village where they'd meet the healer, who she hoped would become her teacher. After weeks of travel, and stopping to perform in a handful of tiny villages along the way, they were finally about to reach their destination. A tingle of excitement stirred in her breast.

They roused the others, packed camp, and set out, heading west. Lark hefted the pack on her back, her shoulders already protesting the familiar weight. Each of them carried all their belongings with them. There were no beasts of burden that could survive the dangers of Raimire.

But though the constant hiking was not ideal for her comfort, the constant activity strengthened her muscles and boosted her endurance, leaving her fitter than at any other point in her life. Hopefully, her physical transformation would be beneficial in the days to come, as she learned to control her talent.

Soon, the warm morning yielded to another sweltering day. Sweat trickled down her back underneath the heavy pack. When Gia called for a stop at the top of a tree-covered ridge that was home to an enormous waterfall, Lark sighed with relief. She shucked off her pack and slumped down on the roots of a massive diquat tree to rest in the shade.

"That's the Shore River." Gia pointed north at the waterfall. "Stoneshore rests along the river's southern banks, just west of this waterfall. We'll rest for a bit, then all that's left is to climb down the ridge, and we're home."

Tiora collapsed next to Lark on the diquat roots, gazing down the ridge's edge. "We have to climb down there?"

Mata Moyra scoffed. "If my old bones can handle the climb, then you shall, too, child."

Dausius stopped beside Gia. "I'm sure our guide will know the easiest way to the bottom."

Gia only smiled in response, her tanned cheeks reddening. She and Dausius had become rather cozy during their trek through the jungle.

Tiora leaned closer to Lark. "Hey, I need to make a stop in the woods. Care to join me?"

Lark nodded, pushing to her feet and leaving her pack on the ground. She followed Tiora through the trees the way they'd come, far enough from the main group they could be afforded a bit of privacy. She waited with her back turned for Tiora to take care of her business, scanning the trees for any sign of danger.

For all Mazen's teasing about snakes, jagoths, and the many other predators rumored to inhabit Raimire, they'd trekked across the jungle without trouble. There'd been a few times she'd spotted a scaled tail slithering through the underbrush or dangling from a tree, but the snakes seemed happy to allow their group to pass through their territory unmolested, preferring to hunt smaller game.

The jagoths—the creatures that made the hammocks a necessity—they'd not seen, but they'd heard their unmistakable growling mating calls countless times in the night. Luckily, the beasts rested most of the day. And so far, they'd been lucky enough not to run into any of the vicious cats sleeping in their dens. Still, she kept a wary eye on the jungle, not willing to press her luck by being less than vigilant.

"I'm done." Tiora popped up beside her. "Did you need to go?"

"No, I'm al—" The word snagged in her throat as she glimpsed something moving in the jungle ahead of them. She grabbed Tiora's luct sleeve. "Did you see that?"

Tiora frowned, peering into the distance. "No. Maybe we should head back, just in case."

Visions of jagoths flashed in Lark's mind. Could that be one of their dens?

She nodded, and was about to turn back when she spied another glimpse of movement. This time, the image appeared from within a small break in the foliage, close to the ground.

She gasped. It was a little girl, her long brown braid dangling in the dirt as she scrambled backward on her hands and knees, her face full of terror.

"What is that?" Tiora squinted into the distance, her lips pursed.

Lark heard the question, but as if from a distance. Her breath hitched, then flooded her chest, quick and shallow, her hands shaking. Then her feet flew forward as if they had a life of their own.

"Get the others, now," she yelled, not bothering to look back to check if Tiora was listening.

"Muse. I need you!"

"I'm coming," Muse replied, without hesitation.

Lark hurtled through the jungle. The glimpse she'd caught of the girl had quickly vanished, but she shot straight for the spot she'd last seen her scuttling through the underbrush. The fear on her face was branded in her mind's eye.

What was she running from? She had to save her. There was no way she was going to watch another child die. Not today. Never again.

She ran for so long. It didn't make sense... She should be there. How had she even seen this far?

She shoved the thought aside. Her lungs burned, and her legs wobbled like jelly when she finally arrived at the break in the foliage. She dove between bushes, adrenaline raging within her as she took stock of the scene.

The girl was there, cowering back against the gargantuan roots of a massive kapok tree. And there before her, poised to strike, was a red and black-striped snake.

The snake was huge—at least as long as the girl—and a thousand times more vicious. Its mouth opened, emitting a toe-curling hiss. Its head spun in Lark's direction as she stood there, fighting to catch her breath, soaked in sweat and dizzy with terror.

For a heartbeat she paused, eyes widening as she fought the panic and fear racing through her body. Then the serpent swung back to the girl, raising its head high off the ground, coiling back to strike.

Lark didn't think. She jumped, kicking the snake as she leapt, and rolled to a stop in front of the girl. Pain shot up her leg.

The snake slithered back from her strike, hissing louder than ever.

She gulped and positioned herself between the child and the snake as it recoiled, ignoring the pain stabbing her leg when she placed her weight on it.

The snake was angry now. Even angrier than before. Its scales rippled, and venom dripped from within its open jaw as it hissed.

Lark's heart hammered. She couldn't see a way out of this. It was her and a child against a pissed off predator, and she was out of ideas.

Wait. She dug her fingers into the soft soil, praying she could use the magic the same way she had to stop Gael.

Sink, snake. Blazes. Sink!

She waited for the vibration to fill her the way it always did when she used her talent, but all she could feel was panic, pain, and fear. It was too late. The snake drew back to strike.

Muse tore into sight, flashing down from the sky. She dove with expert precision, aiming for the massive snake's neck and latching onto its throat, tearing at its skin.

Worry swamped Lark for her bondmate, but she seized her chance. She pulled the girl to her feet and raced away. Lark shoved her through the hole in the underbrush and spun back to where Muse and the snake grappled.

"I got her. We're safe," she screamed in her mind.

Muse pulled free, abandoning her attempt to attack the back of the massive beast's neck and rose into the air.

The snake looked dazed for an instant. Then it bolted into a hole in the same kapok tree the girl had cowered under. Lark's lips quirked up in a crooked smile as she backed away through the underbrush.

So, the girl had been blocking the snake's den. Wonderful.

Now that the adrenaline and fear had passed, the pain in her leg started screaming. She glanced down, examining the wound on her leg for the first time. She had two lines of blood leaking down her right calf, topped with a pair of circular puncture marks. It was the same leg she'd used to kick the snake out of the way. The wound burned and was already starting to swell.

Had the snake bitten her as she kicked? Her stomach clenched with dread. She remembered Mazen's warnings of how quickly Raimish snakes' venom could kill.

Was she going to die?

She collapsed to the ground, a wave of dizziness washing over her.

"Lady, are you all right?"

A pair of curious brown eyes stared down at her. It was the girl. She was thin, wide-eyed, and dressed in the typical luct outfit, minus the undershirt. Now that she hovered above her, her brows knitted together with worry, Lark could see she wasn't a child at all. She was a girl on the cusp of womanhood, perhaps twelve or thirteen years old. Still, Lark's heart warmed all the same, seeing the young girl perched above her whole and unharmed, not bitten by that awful snake.

Muse landed beside her, and the girl hopped back in alarm. *"Lark. What's wrong?"*

"The snake, it got me." Her head swam with fuzziness as the pain radiated up her leg.

The girl snatched a stick off the ground and swung it at Muse. "Get away from her," she yelled.

It was Muse's turn to hop back. She screeched angrily, lifting off the ground and landing on a branch of a nearby tree, out of the girl's reach.

Footsteps pounded on the ground. A moment later, the faces of Lark's friends appeared in the jungle behind them.

"Ravenna?" Gia was the first to arrive, the name tumbling off her lips as she spotted them.

"Gia? Thank the Mother!" The girl—Ravenna—shot up from where she crouched beside Lark and dropped the stick. "A snake had me cornered. This lady saved me, but I think she got bit." She grimaced, glancing back at Lark. "It was a hexer."

"Rot and decay." Gia pressed a hand to her chest. "Find Mika. Have him meet us on the ridge. We'll carry her down the trail. Run!"

Ravenna sped off without another word, quickly disappearing in the distance.

Lark tried to speak. She tried to stand. But her body wouldn't listen. Panic struck her again, spreading through muscles as limp as old lettuce. Tiora knelt beside her and grabbed her slack hand. Aren and

Dausius crowded around her. Mazen and Meital paced on the trail, gazing at her from a distance. All of their faces mirrored the shock and disbelief raging within her.

Aren turned to Gia, his voice wobbling. "What's happening? Tell me what to do."

Out of all of them, Gia was the only one who held her cool. She strode forward, grabbing Lark's brown leather boots and lifting her legs. "Grab her shoulders. We'll all take turns carrying her. We have to bring her to the healer, now."

Aren nodded, and soon Lark found herself lifted in his strong arms. They hurried through the jungle in silence until they reached the spot where Mata Moyra and Sunny awaited them.

"I saw Ravenna tear through. What's happened?" the old woman called out in question.

Gia didn't slow, only grunted out a single word as she hustled forward, struggling under Lark's dead weight. "Hexer."

Moyra gasped and grabbed Sunny's collar, holding her steady. "Go. I'll bring the dog so she's not underfoot. Don't wait for me if I fall behind. I know the way."

The urgency in Moyra's tone sent another wave of panic through Lark. She did her best to stay calm, but her mind was screaming. Why couldn't she move? Why couldn't she speak? Tears leaked out of her eyes, the only physical sign of distress in a body out of her control.

"Muse? Blazes, I'm in trouble. Please, tell me you can still hear me."

"Yes, yes, I'm here. Lark, you're going to be all right. The healer from the village will come." Muse hopped from tree to tree, shadowing their movements.

Hearing Muse's voice in her mind calmed some part deep within Lark. Her heart still raced, but the comfort of her bondmate swept over her, soothing the voice inside that screamed until it was merely a whimper.

Muse was right. She would survive this. Her friends would save her.

They reached the ridge. Gia barked out orders, having each of them climb a little lower and stand in a line so they could pass her down the hill. It was the same method the people in her village used to haul buckets of water to battle the flames of a house fire. Lark found she didn't enjoy being the bucket. Her body was constantly jostled, and the pain exploded within her leg and radiated up her thigh every time her leg was bumped.

Worse still, she had to glimpse the worry and fear painting each of her friends' faces as they shuffled her between them. Though they tried their best to disguise it, there was no mistaking their pallid complexions, shaky hands, and trembling lips. Her heart broke seeing the pain and anxiety behind their eyes. If only she hadn't been so impulsive… but no, then the girl would be dead.

They arrived at a craggy spot on the ridge. Gia's method wouldn't work here; the ground was far too steep. The group paused, each of them breathing hard.

Then the clatter of rocks falling greeted them from below as the heads of two people emerged. It was Ravenna and a handsome young man with wild brown locks carrying a satchel.

"There she is, Mika." Ravenna pointed up at where Lark rested, cradled within Dausius' lanky brown arms.

Mika sprang forward, closing the remaining distance in an instant. "Toss her down," he yelled, staring up at Dausius and holding out his muscular olive arms. "Do it! I'll catch her."

Aren's voice rang out from behind her, full of alarm. "Wait, are you mad?"

Lark couldn't see him. She only saw Dausius gaze down into her face and whisper, "Help her fly..." He winked at her. The next thing she knew, she was soaring through the sky, weightless.

She landed in Mika's arms. He wasted no time setting her on the ground and reaching inside his satchel. He pulled out something small, spindly and brown. It looked an awful lot like the plant roots she'd tended in the herb garden with her mother. He pressed the roots to her leg, his brows lifting slightly as he stared down at her calf.

A tremor whispered over her skin. The pain receded, and she almost cried out with relief, but—she couldn't.

The pain surged back. Mika let out a heavy sigh and shook his head. "I'm sorry," he whispered, lifting his hand. "It's too late. I don't have the strength to save you."

Aren jumped down beside her and cradled her head in his arms. "No... no, you have to save her. Please." Tears streaked his face.

The rest of the group climbed down more slowly, but within moments, they all crowded around where she lay on the ridge side.

Mika's shoulders slumped. "It's too late. The venom's spread too far. I haven't the talent to pull it all free."

"No." Dausius moaned and clutched onto Gia, shaking his head back and forth slowly.

Tiora started wailing. Mazen and Meital pulled Tiora close, their backs shuddering. From the air, Muse and Whisper both circled, Muse's shrieking cries ringing through the air.

"Please." Aren lifted bloodshot eyes to Mika. "We brought her here to meet you, so you could teach her. You have to do something!"

Mika's shoulders lifted and his eyes brightened. "She has talent? Why didn't you say so?" He slapped the hand with the roots back on her calf, his gaze zeroing in on her hazel eyes. He snapped at Aren with his other hand. "Her name. What's her name?"

"Lark."

"Listen to me, Lark." Mika leaned so close to her face her world narrowed down to his golden-brown eyes. "I need your help. Call on your talent. Lend it to me, so I can heal you."

Damn it! That was the problem. She would've cried if she had any control over the muscles in her face.

"What's happening? Is he healing you?" Muse asked.

"He needs me to use magic. But I don't know how. What am I going to do, Muse?"

A scoff sounded in her mind. *"That's all? Ha. That's nothing. You got this. You can do this!"*

She could do this. She would do this.

Lark stared back into those warm golden eyes, and she wished. But she didn't wish for herself. She wished with all her heart she could wipe the sorrow and pain off her friends' faces.

She felt it then. First, a spreading warmth on her calf where Mika's hand rested. Then the magic rumbled through her blood, shaking her from her very core.

Mika sucked in a breath. His eyes bulged. And Lark shot up from Aren's arms, gasping and nearly slamming her head into Mika's chin.

Then a wave of exhaustion crashed into her. She slumped back, and the world went black.

Chapter 8

The horizon slowly brightened in the dawn sky, pale blush and amber streaks banishing the inky black night. Kayda climbed above deck and made her way to where her bondmate rested.

"You ready, Dru?" she asked.

He cocked his head sideways, crimson eyes shooting open. *"Are you?"* he asked in return, his gaze lingering on her attire. She wore the same plain cotton trousers and a white shirt, much the same as the yellow she wore yesterday.

"Just about. I only have one more thing to take care of."

Druturion's eyelids drooped closed again. *"Wake me when you're really ready."*

Kayda rolled her eyes. One would think someone who spent the better part of a millennium sleeping would want to rise with the dawn.

Her boots tapped on the wooden boards as she strolled across the deck. She shuffled around a handful of sleeping forms. The former slaves were all still on board. Most had slept out here in the open air rather than roasting in the stifling rooms below deck.

Finally, she found the man she was looking for. Jayan stared beyond the back rail at the open ocean. His feet were still bare beneath his cotton shorts, but he wore a tan shirt this morning. Half the buttons were undone, allowing the warm breeze to blow through, billowing the fabric like a sail.

She joined Jayan at the rail and gazed down into the dark water. "Morning."

"Morning, Princess." He sent her a bemused smile.

"I've a journey I need to make. I'm not sure how long I'll be gone... a few days, maybe a week. Can you keep a handle on things here while I'm gone? Make sure the others know they're free to leave if they wish or free to stay."

"Aye, Princess. I can do that." He sighed.

She cocked a brow, shifting to look at him closely. "You miss the sea?"

"Yes, and no. I love sailing. Even as a slave, being out on the ocean, one with the waves and the sky, brought me such peace. But another part of me misses home. I never thought I'd have the chance to go back... now, thanks to you, I do." He pursed his lips and stared at the sea.

"Who says you can't have both?" She squeezed his arm. "Go, find your family. I'll leave someone else in charge. Come back when you're ready. Or never. The choice is yours to make."

He finally turned from the ocean, his brown eyes glossy in the dawn light. "It's a funny thing. I've spent so long without a choice, now that I have the chance to make one of my own, I can't make up my mind." He chuckled, rubbing the wooden rail.

"Hello," called out a familiar deep voice, as steps pounded on the gangplank.

Kayda and Jayan spun around, ambling toward the center of the ship to meet their early morning visitor.

It was Wyll, wearing a cream-colored suit and a bright smile. He carried a rolled parchment and a paper-wrapped package.

"Good morning," Kayda said.

"I told you I'd have the papers drawn up. Here they are." He handed the parchment to her and pulled a charcoal writing stick from his pocket. "I figured I'd get your signature before you headed off on your search."

Kayda smiled. "That's very thoughtful of you, Wyll." She scanned the pages quickly, and seeing all in order, she adjusted the charcoal in her hand, motioned for Jayan to spin around, leaned the parchment against his back, and signed.

She rolled the parchment back up and handed it to Wyll. "I wonder, could I trouble you for a favor, *cousin*?"

Wyll lifted a brow, clearly not mistaking the emphasis she put on the final word. "What might that be?"

"Could you keep an eye on my ship and my crew while I'm out of town?"

"I can handle that for you." He smiled. "So, you're all set to search for the elusive Sul, then?"

"As ready as I can be. Though I can't help but feel like I'm forgetting something."

"Perhaps this will help." Wyll handed her the paper-wrapped bundle. "Just a little gift. From one cousin to another."

Kayda blinked in surprise. He'd gotten her a gift? She tore open the delicate tissue, revealing a flash of gold. It was the beautiful golden gown she'd spotted in the store window yesterday. Blood rushed to her cheeks. "Thank you, it's lovely. Though this might not be what I need for a trek through the Suland Waste."

Jayan cleared his throat loudly. "I know exactly what you're missing, Princess."

She raised a brow. "You do?"

He took a step forward, wedging his way between her and Wyll. "You need a guide. Someone who's been there before."

Wyll scoffed. "Good luck with that."

Jayan's jaw clenched, but he didn't respond to Wyll. He kept his focus on her and her alone. "I'm ready to go home, Princess. I'll take you."

Jayan was Sul? Kayda smiled, pleased with this stroke of luck. Maybe now she wouldn't have to spend days flying over sand dunes, searching for the hidden people who were rumored to be as hard to find as a shard of glass in the shifting sands.

"Dru?" From the corner of her eye, she saw him lift his head again. *"How many people can you carry?"*

"I've never had cause to test my limits, but I expect I can handle you and the captain just fine." He dropped his head again. *"Wake me when you both are* actually *ready,"* he grumbled.

Kayda slapped Jayan's shoulder, her smile widening. "That sounds like a wonderful idea, Jayan. Why don't you go gather your things below deck? Would you drop this in my room while you're down there?"

Jayan grinned, taking the bundled dress and heading for the stairs.

"Oh, don't forget your shoes," she called after him.

He stopped in his tracks and swung a sheepish grin her way. "That's gonna be a problem. I don't have any."

His admission needled her heart. What kind of beast forced a man to captain his ship for years without even providing him with a simple pair of shoes?

She waved him off, shaking her head. "I'll take care of it. Go, grab whatever else you need."

Wyll remained at her side, casually leaning against the rail as Jayan disappeared below deck.

She bit the inside of her lip, an idea forming. Jayan had not belonged to Wyll. He'd been the *Sea Silk* captain's personal slave. But Wyll had employed that monster for years. He'd watched countless slaves be loaded and unloaded from within his ship's holds. She wasn't foolish enough to imagine she could balance the scales between them, but maybe she could tip them in the right direction. Her gaze lit on Wyll's expensive brown boots.

"Care to do me another favor, *cuz*?"

***

Hot, dry air flew through her long red hair from her perch upon Druturion's back. Sand spread out below them in all directions, as far as the eye could see.

Despite the heat and the desolate landscape, Kayda breathed in deeply and smiled. She was at home in the sky. Floating through the air like one of those delicate, shimmering, Jorian butterflies.

It would've been relaxing, if not for the set of shuddering arms latched around her waist like a child afraid of being torn from its mother's arms. She suppressed a smirk as Dru picked up speed, and Jayan's hands clenched even tighter. It was safe to say he wasn't a fan of flying.

"There," he yelled in her ear.

She swiveled her neck around but saw nothing out of the ordinary. Just an endless expanse of dunes. "Where?"

Jayan lifted his hand from her stomach, enough to point his finger slightly to the left. "Over there, on the horizon. Those rocky hills. That's home."

Kayda squinted. He called those hills? A handful of specks rose in the distance, barely distinguishable from the surrounding sand.

Druturion must've heard him, too. He banked to the left, and soon, they hovered above the rocky outcrop that was barely big enough to be called a hill and made of a stone the exact shade of burnt-orange as the ever-changing dunes.

No wonder the Sul were so hard to find.

Druturion swooped down for a landing. Kayda's nose twitched as sand sprayed up to greet them with each beat of his huge black wings. Then she gently pried Jayan's hands off her waist and hopped down from Dru's neck onto the hard sandstone.

Shading her eyes from the hot midday sun, she spun in a slow circle. A frown tugged at the corners of her mouth. "You sure this is the place?"

Jayan's new, expensive brown boots smacked down on the sandstone. "Yes. Home sweet home." He laughed. His voice boomed in the arid wasteland, loud and wild.

Kayda's stomach turned at the hint of madness in his laughter. Was she destined to be surrounded by people who were half-mad?

She stole another long look at the barren landscape. There was no sign of civilization. No village. No people. Was her intuition wrong to follow this man she'd only recently met into the middle of nowhere?

Then she heard something. A skittering murmur below her feet. A heartbeat later came the scrape of rock on rock and a dozen holes appeared in the craggy hillside. Countless people poured out, all of them dark-skinned, their hair braided in hundreds of tiny, neat braids wreathed around their heads like dark halos. The Sul.

It only took moments for them to be surrounded. The Sul circled them with weapons drawn. Most held long staffs with curved blades latched at the tips; a few bows and knives were sprinkled in. All of them wore the same rust-orange attire, long-sleeved tunics, and pants that matched the sand's color perfectly.

Despite their battle-ready stance, she couldn't mistake their amazed reactions when they gazed upon Druturion. They crowded around him, openly staring, glancing at each other as if confirming to themselves what they were seeing was actually there before them. He sat upon the rock in a relaxed stance, his neck and wings spread out, his eyes closed, soaking up the heat like a kitten lounging in a sunbeam.

She resisted the urge to roll her eyes. *"A greeting for our new friends might be in order. Maybe you could look a touch more menacing?"*

Druturion's crimson eyes snapped open, and he shot up on his hind legs, unfurling his wings to their full length before tucking them close to his body and sitting once more. His scaled tail flew around, curling before him like a whip.

The display made the Sul fall back in unison, their boots skidding on the rock, each of them staring in awe at the massive black dragon.

A man broke free from the pack, striding forward and targeting Jayan. "Who are you interlopers? Why do you pound upon our roof, uninvited?" The man was no larger than most present, but something about his bearing, the way his shoulders stood tall and strong, marked him as a leader among these people. His brown eyes bored a hole through Jayan, his full lips set in a grim line.

"Lazar, it's me, Jayan, son of Akilt. I've come home."

Lazar sneered. He circled around Jayan, scanning him up and down with undisguised disgust. "Lies. I knew Jayan, son of Akilt. He was a warrior. A Sandspear. Not this braidless, scrawny bag of bones I see before me."

Laughs rose from the gathered Sul. The sound sent a pang of sympathy through Kayda's chest as Jayan's shoulders slumped with the weight of their mockery.

What was happening? Was Jayan lying? She didn't think so. She'd watched recognition light on several faces in the crowd when he'd supplied his name. Was this the start of some strange ritual these people had for those who ventured out and returned? Or was something else going on underneath the surface she couldn't quite grasp?

Whatever it was, she didn't like it. Not one bit.

She stepped forward, pitching her voice loudly, not bothering to hide the anger tinging her words. "You're the liar. This man has battled more than you could imagine. He's a warrior in truth."

Jayan's eyes widened as Lazar swung to face her. "Still your tongue, dust eater. Your words hold no weight here. You're not sandborn. You're lucky we didn't skewer you on sight."

Kayda's skin thrummed with the force of the rancor behind the man's words, but she refused to cower. One of Lazar's words struck a chord within her. Sandborn. Hadn't Izora told her in that tower room her mother was born of the sand? "You're wrong there as well. My mother was Sul."

Gasps spilled into the air. Dozens of curious eyes lit on her, searching her features as they whispered among themselves.

Lazar's brows shot up in the air. The silver streaks in his dark brown braids glinted in the sun as he shook his head. He barked out a laugh, the deep boom echoing across the dunes. "It doesn't matter whose loins you sprang from. You're not one of the sandborn until you prove it."

A chill darted up her spine. Was that a threat? But no matter what these people asked of her, she would face it. She wasn't leaving the Waste until she uncovered the secrets of her mother's past.

Her hand clenched into a fist. "Then we'll prove it."

Jayan's face turned ashen as whoops rang out from the Sul. A flurry of motion began, some of the people already heading off in the distance, racing down the dunes in the opposite direction from which they'd come.

"After you," Lazar said, finally smiling. He held his hand out ahead of him in invitation. Then he frowned again and glanced back at Druturion. "The dragon stays."

Kayda nodded and strode forward. *I'll be back. Don't have too much fun without me.*

Druturion snorted, shaking out his wings and lounging back in the sun. *Don't go getting yourself killed, Princess.*

Kayda shrugged, catching up to Jayan. Whatever this test was, these *sandborn* could handle it. They'd handle it, too.

"Hey, Jayan. What did kind of trouble did I land us in?" she asked, her voice so quiet it could barely be heard over the sand shifting beneath their feet.

His face screwed up in a grimace. "It's all right. I'll walk you through it. The silk harvest—it's a two-person job." He rubbed his neck, gaze flicking to the ground. "It's been years since I've done it, but I still remember how... It's not something you'll ever forget."

Well, that sounded ominous.

"Wait, silk harvest? I thought the silk came from the river butterflies' cocoons?"

Jayan shook his head. "That's where most silk comes from. But the really fine stuff—like on that golden dress you were gifted this morning—that can only be found out here in the Waste."

Kayda scrutinized the scenery, her head tilting slightly. "There are no butterflies out here..."

"Butterflies aren't the only creatures that spin silk. Think bigger. Scarier."

Dread stole her breath, her stomach sinking like she'd swallowed a belly full of sand.

"Don't worry, Princess." He leaned close, sending her a wobbly grin. "You can be the bait."

Chapter 9

"Here we are." Taul guided his black stallion to the top of a small hill. "Norwich. It ain't much to look at, but at least there's an inn."

Conall led his white stallion to a stop beside him. Delyth's brown mare nickered behind him. He stared down at the tiny village perched on the Northern Depths' edge beside the mouth of the Gran River. The town couldn't have held more than a few dozen ramshackle wooden buildings, all of them dusted liberally with snow.

This far north, the snow never melted, and this late in the fall, blizzards were common. They'd been lucky to only encounter one so far. Taul shrugged it off, claiming it was milder than most, but the blistering wind and near blinding snowfall had been worse than the strongest winter storm in Dracwood. Still, they'd survived. Pressing on doggedly through the storm, hunkered down in their thick furs.

Even the horses were coated in furs. Bred for centuries to survive the harsh winters; they sported thick coats all over their bodies. They'd even adapted to accept an omnivorous diet, although given the choice, they still favored grain like the short-haired horses of his homeland.

They still had one thing in common with their southern cousins. An uneasy relationship with wolves. Shadow had trailed behind them for most of the journey north, only slinking into camp at night to avoid upsetting the skittish mounts.

"Brother. We've reached Norwich. How soon can you catch up?"

"Not long. I'm just behind you," Shadow replied.

Conall dismounted, his boots sinking into the soft snow. He handed Taul his reins. "I'll wait here for Shadow, and we'll meet you at the inn."

"All right." Taul pointed his gloved finger at a large building on the eastern edge of town. "That's the Hearth's Rest Inn. I'll see the mounts find a spot in the stable, and we'll all meet for a hot meal."

Delyth nodded in agreement, leading her mare to trot beside Taul down the hill into town. Soon, they disappeared between buildings, and Shadow materialized beside Conall, his gray fur crusted with white frost.

They headed into town silently. Conall trudged down the hillside, admiring his bondmate's nimbleness even when navigating the thick snow.

Frankly, he was sick of the cold. He kept his stare locked on the little inn as he stumbled through the snow and ice, images of a blazing fire and a warm bed playing in his mind.

Soon, they approached the Hearth's Rest Inn. Music and laughter leaked through the walls, bubbling up in the air as Conall shoved open the heavy wooden door and stepped inside. The heat from the enormous brick fireplace hit his face, and he sighed.

The place was crowded with people. The wooden tables were almost all occupied with rowdy villagers chugging ale and talking boisterously. In the far right corner, a bearded man plucked a lute, his long fingers dancing over the strings merrily. A smile pricked at Conall's lips as his cheeks tingled with warmth, and the delicious scent of hearty stew made his stomach rumble.

"Ho, Conall." Taul waved him over to a table near the hearth.

Conall stomped the snow from his boots, strode over, and sank down into a seat, removing his gloves. Shadow shook the snow from his fur and followed but turned at the last instant and curled up to rest beside the fire.

The innkeeper eyed Shadow as he hustled over to their table. "That a wolf?" The old man tugged his gray beard, blinking rapidly. "I don't need my patrons being hunted."

Delyth smiled and flicked a coin on the table before Conall had the chance to answer. "He's trained. You won't have to worry about Shadow. I imagine he's better behaved than half your patrons."

The innkeeper's blue eyes gleamed, a laugh falling from his lips. "I imagine you might be right on that count. What can I get you folks?"

"We'll need rooms for the night. Food and drink. Whatever you recommend, as long as it's hot." Delyth pulled more coins from her coin purse, and the innkeeper nodded readily. He pocketed the money and rushed off to arrange things.

Taul laughed. "He's going to wait on you hand and foot all night. That's likely more money than he sees in a month."

Delyth shrugged. "I won't be here long enough to be a bother to him. As soon as I eat and the rooms are ready, I'm heading up for a decent night's sleep. We leave on the morrow, Conall. There's no time to waste."

Conall nodded once, meeting Delyth's eyes.

"I still can't believe you're heading to the Witch this time of year." Taul leaned back in his chair. "The Depths are impassable after the frost sets in. Not even the bravest fishermen are willing to sail now. I mean, why'd ya think this place is so busy in the middle of the day? I bet in the spring and summer this inn doesn't get a lick of business until the sun goes down."

Delyth shook her head. "I'm afraid it can't wait that long. We'll make our way alone. All we need is someone willing to rent us a boat."

The innkeeper returned, carrying three flagons of ale. "You need to rent a boat? I've a row boat I can part with for another one of those coins."

"Thank you. That would be most helpful." Delyth smiled, handing off another coin.

Delyth was true to her word. She quickly ate the hot stew and disappeared into her room, leaving Conall alone at the table with Taul. They sat listening to the lutist for a time, slowly sipping their ale.

It was a strange feeling, to rest in an inn, enjoying a hearty meal and entertainment, surrounded by people chatting happily, and not running for their lives or on a mission to save the world. For so long, all he'd known was hardship and fear. First, the fear for his sister. That familiar wash of worry he'd been unable to quench. And now, fear for his country. For the entire world even, if what Delyth said about the *ichneumon*, the scourge, came to pass.

For once—for this one single moment in time—he pushed his fears aside and grabbed this tiny sliver of normalcy. After all, this was what he'd fought for. The chance to one day be one of those old men gathered around a table, his belly full and his heart filled with laughter. Those days would come again for the people in his country. He would make sure of it.

They departed the inn early the next morning. Conall's breath fogged the air as he trudged with Delyth and Shadow down the snow-covered streets to the docks.

Taul had agreed to wait in Norwich for two weeks, although the dubious way he rolled his eyes at their plans gave the impression he didn't hold out much hope of the two of them returning. When Conall took his first glance at the Northern Depths' waters, he could see why.

Ice floated everywhere on the shifting waves. Chunks as small as a grain of sand joined larger flat sheets that shined like glass in the morning sun. In the distance, dozens of gargantuan icebergs slammed about in the surf, twisting, tumbling, and occasionally smashing together with such force they cracked through the air like thunder.

Delyth led him to a tiny wooden rowboat tied to a rickety wooden dock. His stomach buckled as his gaze shifted between the small craft and the dark, frozen waters.

"You want to take that... out there?" His brows rose, and his chest tightened.

She chuckled, tossing her bag on the front bench and seating herself beside it. "Yes. You take care of rowing. I'll navigate."

Conall shrugged. It was too late to turn back now. He hopped in and seated himself in the back of the boat He stashed his bag on the floor and grabbed the oars.

"I don't like the looks of that water. Or that boat." Shadow backed up down the dock, his tail tucked between his legs.

"C'mon, Shadow. Delyth knows what she's doing. Hop on board."

Shadow crept forward slowly, for once looking less than fleet-footed on the shifting dock. *"Fine. But if we sink, I'm swimming back to shore without you."*

Shadow jumped aboard. He crouched on the boat's bottom by Conall's feet.

"Which way should I head?"

"You'll see. Just a moment." Delyth's hand slipped over the side of the boat and hovered above the water. She took a deep breath and closed her eyes.

When her lashes lifted a heartbeat later, the air flooded with moisture, and Conall's skin prickled like he'd fallen in a pricker bush. A path opened before them in the icy water, wide enough for three boats their size to slide through abreast.

So that's why Delyth didn't fear the Northern Depths.

"I didn't realize you had water talent as well as air," he said.

"I've a touch of earth talent, too." She smiled and stared off into the sea. "My family has been blessed. For generations, they've sought other talented folk to be their partners, and that's led to a generous inheritance."

"Huh." Conall rowed, steering through the hole Delyth made in the ice.

A quiet sigh escaped her.

Was she reminiscing about her daughter? Ereni's absence had affected both of them in different ways. He couldn't imagine what Delyth must be feeling, to have been betrayed by her own child.

At the same time, he was nursing his own wounds. Was that all he'd been to Ereni? A talented partner to add to the family inheritance?

He would be lying if he said he never thought of her. Though he wished it wasn't the case, her face was still fresh in his mind most nights when he closed his eyes. Was she out there somewhere, still fighting?

Or had she been lost to the first wave of the creatures she'd helped to unleash on the world?

They sailed for ages. Conall's arms ached from rowing. Delyth's shoulders slumped, the energy she used to maintain their clear path through the water weighing on her. The width of the clear water before them slowly decreased until flecks of ice stuck to the oar's tips.

Thankfully, they arrived at a spot where the ice grew thick enough to walk on. They clambered out of the boat on top of the slick ice. He helped Delyth pull the boat free from the sea, and they dragged it behind them across the snowy wasteland.

It took them long hours to cross, each of them taking turns pulling the heavy wooden boat, only to arrive at more icy water. They crawled back into the boat, setting sail once more as the sun sank down in the sky.

Conall's fingers twitched beneath his thick gloves as he rowed. Would they reach their destination before nightfall? His toes had long ago gone numb with cold. The temperature continued to sink the farther they traveled. Even Shadow shivered, curling into a tiny ball on the chilled wooden boards. How long could they last in this bitter water once night fell?

Of the three of them, Delyth fared the worst. She'd started to cough as they'd trudged across the ice. Now that they sailed again, she'd begun to shiver violently, her teeth chattering and her whole body quaking every so often from a rattling cough.

The path before them through the water was so narrow tiny specks of ice jostled the boat's sides with every stroke. Conall's shoulders ached, and his nerves jolted every time they came close to the larger chunks of ice floating just out of reach.

Blazes. If only he'd not been so stubborn, maybe he'd have already figured out how to overcome his block and he could've helped to clear the way instead of just rowing blindly.

As the sun dipped down below the waves, painting the sky in shades of pink, purple, and orange, a spit of land emerged on the horizon. On it, a tiny shack sat, lit from inside with a warm glow seeping out the windows. Conall breathed a sigh of relief, rowing with renewed vigor toward the succor of the single spot of civilization on the frozen island.

The sky darkened, turning the water pitch black. By the time they trudged to the shack, stars twinkled, and the full moon shone down on the ice.

Delyth strode to the door and knocked firmly on it.

Conall's heart sped up as tapping footsteps drew closer, and the doorknob slowly spun.

Warmth and light escaped the building. He shielded his eyes from the sudden glare. A young woman stuck her head out, her sharp blue eyes sliding over each of them before she threw the door wide open and disappeared inside without a word.

Delyth didn't waste any time following her inside. Shadow bounded in on her tail, leaving Conall to slip in last and pull the door closed behind him.

He inhaled as he entered. The pungent scents of wood smoke and fish filled the tiny shack. The wooden walls were unadorned and the room practically bare. Stacked beside the door, a few sacks and boxes burst at the seams with all manner of things. Aside from the hearth, which Shadow had already curled up next to, and a small wooden table and single chair, the only other thing of note in the shack was its lone occupant.

The woman wasn't at all what he'd been picturing. She sat by the far wall, on a bed piled with furs, her legs tucked beneath a plain brown dress. Long golden curls spilled down her shoulders, framing a face of staggering beauty.

This was the Winter Witch? She appeared barely older than he was. Rather, how he would look had he not been prematurely aged. Yet Delyth claimed to have met her before, many years ago. How was that possible?

Delyth was the first to break the silence. She sighed as she sank down on the lone chair, her eyelids drooping with fatigue. "Freya has awakened, I take it?"

Conall cocked a brow at the odd question.

The young woman nodded solemnly. "Yes, Freya dreamed her last dream this past spring. I am Halynn. The new dreamer."

"I am—"

"I know who you are, Sade Prim. That you travel with shadows and trapped boys." Her gaze flicked to him.

He stared into the icy blue depths of her eyes. Something strange glittered back at him. An ageless wisdom that belied her youthful features. His breath caught until she looked away.

She patted the furs beside her in invitation, a smile spreading across her lips. "Come. Sit."

He crossed the room and sank down on the soft mattress beside her. Delyth, her head resting on her hands on the table, softly snored. The exhaustion of clearing their path through the ice had caught up to her.

It left the two of them, essentially, alone. Not many beautiful young women would be keen to have a strange man on their bed. But Halynn did not cower. She leaned forward, closing the distance between them, and peered straight into his face.

She laughed. It wasn't a girlish giggle or a simple chuckle, but an explosion of mirth, like his face was the most amusing thing she'd seen in her entire life.

Conall's ears heated as he stared back at her.

"I'm sorry," she said finally, wiping a tear from the corner of her eye. "It's bizarre, is all, seeing someone in the flesh you've only seen before in your dreams." She patted his knee, her eyes twinkling. "Don't worry. Soon, you'll understand."

Chapter 10

Lark awoke slowly, lying flat on a soft mattress. A wooden roof shaded her head, and all around her, green fabric floated. She groaned, stretching. Relief flooded her as her muscles complied. All except for her right hand.

She twisted away from the ceiling and spotted why. "Aren?"

He perched on a wooden stool, gripping her hand tightly, his eyes closed. At the sound of her voice, he jolted, eyes shooting open, a smile lighting his face. "Lark, you're awake." He leaned forward and squeezed her fingers. "How're you feeling?"

She met his gaze, her cheeks heating. "I can move, at least."

What about her leg? The pain was gone, but she was covered with a thin sheet. She started to sit, easing up on her elbows.

"Here, let me help you." Aren dropped her hand and slid an arm around her shoulders to lever her up.

She sucked in a breath, peeking at him from beneath her lashes. "Thanks." Then she flicked the sheet off her legs, certain she would see a bloody mark where the snake bit her, but there was nothing. Just perfect, intact skin. If it wasn't for the jagged hole torn into her sheer pants, she could almost convince herself it had all been a dream.

Incredible.

"Muse?" she reached out with her thoughts. *"Where are you?"*

"Good, you're awake. I'm outside. That rude healer wouldn't let me follow you in. If he hadn't just saved you, I would've clawed his eyes out."

She resisted the urge to giggle at her bondmate's indignant tone. *"I'm glad you didn't before I got the chance to thank him. I'm feeling much better, Muse. I'll come find you soon."*

She smiled and took another look around. Except for the cot she lay on, and the stool, she couldn't see anything beyond the curtains except for the occasional shadowy movement somewhere beyond their little private bubble. "Where are we?"

Aren stood right next to her, his strong arm wrapped around her shoulders. She leaned against him, taking comfort in his strength.

"We're in the healing hut, in Stoneshore." He gave her shoulder a squeeze. "The others are with Mata Moyra. She offered to show them where we'll be staying while we're here."

"Oh. You didn't go with them?" She stole another look at him. Her heart sped up. He was so close.

He met her gaze and slowly shook his head. "No, I—"

The rattle of hooks sliding and the swoosh of fabric interrupted him. Light streamed in as the curtains were drawn back. The man from the mountain glided in—the mage she'd come here to meet—her savior, Mika.

"Hello, Lark." Mika offered her a polite smile. "I thought I heard you two talking. I'm happy to see you're awake. How are you feeling?"

Aren kept his arm wrapped around her, a tiny frown flashing for an instant before he smoothed his features.

She swallowed and turned to Mika. "I'm great, thanks to you." She grinned, sticking out a hand. "Thank you for saving me."

He shook her hand, nodding perfunctorily. "Yes, of course. It's what I do." He dropped her hand and strode closer. "Let me just check a few things." He slid a glance at Aren, nodding toward the stool. "Do you mind?"

Aren's arm tensed slightly, but he released her shoulders and sat on the stool without a word.

Mika drew closer and stared into her eyes. He placed two fingers gently on her neck. "Are you experiencing any dizziness?"

"No."

He nodded, moving to examine her leg. He skimmed his fingers over her calf, firmly prodding her flesh. "Do you feel any pain?"

She shook her head. "Nothing." She smiled.

Mika nodded again, seeming satisfied. "You need to take it easy for the rest of the day. Get plenty to eat and a good night's sleep. You're going to be just fine." He turned to leave.

"Wait." She grabbed his sleeve. "I came here to learn how to be a better healer. Mata Moyra said you—"

He shook free of her hold. "Yes, we've spoken. I'll teach you, but not until you've rested." He grinned and turned to leave again. "I'm here every morning just after dawn. Don't be late." He grabbed the curtain, and instead of pulling it closed, he slid it open fully. "Go. You don't need to stay here any longer."

Aren rose to his feet. The wooden stool clattered across the floor as he rushed to grab her arm. "Let me help you."

She hopped down off the cot. "I'm all right, Aren." She let him steady her all the same, then linked their arms together.

She half expected her leg to buckle when she shifted her weight onto it, but it held her with no pain. She let out a sigh and glanced around as

Aren led her across the room. The healing hut was a large rectangular building, lined with cots and filled with a multitude of potted plants.

She only gave it a quick look, pleased she'd have the chance to examine it more tomorrow. Finally, she'd found the teacher she'd been searching for. The thought had her smile widening as they opened the screened door and slipped out into the late afternoon sunshine.

The village looked much the same as all the others they'd passed through during their time in Raimire. The jungle loomed on all sides, shading the wooden huts crowded inside the town clearing. There were people all over, gathered together chatting in small groups. An air of excitement pervaded the village, no doubt due to their group's arrival and the promise of live performances.

"Lark." Tiora rushed to her side. "You're all better?" She tilted her head, examining her leg beneath the torn green fabric.

"Yeah, I'm all right." Lark sent a smile to Tiora and a nod to Mazen and Meital as they joined them.

Tiora grabbed her arm and tugged, pulling her away from Aren. "C'mon, you've got to see where we're staying. It's so cute."

Mazen fell in beside Aren. "I'll take you to our hut, Aren. It's this way."

"Don't let her do anything strenuous, Ti. She's supposed to be resting," Aren called out.

Tiora waved him off. "I won't, I promise."

Tiora led the way to the village's center. Meital trailed just behind them. Muse shadowed their movements, hopping from hut to hut. Soon, they found themselves in front of a small hut, practically identical to all the others from the outside, except for a dagger sticking out of the wooden door frame.

Lark raised a brow at Meital.

"What? These huts all look the same to me." Meital chuckled, making no effort to hide her smug smile.

Lark held back the screen so Muse could fly in, then followed the others inside. Sunny hopped up off the dirt floor and bustled over to greet her, tail wagging. Lark leaned down to tussle her ears as she took her first look around the wooden structure.

This hut was smaller than the healing hut, with three cots and a wide wooden bench serving as furniture. Brightly colored sheets and pillows adorned the beds, and the sun shone through green-screened windows, giving the space an earthy feel.

"Here, Lark. I put your things over here." Tiora pointed to the cot that sat beside the bench.

Lark sank down on the bed with a smile. The short hike across the village had her more worn out than she should be. Maybe Mika had it right when he said she still needed to rest.

Muse settled on the bench beside her. *"You got anything to eat?"*

Lark didn't bother holding back the giggle that bubbled up. When Tiora and Meital peered at her in question, she sent them a crooked smile and dug in her pack. "Sometimes I think Muse just sticks around me for the snacks."

She pulled out a pouch full of dried meat and placed a handful on the bench. *"Here, have at it."*

"Ha. That'll do till I get my claws on one of those monkeys in the morning."

Lark rolled her eyes, grabbing a piece of jerky for herself. "This is kinda cute." She popped the bite in her mouth, then tossed the pouch to Tiora.

"Yeah, real cozy." Meital lounged back on her cot and kicked off her boots.

Tiora pulled out a piece of jerky and lifted the pouch to toss it to Meital, but Meital shook her head and leaned further back on the bright pillows.

"I bet you lived somewhere like this when you and Mazen were kids." Lark caught the pouch and stuffed it back in her pack.

Meital sighed. "Not as long as I would've liked."

"What do you mean, Mei? Isn't all of Raimire like this?" Tiora asked.

"Not Slinas, the port city to the east. That's where our father brought us to live after our mother died." She wrapped an arm around her chest. "He was a seeker. Spent all his time trekking through the jungle, searching for rare flowers and exotic creatures to fill the menageries of foreign buyers. We were eight when Ma got sick." She scowled. "Da couldn't be bothered to travel all the way north to our little village after she passed, even though some of the villagers would've been happy to take us in. He stuck us in a boarding house in Slinas instead, with a bunch of other kids of seekers."

Her admission tore at Lark's heart. "I'm so sorry. You lost your mother and your home all at once."

"I'm sorry, too." Tiora spun the meat in her hands, her brows drawing together and features softening.

Meital forced a smile. "I had Mazen there with me. It wasn't so bad. At least, not at first. They left us alone, mostly. That's where me and Maz got so good with our knives. Da gifted us each a set before he dumped us there." She flashed a crooked grin. "We had a lot of time to practice."

Lark sat silently, not pushing, waiting to see if Meital would finally share the whole of their story. She and Mazen had shared dozens of stories about their pasts in the time they'd spent together, but they were always lighthearted and adventurous. This was the first time either of them had opened up about the hard times they'd had to face.

Dausius always introduced the twins during the show by spinning a tale of how he found them, living by their wits, dodging jungle cats and venomous snakes in Raimire. Neither of them refuted his claims. Was it just an exaggeration played out for the crowd, or was there a kernel of truth to his tale?

Meital sat up and folded her legs, gripping her knees tightly. "Me and Maz kept to ourselves. It was a few years before we noticed what was happening there. That the people who ran the place weren't the gentle caretakers they made themselves out to be to Da."

Lark's eyes widened. "What was happening?"

"Being a seeker is a dangerous job. Lots of kids lost their fathers. To make up for it, they demanded a premium. The contract our father signed, and the huge down payment he made, provided we wouldn't be tossed out on the streets should he not make payments, for whatever reason." She pulled her knees closer, her head tilting down. "We began to notice something strange happening to the kids whose parents disappeared. After a few missed payments, they suddenly had an endless stream of uncles appearing for late night visits. Uncles that usually looked nothing like them."

Lark's stomach turned. She could guess what was happening. To poor kids with no one there to look out for them, no less. It was sickening.

Tiora's face blanched. "That's awful."

Meital nodded, staring blankly out the screened window. "We were fifteen the last time we saw Da. By then, we didn't just suspect what was happening. We knew." She grimaced and shook her head. "We didn't stick around to meet our long-lost uncles."

"Where did you go?" Lark asked.

"We spent a few months living on the streets in Slinas. It's a whole different world there. Slinas is the one place in Raimire the Matas hold no power. The city's overrun with rough men and women who only care about coin." She turned from the window, a wry smile on her lips. "We had nothing. Just each other and our knives. We ended up doing whatever odd jobs we could find to survive. Picked a few pockets when we had to."

Tiora frowned. "That sounds terrible. Why didn't you go back to the village you were born in?"

"That was our plan." Meital shrugged. "But you've been in the jungle. If you go anywhere without a guide and the proper supplies, you won't last the night. We saved every spare coin we could scrape together, but it was never enough."

"And that's when Dausius found you?" Lark asked.

"Yep." Meital wrinkled her nose, tilting her head sideways. "He saved us, really. Caught Mazen red-handed, lifting his coin purse. He could've turned us in, but he offered us a job instead." She grinned. "The rest is history."

Lark smiled and rose off her cot, plunking down next to Meital. "I'm glad he found you." She slung an arm around her and pulled her close.

The bed sank an instant later as Tiora joined them. "Me too." Tiora joined in the hug, and they all started giggling.

"I think they put me in the wrong hut," Mazen announced as he slipped in the screened door, his arms loaded with bowls filled with something steaming and fragrant. He offloaded the bowls onto the bench next to Muse and approached his sister's cot as the girls pulled apart. "Hey, no fair! I missed cuddle time?"

Aren popped in behind him, a smile lighting his face, carrying more bowls. "Don't worry, you can cuddle with me and Whisper later," he offered with a wink. That set off another round of laughter.

Mazen shrugged, his smile mischievous. "Can't blame a guy for trying." Then he scooped up a bowl and handed it to his sister. "We brought stew. Smells pretty good."

Lark stood and grabbed one of the bowls Aren carried, then sat back down on her cot and patted the mattress next to her. "Have a seat."

Aren sat beside her. Mazen with Meital and Tiora. The stew melted in her mouth, and laughter filled her ears, warming a place in Lark's heart that lived for times like these. There was nothing like sharing a meal with friends.

Once again, she found herself marveling at the amazing friends she'd found. She wasn't sure what she would've done without them. At every turn, they'd been there to support her in her mission to learn more about her earth talent.

As much as she loved spending time with them, a small part of her was worried about what would happen now. After all, her journey had ended, for now at least. She'd found the mage she'd been searching for and would need to stay here to train. What would happen to her friends? Would they stay, or would they move on?

Lark sighed, finishing her stew and forcing the thought aside. There would be time for those worries later. She planned to enjoy every moment she had with her friends and save the questions for another day.

Chapter 11

Kayda had sand everywhere. A fine layer dusted her entire body, chafing her sweat-slicked skin. It snuck into her boots, crunching between her toes as she followed the crowd of Sul across the Waste's dunes.

"Not much farther now," Jayan said at her side.

She shaded her eyes, blocking the setting sun's glare. "How can you tell? There's just dunes and more dunes."

Jayan pointed to the sand. "Look, tracks. We're getting close to the mountains if we can see azaros prints."

"Azaros?"

"They're small lizards, no bigger than your forearm. They come down from the mountains at dusk to feed on the sandflies."

Sandflies... could they be the creatures whose cocoons they'd come to harvest? Kayda frowned. "I haven't seen any flies."

"You wouldn't have." Jayan grabbed her elbow as she struggled to climb an especially steep dune. "They're nocturnal. Most creatures of the Waste are." His eyes lit up as he reached the dune's top. "What did I tell ya? There they are. The Anaraine Mountains."

Kayda shaded her eyes again as she clambered atop the shifting sand. As she crested the rise, the sun sank below the mountains, and her hand dropped slack at her side.

The Anariane Mountains stretched out diagonally across the horizon in all their majestic glory. Now this was what she thought of when someone said mountain, not the sorry excuse for hills the Sul called home. The range spanned the horizon and rose high in the air, taller than the highest trees of her homeland.

Kayda sucked in a breath, gaping at the colossal jagged peaks. Much of the rock was the same burnt orange as the dunes they'd just traversed, but layered in between were a myriad of other colors. Copper, rust-red, and even hints of pearl and silver abounded, sparkling in the places where the sun's dying rays peeked through the multitude of holes in the rock.

Some of the Sul had already mounted the mountain's lower slopes and prodded the ground with the bottoms of their wooden staffs, searching within the craggy landscape for—something.

"Is that where we're headed?" she asked.

"Yes. Quickly now, we don't want to be out on the dunes unprepared after dusk."

Kayda gulped, then half running, half sliding, she followed Jayan down the dune and scrambled atop the rock wall before her. Luckily, the slope was modest this close to the ground, and it was an easy climb. Still, she was out of breath by the time Jayan bid her stop and turn, not used to such physical activity in the heat.

Kayda tugged the neck of her billowy white tunic, attempting to cool her heated skin. Whoops echoed from somewhere further up the slope, followed by an animal shrieking and hissing. "What was that?"

"Sounds like they found a duncoon."

Her brow furrowing, she opened her mouth to ask for further explanation, but snapped it closed as Lazar vaulted over a rock and landed beside Jayan.

"Will you be the harvester?" the Sul leader asked, his stare locked on Jayan's face.

"Aye." Jayan replied.

Lazar tilted his head, glancing at her face before flicking his gaze lower, down her torso. "Do you bleed?"

"Excuse me?" she asked, unable to hide the hint of incredulity in her tone or the blush warming her cheeks.

Jayan squeezed her forearm, leaning close, his voice soft. "It's important we know, Princess. You have to answer, truthfully."

She glared at Lazar, meeting his dark brown eyes. She could feel her cheeks burning but refused to drop her gaze. "No."

Lazar grunted, then reached down on his belt, pulled free a dented metal flask, and thrust it toward her. "Drink this."

Kayda backed up a pace and grabbed her own belt, jiggling her waterskin. "I brought my own water."

Jayan jumped in. "It's not water. You're gonna want to drink it."

Kayda frowned, her gaze flicking from the flask back to Lazar's face.

Lazar stared back at her, his expression flat, making no move to retract his hand. "Drink."

She plucked the smooth metal from his fingers, twisted off the lid, and took a sniff. The liquid sloshed within, giving off an odd metallic scent, no doubt from the container. If Jayan hadn't said otherwise, she would've guessed it water, but it was clear from the way they both watched her expectantly it was anything but.

She lifted it to her lips and took a tentative sip. When the liquid touched her tongue, she grimaced, wanting nothing more than to spit out the bitter brew. But she resisted the urge and swallowed. "Ugh, what is that?"

Lazar stared back at her, stone-faced. "More."

She glanced at Jayan. He nodded to the flask.

She scowled but lifted the liquid to her lips and took another swallow. The fluid was thicker than water, coating her tongue with a layer of foul, syrupy goo. She gulped it down hastily, praying the man wouldn't insist she drink more. But that amount seemed to satisfy Lazar. He jerked the flask from her hands and hopped upon a nearby rock, vanishing as quickly as he'd arrived.

Kayda spun to face Jayan, hands on her hips. "What was that vile drink? Why did he ask me *that*? What's going on here, Jayan?"

The scrape of a thousand claws on rock interrupted his answer. A sudden symphony of scratching and scrambling assaulted her ears as the sun slipped down below the horizon and the azaros emerged. The small orange lizards climbed free from the holes in the ground in the hundreds and raced for the dunes.

Jayan slid up beside her. They stared at the dunes as the cacophonous scratching died down. "Watch. The sandflies will be next."

Kayda squinted in the dimming light. "I don't see any—"

She gasped. Thousands—no, more like hundreds of thousands—of tiny specks broke free from the sand. They shot into the air, forming a cloud of glittering dust and fluttering wings. The azaros went crazy, their tongues flicking out, stabbing into the cloud and crunching down flies like starving children let loose in a sweets shop.

The sky brightened behind her. She started to turn, but Jayan shook his head and clasped her arm.

"Don't look at the torches. You'll want your eyes adjusted to the dark."

She stared down at the dunes again, watching the cloud of tiny flies thicken. "I thought you said the silk spinners would be bigger?"

"Oh, they are." He pointed to the dunes' edge. "Look, here comes a duncoon."

A hound-sized creature crept across the mountain's bottom edge. It was short-haired, similar in build to the foxes of Dracwood but longer and wider, with dark brown fur, pointed ears, and a long, skinny tail.

"The azaros come for the sandflies. The duncoons, for the azaros," Jayan explained, as the duncoon leapt forward, snatching a lizard off the sand and lifting it to its mouth with its clawed fists. "The creatures we're here for, they hunt the duncoons." He pointed, just behind the furred creature. "Look, in the dune."

The sand on the dune shifted, unbeknownst to the duncoon who'd viciously snapped off the lizard's head. Something was preparing to break free from the dune. Something massive. The pointed tip of a hairy brown leg poked free from the sand.

Kayda's eyes widened so much they ached within her skull. There was something familiar about that appendage. A cold sweat broke out on her neck.

The sand stopped shifting, with just that one leg peeking out. Then it blasted outward in all directions as the creature within burst free.

Blazes. Bloody blazes! Kayda stared in horror as goosebumps spread across her skin. It had to be a spider. Of course, it was.

The massive beast attacked from the air. Spiny hairs shot free from its abdomen and pummeled the sand like a hail of nettles. The duncoon only had time to look up and squeal before it was stabbed with the barbs and dropped on its face, motionless. Dozens of the lizards were caught in the crossfire. A few escaped and scampered away across the dunes, but a handful were impaled with barbs and fell down to the sand.

All of this happened in the fraction of an instant the spider flew through the air, scattering flies in every direction. It landed in a slide, then it clambered across the sand straight for the poor duncoon.

It swept it up with its spindly legs and twisted and twirled the creature, covering it in layer upon layer of the sticky silk that it exuded from the bottom of its abdomen.

"The tetrela. They're ambush predators. The spider silk is fine enough the duncoon can breathe, even while buried under the sand, but strong enough to keep it trapped after the barbs' poison wears off in a few hours. The tetrela will pull it underground and keep it alive for a few days, slowly sipping on its blood until it drains it."

Dread coiled in Kayda's belly as the helpless duncoon disappeared under layers of sheer silk. "Those things were under the sand the whole time we walked here?"

"Yes. But they only attack at night. Look at their eyes."

Kayda lifted her gaze to the creature's face. It had four pairs of huge black orbs.

"They're made for hunting in the dark," Jayan explained. "The sunlight can blind them."

Movement caught her eye near the tetrela's feet. An azaros, pierced in the back with the tetrela's spiky barb, struggled up on shaky legs and scampered off.

"I thought you said the barb's poison lasted for hours?" Even more of the impaled lizards lurched to their feet and bolted away from the tetrela as fast as their wobbly legs would carry them.

"The azaros have something in their blood. It counteracts the barbs toxin." Jayan smiled.

Kayda's hand rose to her lips, recalling that viscous liquid on her tongue. "Please tell me that's not what I just drank..." She shuddered, revulsion mingling with fear in the pit of her stomach. He'd said she would be the bait. "Jayan, how exactly do we harvest spider silk?"

"The tetrela prefer to drag their prey beneath the sand." As if on cue, the giant spider stopped spinning and dropped the silk-shrouded duncoon to the sand. Holding onto a length of silk like a rope, it dove back into a dune. Submerging itself beneath the dune, it tugged the bundled creature behind it. "It will climb back to the top of the dune and wait for more prey. The only time they break this cycle is if their prey is injured during their fight. If it smells blood spilling on the sand, it will drain the duncoon dry then and there."

"That's why you had to know…" Her cheeks warmed again.

"Yes. But we use this knowledge to our advantage. One of the Sul will march out on the sand. Let the tetrela cover them in silk. The harvester will follow, carrying a duncoon."

Kayda's eyes widened, recalling the Sul stabbing the rocks as they arrived. The animal shrieking she'd heard soon after.

"The harvester slices the duncoon and drops it nearby on the sand. When the tetrela scents the blood in the air, it abandons spinning, and heads for the quick meal, content to finish spinning its prisoner after. Then the harvester can sneak in and rescue their partner, silk and all."

Kayda trembled. "I'm just supposed to go out there and let that thing smother me?" Her voice rose, ending on a shrill note. She narrowed her eyes. "Why am I the bait?"

Jayan rubbed the back of his neck. "A successful harvest is a matter of timing—precision. There's only a short moment for the harvester to drag his partner away from the dunes. You're much smaller than me, Princess."

Kayda exhaled and clenched her hands together. He was right, of course. She'd struggle to pull him across the dunes, whereas he'd have little trouble lifting her scant weight. But the fact didn't help calm the tingling sensation swarming across her skin when she imagined that disgusting spider having her within its grasp.

She drew a deep breath and did her best to ignore the visceral terror quaking through her body. She had to pass this test. It was the only way to uncover the secrets of her mother's past.

Lazar appeared with a squirming duncoon slung under his arm. The Sul had tied a length of rope around its muzzle and each of its legs. But though the creature couldn't snap its jaws or scratch with its claws, it continued to buck and moan. Its short fur bristled and quaked with fury.

Lazar dropped the critter by Jayan's feet. Then he targeted his glare on her. "It's time."

Jayan grabbed her hand and slipped something small and hard into her palm. He pulled her close, his breath whispering over her ear, sending a tingle down her spine. "Just in case."

Enclosing the tiny object within her fist, she met his eyes one last time and fought the urge to scowl at the gleam of excitement she spied within their depths. Then she turned and climbed down the rocks toward the dunes.

It wasn't until she'd almost arrived at the sand that she unclenched her hand and took a peek at her mystery gift. It was a tiny switchblade. She'd seen Jayan use it countless times onboard *Nova's Champion* when handling repairs to the rigging. She shoved the small blade into her pants pocket, but it didn't bring her much relief. It would barely be enough to scratch the behemoth tetrela.

She paused on the sand's edge and squinted into the darkness that had only grown thicker since she'd reached the bottom of the mountain. Her skin itched as sweat trickled down her back, her mouth dry as she swallowed for the hundredth time.

Was she really about to do this? Allow herself to be struck with a barb, imprisoned by that monster, and wait to be rescued?

Yes. She had to.

Kayda blew out a steadying breath and lifted her foot, striking out across the dune. Raising a hand to her face, she swatted the air, trying to clear the space in front of her of the tiny sandflies.

Now that she was within the cloud, the reason for the insect's strange frenzy became clear. Hundreds upon hundreds of the bugs were clasped together as they floated, copulating in mid-air. Even more flew in erratic patterns, attempting to attract the attention of a mate, no doubt.

Kayda shuddered, pushing down her disgust. It was not bad enough she was about to be manhandled by a mammoth arachnid; she was barging into the middle of a fly orgy as well. Yuck.

She stared at her feet, watching her boots sinking into the sand, and tried to ignore the countless fluttering wings jostling her skin as she barreled through the cloud of randy insects.

Before long, the shifting sand on the dune caught her attention. She gulped and crouched down on the sand, making herself as small a target as possible, preparing for the fall to the ground.

Even though she knew it was coming, nothing prepared her for the blast of sand and the tetrela's emergence. Her heart hammered against her ribs, her arms instinctively covering her head against the rain of barbs streaking through the sky. A barb pierced her in each of her arms, and a third stabbed into the back of her neck.

The effect was instant. A sharp, fleeting pain, followed immediately by her limbs shooting out, suddenly as stiff and unyielding as the stone mountains she'd just stood on. She slammed into the sand face-first. All of her muscles contracted painfully, and her body locked up.

With her face pressed into the ground, she didn't see the tetrela approaching. But she heard the sand skittering in her ears. She felt the vibrations surrounding her as its huge hairy legs pummeled toward her.

Revulsion and fear swamped her. She fought to cope with the panic ricocheting within her chest as the beast lifted her prone body from the dune and spun her with its gargantuan legs. Her chest was tight, and her breath hitched, her throat suddenly locking up like she was choking.

Her eyes bulged as the beast flipped her, and she got her first close look at it. It was easily twice her size, covered in thick brown hairs all over its body. From where she lay beneath it, she couldn't see its face, but it had a set of sharp black fangs that curved underneath its chin, which sent shivers of ice through her veins.

Though she tried with every fiber of her body to move, she was paralyzed, forced to hang on while the hairy behemoth twirled her. The urge to summon was palpable. If it wasn't for the promise of answers, she'd have called forth the flames; consequences be damned. But she resisted the urge and ignored the voice within screaming at her to burn this massive beast to the ground.

Silk clouded her vision as it spun her. The tetrela moved incredibly fast. Lark's head swam with dizziness, her tense limbs quaked with vertigo. She was swathed in layer after layer of silk, confined in sticky softness. She felt the tension in her muscles subside, the azaros blood working its magic, but by then she'd been so tightly wrapped in the spider silk she could do little more than quiver within the cocoon's confines.

Her breath volleyed in and out in great gasping spurts. Where was Jayan? What if something slowed him, or he stumbled, or he dropped that squirming duncoon? Fear settled deep in her bones. She held on for the ride, twisting and twirling beneath the massive spider.

At long last, the tetrela stilled its spinning. It stopped twirling, and without warning, dropped her. The entire left side of her body slammed into the dune. Her cheek and shoulder took the brunt of the drop. Both throbbed dully as she sank further into the sand, unable to move.

Her heartbeat pounded in her ears. The spider hustled off, bounding away from her. Time slowed to a crawl as she waited for something—anything—to happen.

Was the tetrela preparing to dive into the dune and pull her with it? Her mind flashed back to that underground tunnel in Dracwood, where she was forced to wriggle like a worm through the earth. Lying on the hot sand, blind and defenseless, was so much worse. Would she be buried alive, helpless to do anything as the spider slowly drained her dry? Or had Jayan distracted the beast like they'd planned?

The sand beneath her shifted. Something smacked into the ground by her side.

"I've got you," Jayan whispered.

Relief flooded her. She drew in a sharp breath as the silk covering her face lifted and a blade pierced the cocoon above her brows.

Jayan slit the silk and pulled, ripping a hole large enough for him to peek in at her. He sighed when she locked eyes with him, and winked. Then he hopped away and pointed his blade at the silk near her feet. Another quick cut, and she was severed from the rope-like length of silk tying her to the tetrela.

Her gaze sought the beast. It was halfway across the dune, clutching the bound duncoon within its grasp. Those massive black fangs sunk deep in its belly as blood spilled from the critter's neck and splattered on the sand.

Jayan was already back at her shoulders. He lifted her, still shrouded within the silken cocoon, and hefted her in his arms like she was a sack of grain he was hauling onboard his ship. He sprinted across the dune. Grains of sand sprayed up from his footfalls and pelted her face.

With only the small hole for her to look out of, and her position within Jayan's arms, all she could see was the sand rushing by as he sped away. She held her breath as he slowed, praying the change in speed meant they were approaching the bottom of the mountain range and safety.

Finally, she spotted the first sign of rock beneath them. Jayan hefted her within his arms, twisting her upward, adjusting his grip that had gradually began slipping as they ran.

Slam. She hit the ground hard. Her back smashed into the hard packed sand. The wind knocked out of her lungs and her chest spasmed. Eyes bulging, she spotted the cause of her fall. The tetrela held fast to the bottom of her cocoon, stabbing down on the edge with one spindly leg.

The beast emitted a horrible chirping hiss. Blood dripped down from its fangs. Its gigantic eyes connected with hers and she quaked with fear. She struggled within the cocoon, her arms and legs shoving against the silk but barely moving.

From behind her, an angry roar rent the air. Jayan swung around and leaped forward, tugging her shoulders, trying to pull her free.

The tetrela swiped out a leg and smacked Jayan to the sand like a rag-doll. The tetrela spun to face where he landed and leaned forward, shooting out another batch of barbs. Jayan rolled through the sand, barely avoiding being skewered.

Metal flashed in the sky. The Sul. They sent arrows and spears sailing toward them. Kayda gasped. Didn't they care that she and Jayan might be caught in the crossfire?

She had to do something. But what?

The switchblade! She squirmed and wriggled, sliding her hand into her pants pocket. Even as she seized the blade, the tetrela grabbed her again, hefting her within its grasp, its body tensing, ready to race away back across the dunes.

Jayan lurched back to his feet. This time, he'd picked up one of the Sul pole-knives. He screamed and raced forward, stabbing the tetrela in one of its eight giant eyes.

The beast dropped her and screeched in pain, its head shaking and limbs shooting out to shove the weapon aside.

Kayda's head slammed into the ground, yet again. Stars flashed in her eyes, and her skull throbbed, but she ignored the pain. She flicked open the tiny blade and tore a hole in the cocoon, just big enough to snake her hand and forearm free.

Her arm was free, but the tetrela rounded on Jayan, hissing and dripping blood on the sand. His weapon was nowhere to be seen. No doubt flung far away by the beast's scrambling legs. It pounced atop him and shoved him onto the dune, grains of sand flinging in every direction.

Something flashed above her head and dropped onto the sand beside her free hand. A torch. Yes!

She reached out, the flame's heat kissing the skin of her palm. She pulled at the flames with her talent, faster than she'd ever done. Ice crackled in her veins.

"Hey," she screamed.

The tetrela paused, its fangs a hairsbreadth away from sinking into Jayan's stomach. It swiveled its black eyes toward her, and she shoved out her hand. She lit up the sky with a white-hot wall of flame. The fire burned so bright in the dark. Blindingly bright.

The tetrela hissed and scrambled off Jayan, shaking its head, swinging away from the light. Kayda didn't relent, using the magic to follow the beast wherever it turned, the dazzling fire inescapable.

Jayan hopped up, his gait wobbly. With an arm lifted to shield him from the blinding light, he staggered and slid, but pressed on until he grasped her shoulders and dragged her across the sand. She kept her hand outstretched, her concentration never wavering while they raced away from the tetrela.

Suddenly, a wave of exhaustion slammed into her. The torch. Her source. They'd moved too far from it and she was left with only her own talent feeding the flames. She shuddered and dropped her hand, extinguishing the light. Were they far enough from the beast they could escape this time?

Even as the thought crossed her mind, she was lifted off the sand, pulled into a pair of strong arms. The Sul quickly surrounded them and helped them up the lower slopes of rock, to the mountain's safety.

Within moments, torches blazed all around them, and a tall, dark-skinned woman worked to deftly slice her free from the silken cocoon. Kayda shivered as the silk peeled away by small degrees, all those eyes watching her revealed to the night sky. It was like she'd been reborn in truth; born of the sand.

Jayan sat by her side, holding tight to her free hand. His breath still hadn't calmed, his chest rising and falling erratically, his clothes askew from his tangle with the tetrela. But his eyes glittered nonetheless. He smiled. "What did I tell you, Princess? That was fun, wasn't it?"

She shot him a sideways glare. "Does fun mean something different in the Waste?" She curled a hand through her hair and sighed.

Lazar approached and knelt down beside them. His stony expression was gone, and his eyes had lost their hard edge, shining like dark gems in the night sky. "Welcome home, sandborn." He grinned.

Chapter 12

A rattling cough broke the cabin's silence. Conall's eyes shot open. He groaned from his spot on the wooden floor, stretching his stiff body.

He and Shadow had spent the night curled up beside the fire. His shoulders still ached from all the rowing he'd done yesterday, and the night's rest on the hard floor only worsened the soreness lingering deep in his muscles.

The coughing sounded again. A harsh bark in the quiet morning. Conall grimaced and rolled up to sit, staring across the room to where Delyth lay, shuddering beneath the blankets in Halynn's bed.

"She doesn't sound good." Shadow lifted his head and joined Conall in staring across the room.

"No, she doesn't."

He'd helped Halynn lay Delyth to rest on the large fur-swathed mattress last night. She hadn't stirred as they stripped off her snow-caked fur coat. Nor when he'd lifted her thin frame off the wooden chair and carried her across the room. He shuddered, recalling how frail she'd seemed then.

For as long as he'd known her, she'd always been so strong. She stood by, stolid and unwavering, as she led her people through the mountain passes. Those sharp blue eyes seeing all, always ready with an answer to everyone's questions. Last night, for the first time, he'd glimpsed the fragile soul beneath the force of nature.

He rose to his feet and crossed the room, laying the back of his hand across Delyth's forehead. *"She's burning up."*

A hard pit coalesced in his stomach. He was no healer. If only Lark was here, instead of him. She'd know what to do.

A flash of his own fever, back in that cave in Dracwood, rose in his mind. Hour after hour, he'd lain shaking and shuddering, his mind plagued with unrelenting nightmares. It had been awful. But it hadn't lasted forever. He'd made it through that; surely Delyth would, too.

At least she had them here to help. He strode across the room again. A few short steps and he was at the table. He found a pitcher of water, poured a measure into a wooden cup, then brought it back to the bed.

"Sade Prim. I've brought you some water." He knelt beside her and lifted the cup to her lips. Sweat poured off her brow, soaking the pillow and the wispy gray hairs that snuck out of her braid to frame her face. "Delyth. Wake up and take a drink, then you can go back to sleep."

Her eyes cracked open. Her blue irises were bloodshot and murky, but she stared straight at him before flicking her gaze to Shadow as he padded across the room to his side.

"Bitch whisperer." She laughed. A mirthless cackle that set off another round of coughing.

Conall's brow furrowed. Setting the cup down on the floor beside him, he rubbed her back as her coughing died down, then maneuvered a second pillow beneath her head and lifted her into a reclined position.

"What's she saying?" Shadow asked.

He shook his head. *"Nothing that makes any sense."*

Conall raised the cup again. "Have some water."

She grabbed the cup and drank greedily. He plucked the cup from her fingers after she drained it and rose to refill it.

"Won't have me groveling at your feet like that wicked bitch," she mumbled as he returned.

Conall frowned, ignoring her fevered rambling. "It's all right. You just need to drink." He placed the cup back in her hands. "Then get some rest. You'll feel better soon."

Delyth drained the second cup and sank back into the pillows. She scrubbed her brow and twisted sideways, grumbling under her breath.

Conall sighed, feeling utterly helpless. Where was Halynn? She wasn't inside. There was nowhere to hide in the tiny cabin. She should be in here, helping.

"I'm going outside to look for Halynn. Will you stay with her while I'm gone?" Conall nodded to Delyth as her coughing spilled out again from beneath the covers.

"I'll watch over her." Shadow curled up on the ground by the foot of the bed.

Throwing on his fur and slipping into his boots, Conall cracked open the door and stole outside into the cold. He shivered and pulled his hood up around his unruly gray-streaked brown locks.

He took his first look at the snow-blanketed island in the bright morning light. It looked much the same as it had swathed in moonlight. Barren and cold. The only thing of note was Halynn's tiny shack, and the even smaller outhouse sitting behind it. A massive ice-crusted pile of firewood rested between the two buildings, and beyond that, a set of footprints, leading north.

Conall set off, following Halynn's tracks. It wasn't long before he spotted her, crouched down on the ground at the island's edge, staring down into the sea. She was humming, wrapped in a heavy black fur coat over her simple brown dress and boots. Just out of arm's reach, a wooden bucket floated on the icy water.

He made no effort to walk stealthily. But though she must've heard him approaching, she didn't look up from her task; her stare locked on the floating bucket. Conall watched silently as he strode up beside her.

What was she doing?

Splash. A silver fish emerged from the sea and jumped directly into the bucket.

"Blazes," he exclaimed. "How did you do that?"

She stopped humming and tugged on a thin string, sliding the bucket across the water toward her. Turning from her task, she peeked up at him and smiled. "I asked her to come, so she did."

Conall gaped, his round eyes darting between her and the bucket as she pulled it into her hands. "You talk to fish?"

"Yes." She tsked and dipped the bucket into the water, filling it before lugging it up on the ice beside her. "Surely you understand. It's much the same as you and your Shadow."

"That fish is your bondmate?"

"Not exactly. But we are bonded nonetheless."

"I don't follow..."

She stood and brushed the snow from her skirt. "Carry that back for me. I'll explain while we walk."

Conall grabbed the wooden bucket, gripping the handles carved on either side of the top rim. The fat silver fish popped to the surface and glared up at him with its bulbous black eyes before disappearing back down to the bottom of the bucket.

He lifted, ignoring the twinge in his lower back and the reawakening soreness in his shoulders and arms. He hobbled across the snow, quickening his pace to catch up with Halynn, who'd already started tromping her way back.

"Have you heard of laumarles?" Halynn asked.

"Laumarles?" The word sparked a memory of the bright white oil lamps in the Church of the Dragon back in Flamesmoat. "Do you mean laumarle oil?"

"That's it. Laumarle aren't only useful for their oil. They're the bread and butter for the people of Norwich. They eat their meat and make their living trading their oil and horns."

"Wait, so laumarle oil comes from a creature?"

"A sea creature, yes. They're massive, elusive beasts that live in the Northern Depths."

"I see... but what does that have to do with a fish jumping into your bucket?"

"There are few creatures who can survive these waters." She nodded to the bucket. "The siltreak fish are one of them. Many years ago, they were close to extinction. Their numbers were decimated by a sudden explosion of laumarle. That all changed when the first Winter Witch arrived in Norwich."

How bizarre. The winter witches had the power to save an entire species from extinction? He tilted his head, listening closely as he followed Halynn across the snowy island.

"No one knows for sure how, but she made a discovery that saved the siltreak and opened up a whole new world for those of us who dream." She turned before the cabin and rounded the woodpile's side, stopping in the space between the cabin and outhouse. "Set the bucket down here." She pointed to a spot beside a large flat stump with an old rusty ax leaning against it.

"Isn't that what you said you were last night? The new dreamer. You see things in your dreams?"

She nodded. "It's the siltreak that make it possible. Here, I'll show you."

Halynn knelt down, the breeze blowing her long blond curls as she peered inside the wooden bucket at the siltreak. It floated back up to the water's surface. Those bulging eyes locked on her with an intelligence he'd rarely seen in a land animal, much less a lowly fish.

Shucking off her thick wool gloves, Halynn's hands slid into the water and reverently caressed the siltreak, her touch as gentle as if she were stroking a newborn babe. Then she twisted, sharp and sudden, cracking its neck in a single swift motion. She pulled it from the bucket and slapped it on the log, still twitching.

Conall reared back, swaying slightly. "Blazes! I thought you shared a bond with that fish?"

She pulled a switchblade from within the folds of her skirt, along with an empty glass vial. "I do. Not just with this one individual, but with all of them." Setting the vial down on the log, she flicked the blade open, the metal glittering in the sunlight. She sliced through the fish's neck, cutting its head cleanly off its body with one practiced stroke.

Conall's stomach gurgled as she picked up the head, using her fingers to probe around the viscera within.

"Ah, there it is." She pulled her hand free, withdrawing a small fleshy sack. "This, right here, is what we need. The elixir of dreams." Grabbing the vial, she used the knife to poke a hole in the fish's organ and carefully tipped it over, draining its contents.

Conall did his best not to gag as the thick green goo pooled at the bottom of the vial. "So that stuff lets you communicate with the fish?"

Halynn nodded and stoppered the vial before slipping it back into her skirt pocket. "I told you the laumarle were elusive. They have a knack for hiding from the fishing boats of Norwich. Without a guide using the dream elixir, finding and capturing one is as difficult as catching a solitary snowflake in a blizzard." She got to work again with the switchblade, slicing into the fish's body this time, cutting its flesh into neat even fillets. "An adult laumarle eats hundreds of fish every day. The siltreak help us locate them through the connection, and we keep the laurmarle numbers in check."

"And the fish just come when you ask them to?" He grimaced, recalling the intelligence in the fish's stare. "Do they know what awaits them?"

"They do. It's always a mother who answers the call. It's a sacrifice they are willing to make to ensure the survival of their young."

"I think I understand. But what does that have to do with dreams?"

Halynn rinsed her hands in the bucket, then dumped the water on the ground. "It's a secondary effect of the elixir. Depending who you ask, it's either a happy accident or a curse." She used her knife to slide the fillets into the bucket, then cleaned the blade on the snow and slipped it back into her pocket.

By now, her pale hands were bright pink from the cold. She rubbed them together as she stood, then shoved them back into her gloves. "Do you mind?" She nodded at the bucket.

Conall hefted the bucket once more, the weight much lighter with the water drained. They rounded the cabin as the sound of muffled coughing escaped the wooden structure.

He cringed. Damn. He'd been so caught up with the stupid fish he'd forgotten what he came outside for.

He stopped Halynn on the side of the cabin. "Wait, Delyth isn't doing so good. Can you help her?"

"I saw her state this morning." She cleared her throat, her eyebrows drawing together. "I'm afraid I've no talent for healing. I'll keep her fed and warm, but she'll have to fight off whatever ails her on her own."

Conall scowled and his shoulders slumped. "Can't you get help? Go to the mainland?"

Halynn stared at the sea, eyes narrowing, her voice quiet and laced with a wistful note. "I can't go back to the mainland anymore. My place is here." She turned to him. "Even if I could, the ice is too thick to travel through this time of year. The only people crazy enough to chance it are you mages."

His stomach sank. Delyth had to survive, or he and Shadow would have no choice but to wait for the ice to thaw in the spring. He cursed inwardly, lamenting the block keeping him from accessing his talent. If only he'd started training earlier, he might have some options. For now, it looked like they were stuck on this frozen island until Delyth got well enough to clear a path through the ice with her magic.

They reentered the cabin. Conall sat on the single wooden chair while Halynn busied herself by the fire, and the scent of roasted fish filled the air. His nerves rattled every time Delyth's coughs shook the walls.

Halynn slid a plate of steaming meat before him and rested a hand on his shoulder, giving him a gentle squeeze. "She brought you here like she was meant to. It's time you fulfill your part in coming here. Eat up. We'll begin when you've finished." She left his side and placed a second plate on the ground beside Shadow.

Conall's stomach growled, but even as Shadow began chomping, he made no move to eat. He couldn't stop picturing that fish's bulbous eyes glaring at him from within the bucket. He was no stranger to skinning and eating fresh game, but this felt different. Had she known he was about to eat her when she scowled up at him?

Halynn held no such qualms. She returned to the hearth and speared a serving of fish on a plate, only taking time to blow on the hot meat before taking a bite.

Conall shook his head. "Both of you talk like this was always meant to happen. But you can't possibly know that... It's only by pure chance I even met Delyth. How can you be so sure I'm meant to be here?"

"The dream connects us all. Each person's experience with the dream elixir is unique, but there are things every person, since the days of the first Winter Witch, has reported seeing. Delyth's seen it. I've seen it. You'll see it, too."

He stilled, his muscles tensing. "What is it? What will I see that's so important?"

She pulled the vial from her skirt pocket. She placed it on the table next to the plate of fish. "You want to know? Drink."

He lifted the vial in front of his eyes, the viscous fluid swirling against the glass. Then his gaze slid to his own hands. The deep lines on his knuckles he was still getting used to seeing demanded his attention.

"What about the cost?" He closed his fist around the vial, his gaze flicking to Halynn. "If I've learned anything about magic, there's always a cost."

Her shoulders stiffened. She set her unfinished plate down on the floor beside her, where she sat next to the hearth. "The things you see, you'll never unsee them. But the costs will be minimal for you. It's only with repeated use the effects become binding."

He tilted his head and pursed his lips. "Is that why you can't leave?"

She nodded slowly, her gaze downcast. "It is." She pulled her knees against her chest, wrapping her arms around them. "After so long communing with the siltreak it becomes... painful to be away from the sea. Those who serve as guides for the hunts are careful not to dream too often. But sometimes, mistakes happen." She sighed.

Conall's heart twisted. Was that what happened to Halynn? She dreamed one too many dreams as a guide and now she was stuck out here in this desolate hut, all alone?

Halynn shook herself out of her reverie. She marched over to the table. "It's nothing for you to worry about. One dream or even a handful won't be enough to affect you in such a way." Her voice was firm. She stopped before him with her feet planted and her shoulders pushed back. "If you aren't planning to eat, then let's begin."

She jolted slightly as Delyth, who'd been silent while they ate, coughed again, the wheezing abrupt and harsh, like her throat was full of wet sand.

Conall opened his fist, lifted the vial to his lips, and drank.

Chapter 13

"You're late." Mika glowered at Lark as she slid inside the luct screen of the healing hut.

"Sorry." She smiled and handed a diquat to her new teacher. "Did I miss any new arrivals?"

Mika dropped the fruit into a bowl on top of the large wooden desk near the door. This hut was the largest of all the huts in Stoneshore, even bigger than Mata Moyra's.

Lark peered behind Mika. The rows of cots were empty, the bedding folded neatly and turned down, ready for patients to arrive. A single spot was occupied, the patient within silent, a long green curtain shrouding the cot to block out the bright sunlight filtering in through the luct-screened windows. A pair of young men worked silently in the back corner, sorting through a box of bandages and stacking a variety of bottles and jars filled with unknown liquids atop some shelves on the wall.

"The morning's been quiet so far." Mika leaned back against the table and crossed his arms over his muscular chest, which was visible beneath his sheer luct top. "But that's no excuse to tarry. I've plenty I can teach you while we don't have a whole jungle's worth of sick and injured scrambling for help."

Lark nodded and rocked back on her heels on the dirt floor. "It won't happen again."

It was Muse's fault. Silly bird got tangled in a luct screen trying to fly out the window of their hut at dawn. The corner of her mouth lifted in a smile as she recalled the picture the falcon made, a tangle of feathers and squawking outrage.

Then she caught Mika sending her a scowl, and she pressed her lips into a thin line. "I'm ready to learn. I promise." She glanced back at the young men in the back. "Should we call the others over for the lesson?"

Mika waved a hand. "No. There are a handful of villagers who come help here each day. They're skilled enough to deal with all the minor injuries, allowing me to conserve my magic for the few that need the extra help. They've had all the training they need already."

"Oh. I see."

"All right. So, how much do you know about the art of healing?"

"Not enough." She glanced down at her feet. "I've just got my mother's spell book, really. She was skilled at herbal healing, but she didn't have talent like you and I."

"I'd love to take a look at that book."

"Sure, I can go grab it," she offered.

He shook his head. "Bring it tomorrow. I'm not surprised about your mother. My parents didn't have talent either. Everything I learned came from my Geema."

"Your Geema?"

"My grandmother. Talent skips a generation in our family. We aren't as blessed as you are, either. Talent like you have… I've never felt anything so strong."

"I've been meaning to ask you about that." Lark rubbed her arm, cocking her head sideways. "How did you borrow my talent out on the cliffside? I didn't even know that was possible."

"My Geema taught me. We'd often have to share our talent to heal patients we couldn't handle on our own. I'll teach you how. It's quite simple, only you must be sure to use it sparingly. The person sharing their talent is often exhausted in the process."

That explained why she'd passed out after helping Mika heal her snake bite. "I have a lot to learn." She grinned. "What else is there?"

He smiled and marched away from the desk, further into the hut. He stopped beside a row of shelves lined on the wall, overflowing with pots of plants of all different varieties. Fragrant flowers and herbs sat beside decorative ferns, prickly cacti, and a few ugly, bulbous blooms that looked garish and grotesque next to the rest.

"My Geema taught me everything she knew about tending to jungle plants. Healing with the earth is not just about utilizing the raw talent in your blood. There's knowledge behind it that takes a lifetime to master." He picked up a watering pot and tipped the slender clay vessel among the shelves, watering some and skipping others in a dizzying pattern that had no rhyme or reason she could discern.

A lifetime of knowledge? Her stomach clenched. She didn't have a lifetime. The scourge were already wreaking havoc in her homeland.

Mika continued, "Specific types of plants must be used to heal certain injuries. You can have all the talent in the world at your disposal, but if you don't know what kind of plant to use, it'll be about as useful as slapping a bandage on a sore throat."

"That makes sense. You wouldn't use the same herbs in a poultice to heal a flesh wound as you would for a sprain. Why would this be any different?"

Mika nodded and set the watering pot back on the ground. "I'm sure the herb lore you learned from your mother will serve you well. I expect many of the plants will overlap."

Lark crinkled her nose, a twinge in her right leg reminding her of her own injury. "So, when you healed the snake venom from my leg, you used roots?"

"Roots are amazing for absorbing things from the body. Venom, pus, infection. But roots would be useless for knitting flesh back together. For that, you want something fresh and green. The more alive, the better."

Lark stepped back a pace. Her gaze fell to her hands and flicked back and forth across the surface of her palms. Not so long ago, they were filled with mud and a child's blood. If only she'd known. If only she'd thought to grab a handful of the fresh green grass on the riverside instead.

Mika closed the distance between them and tipped her chin up with a long, tan finger. He stared down into her face, concern flooding his warm brown eyes. "Hey, what is it?"

She gulped, licking her lips. Should she tell him? Would he understand the devastation tainting her soul when she thought of the people she'd failed to save?

A swish of fabric at the door made the question moot. Mika dropped his hand from her chin and backed up a pace, sending a smile to the middle-aged woman and boy on the cusp of adolescence who entered. "Esmar, Nox. What brings you by today? Is your leg paining you again?"

"Mika. Thank the Mother," the woman exclaimed, shoving her way past the screen and tugging the boy behind her. "No, my leg is the same. It's Nox."

Esmar hobbled in, her pace stilted, favoring her left leg. She clutched Nox's hand, her brown eyes wide and panicked. She was slim and tall, her thick brows and sharp nose shared by the boy. Lark suspected the two were mother and son. But the similarities ended there. The woman was jumpy, flushed, and shrill; the boy, calm and silent.

"I woke up this morning and found him like this." Esmar dropped Nox's hand. Her arms flew all over as she spoke, running through her long brown hair, tugging her clothes. "Nox won't speak. Won't move unless you make him. Just keeps staring off into space like there's nothing there inside his mind."

Nox didn't say a word in his defense. He stood there, standing like a statue, giving further weight to Esmar's concern.

How strange. Lark peered at him closely, tapping her fist against her lips. What could cause someone to end up in such a state?

Mika strode forward and bent down, staring into Nox's brown eyes. He looked for a long while, silent and unmoving, then straightened and focused on Esmar. "What of his bondmate? Where is he?"

Lark's hand fell slack at her side, her mouth dropping open. This boy had bonding magic? It figured the first person she'd met that shared the rare ability with her couldn't speak.

Esmar gasped. "I—I don't know. I haven't seen him at all. The two of them are usually tied at the hip. Do you think that has anything to do with this?"

Mika nodded solemnly. "I'm afraid so. Bonding magic can have strange effects on the mind." Mika's gaze lit on Lark briefly before turning back to Esmar. "I'm going to assume something has happened to the poor creature. How many was that now?"

Lark's eyes widened. Questions swirled in her mind, each one louder than the last. He had more than one bondmate? Bonding magic could alter someone's mind? Bonding magic had caused—whatever this was—to happen?

Esmar rubbed her brow. "First there was the pengeen, then the geklit, now the meekrous. So, three?"

He had three bondmates? And different species, too. Meekrous were the cute little orange tree monkeys. As for the other two creatures, she'd no clue.

Lark exhaled, shaking her head. Whenever she thought she had a handle on all this magic stuff, something new came along to shake her understanding.

Mika didn't seem surprised. He sauntered back to the shelf of plants. His finger lifted and traced a line through the air as he scanned the greenery. "Ah ha." He strode forward and plucked a bloom from a light blue flower. He bent down and tore a few thin green leaves from another plant. Then he strode across the room to the front desk, opened a drawer, and plucked free a hairy white mushroom.

Esmar watched Mika's movements, her foot tapping against the dirt floor, arms crossed. "So, you can help him? Nox's father left a few weeks ago for Slinas. I don't know if I can do this all alone." She wrung her hands together, shifting from foot to foot.

"You're not alone, Esmar. I'll do my best to help." Mika set the plants on the desktop and dug into another drawer, his head disappearing as he crouched and rummaged around. "Lark, have Nox sit on one of the cots, please?"

"Sure." Lark hurried to the boy's side.

Esmar grimaced as Lark led him to the bed by the elbow, seeming to notice her for the first time. "I'm sorry, I should've introduced myself. I'm Esmar, and this is my son, Nox." She attempted a smile, but the corners of her mouth wouldn't cooperate.

"I'm Lark of Greenvale. Pleased to meet you. Mika is teaching me about healing."

"Oh. You're the singer who came with the traveling show, aren't you?" She frowned. "Nox came rushing home last night, going on and on about a girl at Stoneshore with a bonded falcon. He was so excited to meet you. I told him he had to wait until morning to make the trek. We live a few clearings away, you see. I've got this damn limp from a bad break I suffered in childhood that healed wrong. I wanted to come with him... now I wish I hadn't made him wait. Maybe he could've made it without me." A heavy sigh escaped her, her lower lip trembling.

Lark finished helping the boy sit on the cot and turned to his mother. "You made the right call. You couldn't have known this would happen. Besides, no one should be out traveling between clearings in the dark." She squeezed Esmar's arm, offering a small smile.

Mika reappeared, holding a wooden cup. Steam escaped from the top and curled through the air. "Lark's right, Esmar. Nox would be worse off than he is now in the belly of a jagoth."

He walked to the cot and held the cup to Nox's lips. "I've brought you some tea, Nox." But though Mika spoke loudly and stared straight at him, Nox made no move to drink.

"Here, let me help you." Lark placed one hand on Nox's chin and the other on his forehead, tilting his head back gently. Mika slid a finger on his lower lip and opened his mouth, spilling a few drops of tea on his tongue.

She was certain the clear brew would come leaking out the corners of his mouth. But then he swallowed, the muscles in his throat working reflexively. That seemed to give his body some signal. His lips clasped onto the cup, and he took slow sip after slow sip until it was drained.

Lark and Mika stepped back after he emptied the cup. All three of them watched the boy silently. Nothing changed. He kept staring blankly off into the distance, his eyes dull and unfocused.

Esmar frowned, her voice shaky. "I don't think it's working."

Mika returned to the desk and swept more of the plants he'd used for the tea into his hand. "We have a few more things we can try." He moved back to the cot. "Help me lay him down, please."

Lark rushed to comply. She rounded the back of the cot and helped Mika gently swing the boy down to lie flat, his brown eyes open and staring at the ceiling of the wooden hut.

Mika laid his hand on the boy's forehead. Crinkling escaped from the plants hidden beneath his palm. He closed his eyes, standing perfectly still.

A tremor spread across her skin. She watched Nox's face, holding her breath.

Still nothing.

Mika opened his eyes and sighed.

"Can I help?" She reached across the cot.

Mika nodded and clasped her hand firmly within his own. "Call on your talent, Lark. I'll do the rest."

Lark inhaled deeply. Having Mika here, guiding her, his hand warm and steady on her own, calmed the panicked part of her mind that always shouted at her when she tried to summon. She closed her eyes, and she wished. She wished for Nox to wake up. To emerge from whatever strange cloud clogged his mind.

A pleasant warmth spread over her palm. Then the tremor returned. Stronger this time. So forceful the cot quaked beneath the boy, swaying side to side like a leaf in the breeze.

Exhaustion came with it. Rolling over her like a wave, pressing her limbs to the ground. It wasn't long before she was swaying, too. Before the weariness consumed her, Mika lifted his hand from Nox's head, breaking the spell.

Her eyes shot open. She studied the boy, praying his eyes would find their focus. That he'd raise his voice and speak. But Nox remained unchanged.

Esmar wailed. "No. No! What am I gonna do? Will he stay like this forever?"

Mika turned to the older woman and wrapped his muscular arms around her thin frame, holding her while she wept.

Lark backed away, leaning against the empty cot behind her. The exhaustion lifted slowly, but she didn't feel any better for it. This poor boy... there had to be something they could do to save him. Her stomach churned with regret and worry. And if she were being perfectly honest, a bit of fear, too.

Was this something she should be worried about in her own future? The thought of Muse dying was enough to make her heart shudder, but having three creatures bonded to her so closely and losing them all? It would be soul-shattering. No wonder Nox was lost.

Mika unwrapped his arms from Esmar and held her at arm's length, gazing down into her face. "I'm not done trying yet. There's a blossom on the spoolwood tree that might help. Stay here with Nox. I'll trek out and retrieve some. There's a few of them growing at the top of the waterfall, a short hike from here."

"I'll go with you." He shook his head and opened his mouth, but Lark spoke up again before he could tell her to stay. "No one should travel alone, right?"

Mika narrowed his eyes but nodded once. "All right. Gather what supplies you need and meet me at the village's eastern edge. We'll be back by midday."

Lark sent a sympathetic smile to Esmar, spun on her heel, and left the healing hut. She rushed past a dozen huts crafted of wood and luct netting. The humidity clung around her like a moist hug. Her ears rang with the noises of jungle creatures and the buzz of insects as she spotted Meital's dagger, still piercing the wooden doorframe.

She slid behind the luct netting into the hut she shared with Tiora and Meital.

"Muse? You in the mood for a little excursion?" Muse wasn't in the hut, just Tiora and Meital, still lounging on their cots. And Sunny, sprawled on the edge of her own cot, her tail waving half-heartedly as she rolled over and went back to sleep. Lark grabbed her knapsack and started scrounging around for what she needed while doing her best to not wake them.

"Hm?" Muse answered. *"Sounds like fun."*

"Meet me back at the hut. I'm almost ready."

"Lark?" Tiora rose on her elbow, her voice groggy from sleep. "What's going on?"

"Hey," she whispered. Lark cinched her sack closed and crouched down beside Tiora's cot. "Nothing to worry about. I'm just taking a hike with Mika to find a flower he needs to heal someone."

"Oh. All right." Tiora sat up fully, swinging her legs off the cot. She sighed.

Lark frowned, squeezing Tiora's knee. "Ti, I know you're dying to see your family in Joria. Just because I have to stay here with Mika doesn't mean the rest of you do. If you and the others feel like it's time to move on, I understand."

Tiora yawned, rubbing the sleep from her eyes. "What? I—"

"Just think about it. Talk it over with the others. I'll be back in a few hours." Lark stood and strode outside.

She squinted and lifted her gaze to the sky, looking for Muse and trying to ignore the twinge in her chest.

She didn't want her friends to leave. Not truly. But she couldn't expect them to put their lives on hold for her. It might take weeks for her to learn all she needed from Mika. And after that, she would return to Dracwood.

She hadn't forgotten the destruction in Bogsmouth or the vow she'd made as she watched the village burn to the ground. But she wouldn't ask her friends to put themselves in danger for a promise she'd made to herself. They weren't even from Dracwood, after all.

She was still planning to defend her home from those vicious creatures. She had to believe she was given her talent for a reason. And she couldn't run from her destiny. At least, not forever.

Muse dropped from the sky and landed on the hut's roof.

"Took you long enough," Lark said. *"C'mon, Mika's waiting."*

"All right, all right. Ha. We don't want to enrage the mage."

She rolled her eyes and started walking. Something told her it was going to be a long day.

Chapter 14

"Wow," Kayda exclaimed.

She stood inside a large underground cavern beneath the Suland Waste. Light shone in from hundreds of holes in the rock above them; the sunbeams bent, ricocheting around the massive chamber between a series of mirrors. Light flashed everywhere. Mirrors angled this way and that to catch the strong desert sun and bend it to the Sul's will.

"Welcome to Sul Hollow," Lazar said. "The jewel of the desert."

People and animals crowded the massive rust-red cavern. There were no tents, houses, or even curtains she could see to separate the folk. Just blankets and pillows spread out on the ground and pens for the animals lining the far wall. Small groups of people gathered together, here and there, none seemingly bothered by the lack of privacy.

Of course, all eyes turned to stare in their direction as they entered. Kayda swallowed. That old familiar tinge of discomfort rose in her chest at being on display. It seemed she would have no choice but to get used to it here.

At least it was cooler down here, shaded from the blistering desert sun. She breathed deeply, sensing a hint of humidity. As they strode further into the cavern, she spotted the reason for the moisture in the air. A slow-moving stream cut through the rocky cavern floor.

Lazar stopped near the stream and hopped up on a rock, raising his fist. "Two new souls join the sandborn this day. Step forward, Jayan, son of Akilt."

A few of the Sul who'd accompanied them on the hunt cheered, shoving Jayan forward. The rest of the room erupted with hoots and applause. Jayan grinned. A young woman burst forward through the crowd, rushing up to him with tears streaming down her face.

"Brother. I thought you were dead," she cried out between sobs. She clutched him tightly, weeping with undisguised relief. Kayda's heart lifted. That must be the sister Jayan spoke of so often, Nova.

Then Lazar's deep voice boomed out again. "Step forward, Kayda, daughter of Chanti." The applause died as the true name of her mother spilled from Lazar's lips, replaced with gasps.

Chanti. Her mother's name was Chanti! At long last, she was on the cusp of discovering the truth of her past. The realization left her feeling buoyant, and for once, the hundreds of eyes on her didn't send unease squirming across her skin. Kayda drew in a deep breath, her pulse thumping beneath her skin, and stepped forward.

Silence reigned. Even Nova quieted her sobs, peeking up at her from within Jayan's embrace. Only the gentle trickling water at her back and the sheep and goat's soft braying at the cave wall remained as evidence that anyone populated the massive cavern. It was as if all the Sul held a shared breath, staring at her in disbelief.

A single clap rang out beside her. Jayan took another step forward, clapping again, even louder this time. It was enough to break the spell of silence. The Sul joined in, clapping, hooting, and hollering, the sound so loud and cacophonous it rattled the stone walls.

A huge mountain of a man hustled through the crowd, dark brown arms wide open as he approached. On his face, he wore a toothy-grin. Tears shone in the corners of his dark brown eyes. "Kayda. You look so much like your mother. My niece, welcome home!"

The man pulled her into a crushing hug. Kayda endured the tight squeeze, her hands trapped at her side.

"You're my uncle?" She tugged the hem of her white silk shirt after the large man set her aside.

"I am. My name is Bamzan. Chanti, she was my sister." A shadow crossed his eyes, but he blinked it aside, shaking his head, his long braids swaying with the motion. "Come, you shall sleep in my circle tonight. I can't wait for you to meet your cousins." He planted a hand on her lower back and steered her through the crowd, toward the cave's far wall.

Kayda peered up at her uncle, keeping pace with him as he barreled through the gathered Sul. "Cousins? I've more than one?"

"Yes, three." He chuckled. "My wife and I, we were very blessed. We have two daughters and a son."

"Will I meet your wife as well?"

The shadow was back, and a frown tipped down the corners of his mouth before he banished it with a grave smile. "I'm afraid not. She was called back to the sands a few years back."

Back to the sands? Did that mean... "I'm so sorry."

"Not to worry, my dear. It was her time. After all, we're all just dust in the end."

Bamzan stopped at a set of brown and tan blankets and pillows strewn together in a large circle. "Here we are." Three children sat among the pillows, busy braiding strands of white thread. "My little sunbeams, come meet your cousin," he bellowed.

Three sets of brown eyes collided with her own. The girls were lovely. Both of them wore their dark brown hair tied up in a simple knot. They were clearly younger than her, perhaps only twelve or thirteen. The boy was younger still, his shoulder length hair unbraided and the exact shade of auburn as her own.

They dropped the threads in unison and rose to their feet.

"Cousin. I didn't know we had a cousin," said the tallest girl. She paced forward, gazing at Kayda curiously.

"Yes, well." Bamzan scratched his chin. "I suppose you'll all like to hear the story. But introductions first, yes? Kayda, meet your cousins. This is Bani." The girl who'd spoken gave her a nod. "Adira." The younger girl nodded next. "And Kai." The boy stared up at her, his brown eyes round.

Kayda smiled. "It's lovely to meet you all. I've never known much of anything about my mother. If I'd known I had cousins... Well, this wouldn't be the first time we'd met, that's for sure."

Little Kai's face screwed up, and he stomped his foot. "Why didn't you tell us, Papasun?"

Banzam bristled, pursing his lips and huffing out a sigh. "It's a long story. Come, let's sit."

Her cousins quickly settled back on their pillows. Banzam plopped down on the largest pillow opposite the children. Kayda chose a smaller brown pillow next to Kai. The plush cushion sank as she settled upon it, cross-legged.

Though there were people all around, no one paid them any mind. All were busy greeting the returning sandborn. A breath of excitement and revelry filled the air, reminiscent of the Harvest Festivals back in

Flamesmoat. Delicious scents wafted toward them, and laughter rang out, boisterous and carefree.

She spotted Jayan talking animatedly with his sister halfway across the cavern. In fact, everyone was talking. The Sul's constant chatter and the animal murmurings bounced off the walls, forming a gentle background noise that made their small family circle seem more intimate.

"We're waiting, Papasun," Bani said.

Bamzan cleared his throat, pointedly looking down at the piled thread in the circle's center. "First... idle hands."

Bani rolled her eyes, but she plucked one of the half-finished braids from the ground. Her siblings followed suit.

Kayda tilted her head, watching them spin and twist the thread expertly. She stifled a gasp. That wasn't thread. It was spider silk.

Bamzan chortled. "Thank you, my sunbeams." He pulled free a handful of silk as well, his hands busy. "To tell the story of my sister, you must first learn the story of my father. It all started one day out on the sands when he met a mirage."

Adira wrinkled her nose. "You can't meet a mirage, Papasun."

Bamzan clicked his tongue. "Do you want to hear me tell it or not?"

Adira nodded hastily, squirming on her pillow.

"So, my father. Back then, he was not yet my father but still a young man. Dechen he was called. He went on a hunt one afternoon and was caught in a sandstorm."

Kai gasped. "A sandstorm? Truly?"

Bamzan grinned, his gaze locked on the braid he threaded in his hands. "To hear him tell it, it was the storm of a century. Dechen was pummeled from all directions. His waterskin lost in the mayhem. All he could do was hunker down in a ball on the ground and pray the gods would see fit to spare him. When the storm blew over and he dug his way back to the dune's surface, he was half mad with dehydration. His sense of direction skewed. He wandered for hours, drifting through the Waste. But when he thought all hope was lost, he saw it. The mirage." His eyes lifted from his braid to glance at Adira. "What he thought at the time could only be a mirage. Only it wasn't. It was real, his savior."

"What was it?" Kayda asked.

"Not what." Bamzan smiled, his grin wistful. "Who. A beautiful young woman emerged from the Waste. She dragged him back to the modest home she shared with her mother. And though she and her mother had barely enough to get by, the young woman nursed him back to health. Dechen was smitten. Mira, he called her, for the mirage that brought them together. My mother."

Bani sighed. "How romantic."

"I imagine it was. For a time. Dechen made Mira his wife. Brought her here to live in Sul Hollow. They were eager to start a family. First came me. Then shortly after, my sister Chanti. It was during Chanti's birth that everything changed. A fire broke out in the middle of the delivery. It was chaos. Somehow, everyone survived. A few days later, Mira disappeared. My father searched for her everywhere, but she was never found. He spent the rest of his years assuming she'd suffered from the mother's melancholy and wandered off into the sands to meet her fate."

Bani's fingers paused. She sniffled. "That's so sad, Papasun. I can see why you don't like to talk about it."

"That's not the end of it, is it?" Kayda asked. "What of my mother?"

Bamzan took a deep breath. "My father died when Chanti and I were still young. He wasn't here on the day my mother returned."

Kai gasped. "So, she wasn't dead?"

Bamzan shook his head. "She wasn't. But she was changed. Aged far more than the lost years could account for."

Kayda's stomach churned. She had a suspicion she knew why.

"At first, the leaders here didn't want to let her in. A strange old woman claiming to be Mira, wife of Dechen? But she knew things. Things only a sandborn would. And when Chanti and I looked in her eyes, we just knew. She was our mother." A wistful smile crossed Bamzan's face. "She told us she'd come back for Chanti. That if she left with her, she would marry a prince in a foreign land. Her child would one day rule. That when the end times came, it would be our blood, one of the sandborn, who would save us all from the great storm to come." He lifted his gaze from his work, staring at her.

The children targeted their gazes on her, too.

Adira snorted. "A prince. Really? So, are you a princess, cousin?"

Kayda glanced down at the floor, then she raised her eyes and stared straight at Bamzan. "Your mother. Your father called her Mira, but that wasn't her real name, was it?"

Bamzan shook his head slowly. "No. Her name was Izora."

Kayda stood abruptly. "I have to get some air. Check on my bond-mate. Please, excuse me." She fled from her circled family without another word, heading toward the tunnel to the dune's surface.

Izora. It all led back to Izora. Her grandmother.

All this time she'd spent searching for her family, only to find out her own grandmother had been there with her, hidden, all along. The knowledge sent a rush of conflicting emotions swirling through her. The relief was immediate and strong, to finally learn the truth. It gave the love she'd always felt for Izora new depth. Izora had stayed with her, watching over her and loving her for her whole life. How hard that must've been on her. Knowing she was her own kin but having to act as a simple nursemaid to her own granddaughter. Forced to love her from the sidelines, in secret.

Behind it all was a bone-deep sense of betrayal. Why keep her in the dark all these years? Why all the secrets and lies? She couldn't wait for the chance to confront Izora. To finally learn the full story behind everything.

She burst out of the cave, the hot sun bearing down like a dry blanket across her shoulders. Druturion was still sunbathing, his eyes closed atop the rocks.

"Dru." She came closer, but still, he didn't respond. *"Druturion."*

His eyelids lifted. Those red eyes connected with her own. *"Hm? What is it?"*

"My family. They're here."

"That's good news." He cocked his head sideways. *"Why don't you sound excited?"*

"My mother was Sul. I know that now." She sighed. *"But I still have so many questions I won't find the answer to here."*

"Shall we leave then?"

"No, not yet. The world won't end if I spend the day here, getting to know my uncle and cousins." She smiled. *"There's three of them, Dru. I've found my family."*

Druturion closed his eyes and settled back on the rocks. *"I'm pleased to hear it. Wake me when you're ready to leave."*

Kayda turned to leave. She paused, sending her bondmate a sideways glance. *"Dru, why are you always sleeping? What aren't you telling me?"*

His eyes popped back open, and his shoulders slumped. *"You're too observant for your own good."* He cocked his head, staring at her directly. *"I told you once before that having so many bonds wasn't a problem for my kind. Well, there's a bit more to that story."*

Kayda returned to Dru's side and rubbed the smooth scale on his cheek. *"Go on."*

"Dragons have been bonding creatures for millenniums. We long ago realized those of us who can bond more than one species could use the boons we receive to our advantage."

Her hand dropped from his cheek, and she bit her lip. *"Boons? You mean like how the scourge let you hibernate underground?"*

"Yes, exactly. Each species brings its own skills. Birds of prey sharpen the eyesight and enhance speed. Humans double their partner's lifespans. But the problems start when those bondmates die. The living partner is left alone with their grief, and the voices in their mind that never leave."

The image of her grandfather, his head in his hands, his room full of scattered disarray, rose in her memory. *"I imagine it's a hard burden to bear."*

"It can be very hard, especially for a species as long-lived as we dragons are. But there is one species that brings a boon that can lessen those effects."

"There is?"

"Yes. Jagoths, the jungle cats of the Raimire jungle. All dragons who could bond more than one species sought jagoths as bondmates. The skill they bring is the ability to block the voices of one's bondmates."

"So, one of your bondmates was a jagoth?"

"Long, long ago. Before even Algernon, I bonded a jagoth. Since then, I've been able to choose when to listen to the voices of my former bondmates and when to silence them."

"That's why the voices don't bother you the way they bother my grandfather."

It made so much sense now. She'd been so worried about Dru succumbing to madness without realizing he had a secret weapon to help him combat the magic's harmful effects.

"Yes." Druturion stiffened and stared off into the distance. *"Only not so much lately."*

She didn't like the sound of that. *"What do you mean?"* She tilted her head and crossed her arms.

Druturion inhaled deeply before answering, his chest rising and falling as he exhaled a deep sigh. *"Since the Palisade fell, the scourge's voice has been becoming harder and harder to ignore."*

"It has?" Kayda gulped.

"That's why I've been sleeping. It's... hard to explain. The intrusions are easier to manage when I don't focus on them with my conscious mind."

Kayda backed up a step, her brows furrowing. What did that mean for Dru? Would he be able to handle the weight of the evil voice in his mind? The voice he'd described as vicious, bloodthirsty, and full of unquenchable hunger?

No. He could handle it. She would help him.

"It's all right, Dru. Sleep if you have to. We'll figure out what to do together." She sucked in a breath, an idea forming. *"The other dragons... Maybe once we find the dragons you're searching for, they'll know how to help. I'm going to head back inside, spend the night with my family. Tomorrow, we'll go hunting for yours."*

***

Kayda struggled to breathe, suffocating under another crushing hug from her uncle.

"Are you sure you can't stay longer?" Bamzan asked as he released her.

Kayda nodded. "I'm sorry." She slid her gaze to her young cousins, lowering her voice. "There's the trouble back in my homeland. I have to help them."

She'd stayed up half the night, chatting and getting to know her cousins by the light of a laumarle oil lamp. Once the children went to bed, she'd called for Lazar. She'd told her uncle and the Sul leader about the devastation in Dracwood. Warned them to keep a wary eye on the horizon for the scourge.

But though she pleaded as sweetly as she could muster for the Sul to take up arms with her against the vermin terrorizing Dracwood, she could win no firm promise of support. At least, not yet. She had to hope, in time, the Sul would agree to join the fight.

Now it was time to leave. As much as she wanted to stay and spend more time with the family she'd discovered, she had to help her bondmate. Then, her country.

"Wait, Kayda, don't you at least want me to finish your braids?" Bani asked.

She'd insisted on braiding her hair in the Sul fashion last night. It was Kayda's right as a Sandspear, now that she'd proved her mettle with the silk harvest. But the Sul braids took a ridiculous amount of time on long hair like hers. Bani only completed half of her head before taking a break to sleep.

Kayda slid her hand across the left side of her head, running her fingers through the dozens of tiny neat braids. "No. I think I like it like this. I'm half Sul after all." She smiled.

After a few more hugs, she set off across the cavern to find Jayan. She tiptoed around countless blanket-shrouded forms. It was just after dawn, and many of the Sul still slept.

She made it to the spot where she'd seen Jayan last, circled together with his sister and a few other Sul. Standing on her toes, she peered around, trying to locate which of the heads peeking out of the blankets belonged to her friend.

She spotted him finally, wrapped in a thin blanket, softly snoring. She crept over, knelt down, and shook his shoulder.

"Princess?" His head popped up, his short hair transformed into shoulder length braids. It looked like the Sul had added some thread to create the extra length. From the way it glimmered in the early morning sunlight, she suspected it was spider silk dyed black.

"Morning. Dru and I are heading back to Joria."

He sat up fully, frowning. "So soon?"

"Yeah. Sorry to cut it short, but I have some things I need to take care of. Are you staying?"

Jayan stared at her, his brows furrowing. "I—"

"Is this her?" a high-pitched voice asked.

Kayda turned sideways and stood. Jayan's sister sat up on her blanket, watching them. She appeared to be in her late teens and was lovely, even with her braids tousled from sleep and the crust of drool on her dark cheek.

"Aye," Jayan said. "Princess Kayda, meet my sister, Nova."

Kayda sent her a smile and a wave.

Nova popped up off the ground, raced across the circle, and pulled her into a crushing embrace. For the second time that morning, Kayda struggled to breathe.

Nova whispered in her ear as she squeezed. "Jayan told me what you did. How you saved him. Made him captain. Named his boat after me. Thank you."

"It was no trouble," she forced out. The tiny girl's hold was even more crushing than her uncle's. "Your brother has been a great friend. He's helped me just as much as I've helped him."

Jayan appeared at their sides. "Nova, give the princess a chance to breathe."

The girl finally released her death grip around Kayda's waist and stepped back, smiling sheepishly up at Jayan. "Sorry. I'm just so grateful to have you back, brother."

Jayan slid a hand behind his new braids, rubbing the back of his neck. "About that…"

Nova's eyes darkened. "You're leaving? Already?"

"Aye." Jayan frowned. "There's evil brewing back in Dracwood. I mean to do my part to stop it."

Her brown eyes glistening with moisture, Nova blew out a breath between her teeth. "I'm coming with you."

Jayan shook his head. "You—you can't. It's far too dangerous."

Hands on her hips, Nova stared him down, stone-faced. "I'll not lose you again. Take me with you, or I'll hunt you down to the ends of the ocean. I swear it."

For a moment, they were locked in a stare, like two gamblers trying to catch their opponent in a bluff.

Jayan was the first to crack. He sighed, turning a quizzical look at Kayda. Kayda shrugged and nodded once.

"All right, all right. You can come," he said.

Nova squealed with delight. She hopped up and bustled about the circle, gathering her things excitedly. "Let me just wake up a friend of mine. I'm sure she won't mind watching Inky while I'm gone."

"Inky?" Kayda asked.

"My pet chumon. Would you like to meet her?" She lifted a small blanket-shrouded cage off the floor and pulled the blanket free, revealing the creature within.

Kayda drew back, her heart slamming against her chest, coming close to slipping on a pillow in her haste. "What are you doing with that thing?" Her voice was thready, quavering.

The creature lifted its head and stared up at her with black, beady eyes.

Nova held a caged scourge.

Jayan and Nova met her reaction with confused expressions. "Princess? What's wrong?" Jayan asked, eyeing her like a kitten needing coaxing off a tree branch.

"That thing. That's one of the scourge." Kayda's lips curled back with disgust.

Nova laughed, cradling the cage against her chest. "Surely not. Inky's a chumon. We Sul have kept chumon as pets for generations. They're excellent hunters, and the only thing keeping the tetrelas in check. Have you seen how many eggs a spider can lay?"

Kayda bit her lip and crept closer to the caged creature. The small rodent was brown and silver-striped with sharp claws. The edges of its sharp incisors rested atop its bottom lip as it lay calmly at the cage's bottom.

Nova might call it by a different name, but there was no question in Kayda's mind this was the same type of creature that was, at this very moment, terrorizing her homeland. She couldn't sleep at night without the malicious beasts haunting her dreams.

She leaned down and stared at the animal, eye-to-eye. Something was different. Absent. That strange feeling, the slithering discomfort she remembered so clearly when she first laid eyes on the vermin terrorizing her country, was no longer there.

What did that mean?

She straightened, still unsure what to think, but letting the matter rest for now. Perhaps Dru could help. Either way, they needed to start moving.

"My mistake," Kayda said. "I'll meet you two outside. The day's wasting."

Chapter 15

"Breathe," Halynn whispered for the hundredth time.

Conall cracked open an eyelid. He sat cross-legged on the wooden floor in the cabin, across from Halynn. She was the picture of cool concentration, her hands loose in her lap, eyes closed, taking slow even breaths.

Why was this taking so long? He closed his eyes again, trying to concentrate on his breathing. Trying not to wonder if this would end up another failure like all his attempts to summon.

"Breathe," Halynn said again. "In and out. Like the tide. Feel the waves lift you. Let them take you away."

Conall breathed. Again, and again, and again.

There was nothing. Just air flowing in and out of his chest.

Wait. There was something. A tickle on his cheek.

Conall's eyes snapped open. Blazes!

His mouth clamped shut even as his eyes opened wider. He was floating. Fully submerged in the near-black ocean, smack dab in the middle of a school of siltreak. The tickle he'd first felt on his face spread all across his skin, along with a frigid chill settling deep within his bones.

Panic filled him. The air trapped in his lungs burned.

"Breathe," a voice said.

No. He was underwater. If he breathed, he would drown. He would die.

A new sensation caressed his skin. Warmth. He turned toward it, and a face appeared in the shadowy ocean beside him. Halynn.

"Breathe," she said, again.

That's right. This was a dream. He wouldn't drown. Just a dream. He breathed.

Water flooded his lungs. The panic was alive now. Screaming he was wrong; he was going to die. But Halynn floated directly before him and met his gaze. She grabbed his hand and placed it over her heart. He felt the slow rise and fall of her chest as the water slipped in and out of her lungs. That was all it took for him to adjust to the strange sensation. He matched the rhythm of her chest with his own, and the panic slid away.

She smiled. "You're all right. See?"

How was she talking? They were underwater, weren't they?

Right. This was a dream. He had to keep reminding himself this wasn't real. Every one of his senses was convinced this was really happening. He shivered at the tickle of scaled fins, quavered with the teeth-chattering cold. His gaze flitted all around, searching the near-black abyss beyond the school. It all felt so *real*.

Even as he marveled at the wonder of being transported beneath the sea, he remembered his purpose. Lark. He had to find her.

"What are we doing here?" His voice rang out through the water, as loudly as ever, even though he shouldn't be able to speak. Shouldn't be able to breathe. He ignored the contradictions and spoke again. "I thought I was supposed to see my future?"

"You will," Halynn said simply. "Breathe."

Conall took a slow, deep breath. Ice-cold water flooded in and out.

A light appeared beneath them. He squinted, trying to see beyond the siltreak to what lay below. What could give off light so deep in the ocean depths?

"Do you see that?" he asked.

"Yes." Halynn dropped his hand. "Come, we must swim."

She pivoted and advanced through the school, swimming deeper down in the depths, toward the light. Conall followed.

After enduring the tickle of a thousand slippery scales on his skin, they emerged from the school. He found himself floating above a scene that played out like a moving painting where there should only be black water. Reflected in the ocean the same way the landscape could sometimes be seen in a lake on a windless day. Only this was not a simple reflection. This was moving. Alive.

It was a battle. A huge, bloody fight spread out before him in all its gory destruction. Humans and scourge locked in combat, fighting on a landscape he barely recognized but still knew all the same. He'd been there before, after all. Saw his fate changed there. The Abandoned Lands.

Amid all the devastation, three people emerged, clear as day. One of them, a young woman with fire flowing from her fingertips, her warm brown skin freckled, hair a red halo on one side and a tumble of braids on the other, he didn't recognize. But the other two, he knew instantly.

"Lark." There she was. Oh, how he'd missed her. And yet, there she was.

Her brown curls floated around her as she raced through the battle, faster than should be possible, her hazel eyes burning with fervor. She flung earth like daggers, felling scourge in every direction. A brown and gold falcon fought at her side, diving, swooping, and clawing like mad.

He wanted to reach out and grab her. Pull her into his arms and never let go. But she didn't see him. She fought on, oblivious to his presence and beyond his reach.

Beside her, fighting just as furiously, was Shadow—and himself.

He turned to Halynn. "Is this my future?"

She shrugged. "I've seen this vision hundreds of times. Everyone who dreams has. No matter what comes next, this one vision always remains. A constant."

"What do you mean, what comes next?"

Even as he asked the question, the picture below changed. The battle spread out before him disappeared, gone in the blink of an eye.

The scene shifted, morphing into a meadow filled with flowers. So many blooms, every color and shape imaginable. The floral aroma smacked him, even in the water—fresh, sweet, and so lovely. And in the middle of the field of vibrant flora, a single woman stood.

"Mother?" Warm tears joined the cold water spilling into his eyes. He felt that same powerful urge to pull her into his arms, but she was beyond his reach.

She spun at the sound of his voice, lifting her beautiful face toward him and smiling. She looked exactly the same, clothed in a simple white dress that stood out starkly among all the bright flowers. Her long brown curls looped behind her ears. Her green eyes shone with warmth and love. "Conall. My boy. I've missed you."

He gasped. She could hear him? Speak to him?

"Mother!" He flew through the water, swimming furiously, trying desperately to cross the boundary separating their dream worlds. Water rushed by, and his muscles ached from the effort, but he could make no headway.

"Conall." She made no attempt to move closer, seeming to understand she couldn't reach him. "Please. We don't have much time."

He stopped. His heart pounded, water flooding in and out of his chest as he floated there in the inky water above her. He nodded. "I'm listening."

"You'll find Lark off the western coast of Joria. There are a series of islands there. She will be on the largest of them."

His heart leapt at her words. Finally! Finally, he knew where to find his sister. Then suspicion crept in, and doubt. "How do you know this? Mother, how are you here?"

Halynn appeared at his elbow, catching up to him in the water. "That's not your mother, Conall. The dream shows you what you need to see. Tells you what you need to hear. Listen."

The dream. Yes. It was all just a dream.

"I love you, son." He turned back to the dream that was his mother. "Tell your sister I love her, too. I don't blame her for what happened when we got sick."

Lark didn't blame herself for their mother's illness, did she? Conall's brow furrowed. "I will. I'll tell her."

"The battle you saw will come to pass. Soon. Very soon. All three of you must be there, or there's no hope." She shuddered and twisted to look behind her shoulder and all around. Like she was afraid. Afraid someone or something was watching her.

He remembered that feeling. The itch slithering over his skin in the void while the Palisade fell. The presence he'd sensed in the back of his mind.

"Who's there?" he asked, his voice shaky.

"There's no time. No time." His mother's gaze shot back to him. It burned into him like a flame, shooting fire through his veins even among all the ice-cold water. "All three of you. Don't forget."

Halynn gasped beside him. He spun away from his mother and saw Halynn's face lit from the light reflecting off the vision, her features twisted in pain. She screamed, pulling her limbs close and dipping her head down to her chest.

He reached for her, but before he brushed her skin, she vanished. "Halynn? Halynn!" Where was she? He swiveled around, searching the dark waters.

The light below him shifted. He wasn't looking directly at it, but he sensed it in the corners of his vision. His skin prickled with gooseflesh. There it was again. The crawling itch. He swung his gaze down below.

He was shown a tunnel. A hovel dug into the ground. Moist brown earth and black decay stung his nostrils. A red light spilled from a tunnel off to the side. Heat came with it, roasting his skin and sending a cold sweat dripping down his back.

Unease swelled within him. What was this place? What was he meant to see?

From within the gloom, a form emerged. A man, his skin blackened and mottled, rose from a crouched position on the ground. His limbs moved awkwardly. Flopping bonelessly, then jerking, like a marionette in the hands of a child. He lurched closer, head lolling on his neck. Then his head jolted upright, and Conall held back a gasp.

"Tarquin?" Though he had only met the man once before, he recognized him. His pale skin was ghostly white beneath smeared dirt and char, but he would know that face anywhere, even before his blue gaze shot to Conall's, and his lips quirked up into a smirk.

"No. Not Tarquin." The words came out of Tarquin's lips, spoken in the haughty voice he remembered so clearly. But it wasn't him. No.

The prickling unease swamping his skin confirmed it even without the denial from his lips. Whatever was speaking to him was not the prince. It was that same phantom presence he'd sensed as the Palisade fell.

Conall fought the urge to heave as the creature drew closer and its sickening effect spread. "You. You've been watching me. Who are you?"

"I am Unseen. The one who watches and waits. The giver of gifts and taker of lost dreams."

Dreams. Yes. This was a dream. The reminder made him bold in the face of certain danger.

"What do you want from me, Unseen?" Conall asked.

"A message. A warning. Heed me." He staggered closer, bobbing Tarquin's head side-to-side. "They don't tell it true. Those witches that caged me, they are the masters of secrets. The spreaders of lies. They can't be trusted."

Conall laughed. "So, I should trust you instead?" Even as the words escaped his lips, he knew he could never. Being in this thing's presence filled his whole body with revulsion. It was like swimming in an ocean full of bile. Like wrapping himself in a blanket of squirming maggots. How could anything that felt that way be trusted?

The thing that looked like Tarquin stilled at his laughter. "I've given you rotting flesh sacks everything!" he thundered, voice full of rage. "You don't know. You don't know the half of what I've given." He laughed, a nauseating chortle that gurgled up from Tarquin unnaturally. "One more gift shall I give to you. Three. Yes, three of you will come. I see that now. But only two will see the next day. Even that will not be enough. Not enough."

Did that mean... was one of them destined to die fighting this thing? He sensed with sudden certainty this Unseen was the true source behind the destruction of his homeland. This creature was responsible for unleashing the scourge to infest the world. Why should he believe a single word that left his lips? Wouldn't he say anything to stop the battle that had been foretold?

"Or perhaps we shall end things now, hm?" His voice was a promise of suffering, doled out slowly and with glee.

Unseen jerked into motion again. Stepping closer and closer to the edge of the vision Conall floated above.

Conall drew back. His stomach churned with disgust as the awful, revolting sensation grew stronger with every step it took. That thing couldn't reach him here. Or could it?

Fear paralyzed him. He should swim away. Fight back. Do something. But his limbs were locked. His stare glued to the jolting body creeping ever closer.

"Conall," a familiar voice whispered in his ear.

"Delyth?"

She appeared next to him, materializing in the water to his right. Confusion filled her face for a brief instant until she opened her mouth and breathed deeply. Then she spun toward the vision and gasped.

"You," she spat, the single word drenched with venom.

"Witch. You've returned." Unseen laughed again, the same sickening gurgle. "I told you you'd live to see me free. Only just." The force of his laughter slowed his advance, glee pouring off him like a torrent.

Conall shook his head, his chest tightening and thoughts freezing as surely as his body had. What did that mean?

Delyth turned to him, ignoring the thing wearing Tarquin's skin. "Conall, you have to wake. Wake from this dream."

A dream. This was a dream. The reminder broke the frozen cage around his thoughts.

"How?" he asked.

"Summon. We must summon. Send this beast back to the darkness that spawned him."

Conall nodded. He tried to clear his mind the way Delyth had taught him. To picture the water surrounding him taking shape in his hands. Nothing. He wanted to scream.

Luckily, Delyth had no such problems. She formed a sphere of water and shoved it at the vision.

Conall gasped.

It crossed the barrier, coalescing around puppet Tarquin in a ball that encompassed him entirely. Unseen jerked within the floating sphere, his body convulsing as water swamped his lungs. He swelled with the force of the water pummeling him, his skin ballooning like a beached whale until it stretched around him unnaturally.

Conall's eyes widened with horror. Tarquin exploded outward in a disgusting eruption of flesh, blood, and bone. But that wasn't the end of it. His flesh molted and transformed with sickening speed into dozens of vicious snarling rodents. The scourge.

Delyth threw more water at the vision. The beasts squirmed, attempting to burst out of the sphere and reach the air, but liquid continued to fill the chamber, flooding in relentlessly until the entire space was filled to the brim with the dark ocean water.

Beside him, Delyth slumped where she floated. Black circles shadowed her eyes, her energy spent. "Rest. I need rest."

Conall lifted a hand, but before he could even reach out, she vanished. Gone as swiftly as Halynn, leaving him alone once more in the darkened sea.

What was he still doing here? The question filled his mind, but deep down he knew. That repulsive itch. It was still there. What Delyth had done wasn't enough.

He whirled around. The scene below him was much the same. The underground hovel still flooded with drowned vermin. Slowly, they coalesced. Turning into something new before his eyes. Something truly terrifying. A dragon.

An ice-white dragon formed beneath him, its scales glittering pink in the red light. Conall squirmed as it grew, sucking up everything in its wake like a whirlpool. Soon, its growing mass forced the dirt to move. The dragon shoved its colossal head through the ground and burst out into a night black sky.

He gawked at the vision as the beast rocketed up. Terror still paralyzed him. He begged his muscles to move, but they wouldn't listen. Then the dragon faced him as it flew past in the moonlight. It stared straight at him and opened its mouth, spewing forth a geyser of molten ice.

Horror speared him as the ice broke through the vision. At the last instant, he dodged. The ice came so close to his skin he shivered uncontrollably as it passed. Two more times he rolled through the water, barely managing to stay out of the path of the creature's blasts. Finally, it circled, racing through the sky, turning around for another pass.

He was done for. Nothing would save him now. He could dodge all day, but eventually, one of those bolts of ice would kill him.

No. He hadn't come all this way, and finally learned his sister's location, only to be destroyed. He would save himself. He had to.

Lark. He had to see her in the flesh. He focused on her face. The picture of her fiercely fighting rose in his mind, and he latched on to it. He would find her. He must.

The next bolt of ice barreled toward him. He stood his ground and lifted his hand. The water around him swirled and danced. The ice slowed. Halted. Then it shot back, slamming into the dragon with such force it screeched and dropped out of the air, careening in a circle and smacking into the ground.

Conall laughed. He'd done it. He'd summoned!

Then the world went black.

Conall's eyes shot open in Halynn's cabin. He lurched forward and coughed, falling out of his cross-legged position. Water spewed from his lungs and splattered across the wooden floor. He landed face-first in the puddle, his muscles like jelly.

"Brother." Shadow bounded over and leaned over his front paws, scrutinizing him with his golden eyes. *"Are you all right?"*

He groaned and forced a shaky hand beneath him, pushing his aching cheek off the wet floor. *"I think so."*

He rolled up to sit, his strength slowly returning, along with a feeling he'd not felt in ages. Triumph. He'd summoned! Alone in that strange ocean dream, he'd found the key to unlocking the talent sealed within him. Clearing his mind didn't work. Not for him. He needed to focus on what he was fighting for.

A hacking cough split the air. Delyth.

Halynn perched on the bed's edge. All the color washed out of her cheeks as she stared down at the woman resting on the sheets.

Conall jolted to his feet. His legs wobbled but bore his weight. A few short steps saw him hovering beside the bed, and the sight that met him made his stomach sink.

"What happened?" He drew closer to the bed, swallowing.

Halynn met his gaze with a blank stare. "I was supposed to be your guide. When that thing ejected me, she insisted on taking the elixir." Her chin trembled. "I shouldn't have allowed it. The water in her lungs... It was too much."

Delyth looked on the verge of death. Her face was drained of vitality, her eyes glassy. Her hair hung lank and stuck to her sweat-soaked skin. Another cough rattled her chest. Drops of blood joined the mucus staining the handkerchief Halynn held to her lips.

The Unseen's message reverberated in his ears. That vision, dream—whatever it was—was no normal dream. It didn't fade into his subconscious the way dreams always did. He remembered every image. Every sickening feeling. Every word.

He was eternally grateful for all Delyth had done. He'd stood silently while the Sade Prim fought that beast on her own, drowning it with the last of her strength. Yet, he couldn't let her fade into the next life without answers. She owed him that much.

Conall sat on the bed beside Delyth. "Tell me. Where is my father?"

She coughed again before she spoke. Her words escaped a throat raw with the scratches of a thousand thorns. "Raimire. Stoneshore."

Conall exhaled, a weight lifting off his shoulders. He had his answers. At long last, he could find his father and sister.

Another cough ripped from Delyth's chest.

He chewed on his lip until she stopped shuddering. "I broke my block in the dream. Let me heal you. Tell me what to do."

Delyth's clammy hand landed atop his own. She shook her head. "You can't. Healing is not so simple. We don't have the right pieces of earth on this barren island."

No. There had to be something he could do. He couldn't sit here and watch her die after the lengths she'd taken to save him.

"We'll head back to the mainland. I can clear—"

Delyth's grip turned crushing. Her eyes lit with fire, and her voice rang out strong and firm. "No." She stared straight at him. "Listen now. There's a book with my things; you must read it. All of it."

Conall gulped, nodding vigorously. "I will."

Her gaze softened. Her grip on his hand lost some of its strength. "I'm sorry. It had to be done. I could see no other option."

He leaned closer, his brow furrowing. "What had to be done?"

She coughed again. Halynn lifted the handkerchief to Delyth's lips, and the white cloth came back stained crimson.

"Ereni," she breathed, her eyes gone wild.

Conall started to pull away, but Delyth gripped him again, harder than before. He couldn't still the gasp that escaped him as her hand locked down on him like a vise.

"Don't blame her. It had to happen this way. You must see that."

Conall's heart skipped a beat. "No."

Delyth's hand fell slack, her voice a pained whisper. "It had to be you three. Now. The Palisade had to fall."

Conall stood, his blood racing through his veins. He held his head in his hands, dizziness washing over him. Had they planned this all along? Was Delyth not some unsuspecting victim of her daughter's betrayal but a willing participant?

He spun back to the bed to demand an explanation, but there would be none. Tears spilled down Halynn's cheeks as she lowered Delyth's eyelids. The Sade Prim's chest no longer rose and fell. She was gone.

Conall and Halynn built a pyre from the stack of firewood she kept behind her shack. As the sun dipped down low on the horizon, they set Delyth's body atop it.

He sighed and stepped back as the fire caught, watching one of the strongest women he'd ever known be consumed by flames. He rested a hand atop Shadow's head, standing as a silent witness while the pyre burned.

"Would you like to say a few words?" Halynn asked.

Conall rubbed his neck, blinking away the moisture filling his eyes from the smoke. He still hadn't wrapped his head around everything she'd revealed on her deathbed. Despite all her scheming, all her plotting and lies, Delyth deserved the honor of a true Dracian funeral.

He drew a deep breath and spoke. "Delyth was many things to many people. A patient teacher. Caring leader. Loving mother and friend. She will be missed."

They stayed out there in the cold, watching, adding wood to the pyre. Doing their best to ignore the sickening scent of charred flesh filling the air. The flame's heat warmed his skin even as the air grew colder and fought to sink deep in his bones.

Tomorrow, he and Shadow would return aboard the tiny rowboat to Norwich to begin their voyage to find his family. Tonight, he took the time to grieve. Not just for Delyth, but for all that he'd loved and lost. He'd lost a part of himself, his youth, his power. His hope for a normal life.

And his mother. She'd been there, too, in that strange underwater vision. The reminder of her loss tore at him anew. She'd been so kind. Such an amazing friend and neighbor to all who knew her. He would make her proud. He would do what needed to be done to destroy the unseen evil plaguing his country. No matter the danger. And not because destiny said so. He would do it for her.

Chapter 16

Lark stared up into the spoolwood tree's branches. A series of wooden stakes lined the trunk, forming a makeshift ladder Mika used to scale the thick tree. He dangled precariously on the highest stake, reaching out to grasp a gorgeous red blossom high in the tree's branches.

"Careful," she ordered, a hand held on her forehead to shade her eyes from the afternoon sunlight filtering in through the jungle canopy.

"Got it." Mika plucked the delicate bloom. "Here, catch." He dropped the blossom, watching it flutter through the air and land on her outstretched palm.

She grinned and lifted the flower to her nose to sample the sweet scent. "I got it. Come down now."

"We might need a few more." Mika pulled another stake from the satchel slung on his shoulder and quickly pounded it into the trunk.

Lark told her stomach to settle as she watched with apprehension. The spoolwood tree was massive, like most trees in the jungle, but its branches were skinny, brittle things, not suitable to hold the weight of a child, much less a full-grown man. Mika insisted the stakes would hold, but his words didn't stop her from picturing him falling and breaking a dozen bones every time the wind kicked up or he hopped from stake to stake.

Mika climbed higher, the added height allowing him to harvest a half dozen more of the colorful blossoms and stuff them into his satchel. Finally, he began the climb down. When his boots sank into the spongy soil, Lark breathed a sigh of relief.

"Ready to head back?" he asked.

"Sure." She tried to hand the spoolwood blossom to him, but he shook his head.

"Keep it. You should add it to your herb collection."

She twirled the lovely red bloom in her hand. "So, you really think this little flower can cure Nox?"

He nodded, starting back down the footpath to Stoneshore. "Spoolwood blossoms contain a powerful poison."

Lark's eyes widened as she followed him down the trail. Her fingers trembled. She'd sniffed poison?

"Don't worry." Mika's hand landed on her shoulder, a playful smile on his lips. "It's only poisonous when ingested."

She exhaled a shaky breath. "I don't understand. Why would a poison cure him?"

Mika dropped his hand from her shoulder. "Nox's problem is having too many bonds. There's only one way I know to break them."

Lark gasped. "You're gonna kill him?"

Mika sent her a crooked grin. "Just for a moment. I'll bring him back." Her face must have displayed her disapproval. "Look, I know it's extreme, but it's the only way I can think to cure him. I'll tell Esmar all about the risks involved first. Let her decide. But it'll work."

Lark frowned. "How did he end up with so many bonds in the first place? He can't be more than, what, twelve or thirteen?"

Mika's nose twitched. "Thirteen, I think. The poor lad's just unlucky. No one's quite sure how bonds are forged. Much less for someone as rare as Nox, who can bond more than one species. As far as I can tell, it has something to do with proximity and danger."

"Proximity and danger," she repeated, rolling the words around in her mind. It made sense, in a way. Muse had first spoken to her to warn her of the scourge. To save her.

"Nox fell into the Stone River two summers past. That was when his first bondmate found him. A pengreen fish saved him from drowning. He was brought to me after he pulled himself free of the river's banks. And I met with him a few weeks later when the pengreen met his untimely end. I helped him deal with the grief and depression that followed." Mika sighed, dragging a hand through his dark locks. "Such a heavy weight for a boy so young."

"That's so sad. The thought of losing Muse..." Her gaze flicked to the sky where she guessed Muse flew, though she couldn't see her with the thick jungle canopy blocking her view. "I don't know what I would do."

"Nox is a resilient boy. He grieved, long and deep, but eventually, he started spending time down by the river, seeking a new bondmate. We were all surprised when it was a lizard and not a fish who answered the bond next. But the jungle is a dangerous place. It's not been easy for Nox to find bondmates—or to keep them."

"I never knew bonding magic could have such a powerful effect on the mind."

Mika nodded. "All magic is intimately entwined in the minds and emotions of the people who wield them." He peered at her closely.

"Tell me, Lark, what's your story? What's in your mind that is keeping you from summoning?"

She sighed. "That's the problem. I don't know what's stopping me from summoning. There are times when I call for my talent, and it's there right when I need it. Then sometimes, I try to summon and nothing happens. I don't know what I'm doing wrong."

He smiled, warmth pooling in his golden-brown eyes. "That's what I'm here to help you with. Can you tell me about the first time you tried to summon and couldn't?"

Dread and shame surfaced from the place deep in her belly where it lurked. A constant ache that she couldn't bury, no matter how hard she tried. She shook her head, not wanting to voice the terrible memory that tormented her.

Mika stopped on the path and trapped her hands in his own. "Lark. You have to face it. I can see from the look in your eyes—whatever it is—it haunts you. If you want to become the healer you were meant to be, you have to work through it."

Her mind fought to rebel at his words. To brush off his concern with a smile and a joke and bury the memory back deep inside. But she pushed the thought aside. He was right. It was past time for her to face it. To own up to the part she'd played in the death of the most important woman in the world. Her mother.

"There was a neighbor, back home in Greenvale. A boy, not much older than Nox. He had a sickness. A choking consumption in his lungs. My mother said he was too far gone. That nothing could be done. But I had to try. I'd just saved a babe with my talent, one on the verge of death." She sighed deeply, her gaze downcast. "I thought I could fix him." Her chin wobbled. "But I couldn't. And whatever it was he had... My mother and I caught it, too. I barely fought it off, but she—died."

Tears pooled in her eyes, her heart twisting. "If we hadn't spent so long trying to save him, we wouldn't have gotten sick. I tried to call on my talent, at the end. To save her. Nothing happened. I couldn't save her either." Her voice was thick with all the sorrow and anguish that burned in her gut. "It's all my fault. I killed her."

He pulled her close. Her cheek landed on the warm, hard plane of his chest. The tears splashed free, moistening his sheer luct top.

"You didn't kill her," he whispered. "The sickness did."

She shook her head, and he loosened his grip around her back, tipping her face up. He stared down into her teary eyes. "It's time to let it go, Lark. The pain you felt was real, but the fault was never yours. The guilt you're harboring will only hold you back."

She stared back up at him, breath hitching in her chest. "I-I don't know how."

Muse careened down from the sky, hovering briefly before landing on a branch to their right. *I hate to break up—whatever this is—but something's happening back at Stoneshore. You two better hurry back.*

Lark shook off Mika's embrace, drying her eyes on her sleeve. "Muse says something's happening back at the village."

"What's happening?" Mika's feet were already in motion, picking up his pace on the footpath.

What is it? Could you tell?

I'm not sure, but it looks like trouble. People running around, screaming.

Lark's stomach sank. "She's not sure, but it looks like trouble."

"We better get a move on then."

Lark nodded, and they took off running. They barreled through the jungle, racing along the path at breakneck speed.

Lark couldn't calm the worry rushing through her veins as speedily as she and Mika darted through the jungle. As they drew closer, the feeling intensified when she recognized that same strange sensation snaking across her skin that she'd first felt in the forest surrounding Mage Keep. The unshakable prickle of eyes on her back.

They'd been running full tilt for ages now, but the foreboding feeling sent her into overdrive. She swept past Mika, leaving him behind on the trail. She ignored her burning lungs and his calls to wait, and burst into the village with screams clogging her ears.

Chaos met her as she skidded to a stop. People lurched between huts, eyes wild and wide, their gazes flitting all over as if searching for something. Some invisible monsters hunting them from the shadows.

At first glance, she saw nothing. There were no enemies, or at least none she could see. Then a blur of fur and gnashing teeth hurtled into sight. It leapt from a tree with a high-pitched snarl, heading straight for a group of terror-struck villagers.

The scourge. They were here! Lark's stomach dropped to her feet. Before she could react, a trio of arrows speared into its back.

She drew in a series of gasping breaths, her chest aching from her run. She spun around in a slow circle, seeking the arrow's source. Finally, she spotted them. Archers—a dozen at least—stationed on rooftops, watched the jungle, eagle-eyed, ready to cut down the enemy.

They'd been ready. She sighed, her heartbeat slowing. Mata Moyra had heeded the warning they'd been given and prepared a plan of defense for the village.

Mika caught up to her at last. He stopped beside her and grasped her elbow. "What's happened?" he croaked out between gasping breaths.

"The scourge. They're here." She pointed to where the beast lay in a small pool of blood on the ground.

Lark's attention returned to the frightened villagers huddled in a group outside a small hut. They clutched each other and whimpered. Where were her friends? She had to find them. Make sure they were all right. She sped off, straight for the hut she shared with Tiora and Meital.

Images of the two of them, torn to shreds, blood spraying the hut's walls, played in her mind. *Please, no. Please let them be there, whole and unharmed.* If they'd been cut down while she was off picking flowers in the jungle, she'd never forgive herself.

Finally, she found herself outside the door. It was deathly quiet within. She tamped down the panic bellowing in her mind and drew a deep breath. Pushing past the luct screen, she peered inside.

Empty. Where could they be? Maybe they'd run to meet with the others?

Mika arrived on her heels. "C'mon, Lark." He tugged her elbow. "They'll need us at the healing hut."

She spared a glance in the direction of the hut Aren, Dausius, and Mazen shared. It was in the opposite direction of the healing hut. "I'll meet you there. I have to find my friends." She didn't wait for a reply, just took off like a shot.

"Muse, I need your help. I'm going to check the men's hut. Can you fly above the village, search for our friends?"

"All right. I'll find them." Muse lifted in the air, circling.

Lark weaved around buildings, her heart racing. Why did they have to house them so far apart? The men's hut sat on the village clearing's far side, close to the jungle's edge, whereas theirs was almost directly in the center.

In the back of her mind, she understood the logic. Keeping the women, the village's future leaders, protected in the center was sound. But right now, when she wanted to desperately know the fate of her friends, she cursed the convention that wouldn't allow the men to be housed more closely to her.

Adrenaline propelled her. She hopped from hut to hut, her gaze darting all around, searching for any sign of the vicious vermin. From somewhere far away, more screams resounded, sending ice through her veins.

Would her friends be there when she got there? The question nagged at her. She had just told Tiora she'd understand if they had to move on. They were a *traveling* show, after all. What if they'd taken their leave while she was gone? They might have set off to find another village to entertain before dark. Would they be caught unaware in a scourge ambush somewhere in the jungle?

Though it only took a moment to travel across the town, the journey seemed to last twice as long. Her mind raced, her nerves on edge at every sound, every scream. Was that her friends, crying out in pain? She had to find them.

At long last, the men's hut appeared. It was perched on the jungle's edge, shaded by a massive diquat tree's branches. No noise and no movement came from within. She burst through the luct screen, her heart pounding.

The hut was empty. She grasped her chest and cursed under her breath.

She spun on her toes and exited as quickly as she'd entered. Sweat poured off her body. With her back pressed against the outer hut wall, she shucked off her knapsack and gulped down a drink from her waterskin.

Had they really left her? Without saying goodbye? One thing was certain: she couldn't keep rushing around out in the open with no weapon. She grimaced. It was a miracle she'd made it this far.

A pair of scourge descended from the branches of the diquat tree shading the men's hut.

Blazes. Lark stood stock still, praying the vermin wouldn't see her.

They slinked down the bark, their sharp claws and lithe bodies working as well as the squirrels of her homeland to scale the rough trunks.

Her skin crawled as they crept closer. Those beady eyes darted all around, searching for prey. The leader reached the ground and shook his brown and silver-striped fur. It lifted its snout, scenting the air.

"Muse?" She fought to ignore the fear paralyzing her. *"Help! Scourge at the men's hut."*

She replied instantly, *"I'm coming!"*

Of course, this had to happen when she had no weapon. If only Mika had taught her more, so she could call on her talent. If they spotted her, she was dead. They'd be on her in an instant, tearing at her skin and feasting on her flesh, just like those poor souls back in Bogsmouth.

Maybe if she froze, unmoving, they would miss her. Maybe they would move on.

For a moment, she thought it might actually work. The beasts made it to the ground and shifted, heading north, away from her. Then the second beast stopped in its tracks and swiveled its head directly at her.

Oh no. It saw her. Her eyes widened.

The beast bared its teeth and snarled. The leader turned at the sound and spotted her, too. Its lips curled back, flashing its wicked fangs. They leaned back on their hind legs, poised to leap at her.

Lark twirled the strings of her knapsack around her hands. She pulled her arms back, preparing to use the bag as a bludgeon to swat them away. If she could hold them off until Muse found her, she might stand a chance.

The scourge leapt. She watched with horror as the creatures sailed through the air, headed directly for her. They were so fast. They bounded off the ground with each leap, reaching the height of her chest easily.

An angry blur caught one of them mid-jump. Muse! The crack of the beast's neck breaking rang out clearly, even as the scourge struggled within her bondmate's grasp.

Lark didn't have time to celebrate. The second scourge lunged for her, its beady eyes locked onto her, mouth opening with a screech. She loosed her sack at the last instant, smacking the creature dead in the face, sending it flying backward, end over end.

Yes! But she swung so hard the bag flew free, leaving her hands empty and her weaponless.

Like a cat, it landed on its feet.

Bloody blazes. Her heart was a tidal wave, pulsing and slamming with the force of a storm.

The scourge turned. It sprang.

Then it fell to the ground, the blade of a knife lodged in its neck.

"Lark?" asked a familiar voice from above.

She lifted her face to the rooftops. "Mazen." She grinned. "Am I glad to see you! Where are the others?"

Mazen hopped down from the roof, joining her on the ground. "They're all back at the healing tent, except for me and Meital. We've been helping with pest control." He leaned down and pulled his knife free from the vermin's neck. "C'mon, I'll take you."

She nodded, grabbing her bag off the ground and following on his heels. *You all right, Muse?*

Ha. Fine. Are you? She hopped up on a tree branch, scanning their surroundings.

Yes, thanks to you. You saved me.

Just then, a thought occurred to her and her stomach clenched. "Wait, Mazen. Why are they all at the healing hut? Was someone hurt?"

Mazen's brow furrowed. "Yeah, but not one of us. It was Fillan."

Lark gasped. "Fillan's back from the Boglands?"

Mazan nodded, twirling a knife in his hand. "He came racing into town to warn us just before the scourge arrived. If it wasn't for him, we might not have been so lucky."

They made it to the healing hut in record time. Mazen dropped her at the door, circling back to join the defense. Muse met her gaze and turned back, too.

It was crowded inside, every bed filled with villagers covered in scratches, bruises, and cuts. Mika and the young men from earlier flitted around the beds, applying salves and bandages.

Dausius, Tiora, and Aren were there, too, crowded around a cot in the back, which held the boy who'd guided them through the Boglands to safety. His face was weary, and he had bandages covering his chest and most of his right arm from view.

She raced back to join them. "Fillan. Are you all right?"

"Lark. I'm glad you made it back. When I got here to warn everyone and heard you were out in the jungle... Well, we all feared the worst."

She spared a glance at Sunny, who lounged beside the cot and clutched Fillan's left hand, her brows drawing together. "Don't worry about me. What about you? What happened?"

"The scourge. No one knew what good climbers they were. We had some unseasonable cold a few days back. It iced over a few of the bog passes near Dracwood. It was enough to give the beasts a foothold through the Boglands."

"Oh no," Lark said.

"We caught on in time. Burned and cut down enough trees that they can't pass any longer. But not before a dozen or so got through. That's why they sent me. I came to warn you."

"It's a good thing you did. We all owe you a great debt," Lark replied.

A scream rose behind the drawn curtain to their right. Mika crossed the room in a few quick steps and shoved the curtain aside.

Esmar stared down at an empty cot. Her words came rushing out, fast and frantic. "Where is he? Where is Nox? He was just sitting there, staring off into space. Then so many people came in with cuts and scratches. I left him to help with the bandages. Where is my boy?" She let out another wail, then her eyes lit with fire. "I'm going to find him." She took a quick step toward the door and landed on her bad leg with a startled sob.

Mika was there to catch her. He grabbed Esmar's shoulders, steadying her and spinning her to face him. "No, Esmar. You can't chase him with your leg. I'll find him. He'll be fine, you'll see."

Mika crossed the room, grabbed his pack where it rested by the door, and shoved aside the luct screen, disappearing outside.

Lark gave Fillan's hand a squeeze and moved to follow. Aren's eyes widened when she started walking, and he departed Fillan's bedside, joining her at the door.

"I'm coming with you." He grabbed a bow and quiver leaning against the wall by the door.

Lark quirked a brow. She'd never once seen Aren with a bow. "Do you even know how to use that thing?"

"Of course. You didn't think I spent my whole life laying around playing the lute, did you?" He spared her a quick half-smile as they burst out into the afternoon sunlight.

They were just in time to see Mika disappearing down a footpath that led west.

"Muse, with me," Lark called out.

Aren had the same idea. He whistled for Whisper to follow. Both birds circled the sky above them as they disappeared down the jungle path.

She'd yet to travel in this direction. She kept expecting an ambush to greet them. Or worse, for them to discover the poor boy being set upon by the scourge. But all they found was more jungle.

A new sound joined the jarring animal cries that never ceased. This was no animal. It hummed low in her ears, growing louder and louder the further they trekked. What was that sound? Then the scent of salt reached her, and her mind connected the dots. Waves.

They burst out of the jungle, finally catching up to Mika at the footpath's end. He stood atop a cliff, overlooking the sea.

Lark and Aren stopped beside him. She raised her gaze to the horizon and gasped.

Out on the ocean, a tiny row boat sailed toward a large island that she could just make out far off on the horizon. Sitting in the boat, his hands busy rowing, was Nox. And on his shoulder, perched there comfortably, like a baby bird in a nest, sat a scourge.

"No." She shook her head. "Tell me I'm not seeing what I think I'm seeing."

Mika sighed, and the words he spoke made her want to cry. "Looks like Nox just found a new bondmate."

Chapter 17

Honeyed shimmering silk slipped across Kayda's fingers. She was back on *Nova's Champion*, below deck in the former captain's study. She couldn't stand the thought of sleeping in that vile man's bed, so she'd made this room her quarters. She sighed, sliding her finger and thumb across the gorgeous dress resting within the paper wrapping.

Wyll had been true to his word while she'd been gone. He'd let no harm fall to the ship and the slaves it held that had once been his own. Now hers as well. She wrinkled her nose.

All was well as they sat docked on the wharf. Once again, she'd urged the people lingering on board to return to their lives. To leave. Except for a handful, they'd all remained. Jayan would welcome them as crew in truth. The *Nova's Champion* would join the fight to save her country. To save the world. As much as she didn't want the former slaves on board to remain out of duty to her, she wouldn't force them to leave. Dracwood needed all the help they could get.

That fact was what had her stroking the lovely silk dress. She frowned and lifted it from the packaging, holding it up in the late afternoon light spilling in the open window.

Would she ever again enjoy wearing this fine silk without her memory flashing back to the terror that was the tetrela silk harvest? Her head spun as she stared at the golden, glittering fabric. It wasn't so long ago she was wrapped in this same silk, quivering in fear beneath a predator's grasp, spinning, just spinning.

She blew out a breath and set her shoulders back. Then she settled the dress back on the huge wooden desk bolted to the floor and kicked off her boots.

Whether she liked it or not, she had to put on that dress. It was time to set aside the part of herself she'd found out there in the Waste. She would wash away the dirt, sand, and sweat and bury the part of her that was sandborn.

Tonight, she needed to be a princess again. She would wear that dress and finally secure the help her country needed. Then she could concentrate on helping Druturion.

She shucked off her filthy trousers and white silk shirt, dropping them onto the wooden boards. Then she got to work scrubbing herself with a bucket of water and a rag.

Dru was above deck, sprawled out on the midship deck, sleeping. How long would he be able to shut out the evil voices in his mind? The hair on her arms and neck stood on end as she scrubbed, giving her light brown skin a pinkish tinge from the force of her strokes.

No. He could handle it. She would make sure of it.

She grabbed a towel from the desk, drying her skin. Her hands slid over the braids covering half of her head. These she was resolved to keep. The corner of her mouth lifted into a grin. She might look a little strange with half of her head done, but the longer she wore them, the more she grew to love the braids. It felt right to have this one little reminder of the family she'd found in the Waste.

The towel joined the pile of clothes on the floor. Slipping into the golden silk, she shuddered as the smooth fabric slid across her skin. But this time it didn't squeeze her until she could scarcely move. She took a deep breath and forced aside the memory of the tetrela's spindly legs wrapping her so tightly.

After taking a moment to tidy her room, she slipped back into her boots and vacated the cabin, emerging into the bright sunlight above deck.

A whistle greeted her. She spun around, her cheeks heating as she spotted Jayan's gaze traveling down her body from her head to her toes. He was back at the helm in his causal state of undress, feet and chest once again bare.

"Princess—that dress—wow." He grinned.

She rolled her eyes. "Keep an eye on things, Captain. I'll be back later."

The smile fell from his face. His mouth opened. Closed. Opened again. "Be careful," he said, finally.

His quiet request sparked a feeling inside of her. One she didn't have time to turn over and examine. She smiled instead, a brash grin full of the confidence his reaction to her dress inspired, and nodded once before heading down the gangplank.

A warm breeze whispered across her bare arms and blew the sleek silk dress against her legs. Dozens of eyes shifted to watch her. She did her best to ignore the dockworker's stares and set her sights on the man who awaited her at the end of the wharf.

"My lady." Wyll offered a shallow bow as she approached, looking as handsome as ever in a dark brown silk suit. His eyes performed the same slow glide across her form as Jayan's had, but his gaze lingered on her head.

She stilled, waiting for him to mention her braids. He didn't disappoint.

"I take it your trip to find the Sul went well?"

She smiled. "It did. Thank you for keeping an eye on things for me while I was gone."

"It was no trouble. I'm so pleased you agreed to join me." He smiled, swiveled sideways, and held out an elbow. "Shall we?"

She slipped her hand into the crook of his arm and matched his steps. "Thank you for the invitation."

When they'd returned to the boat, she'd found a parchment resting atop her desk. A standing invitation from Wyll to join him for dinner upon her return. It was a stroke of luck, to be sure. She still needed to secure allies to defend her home from the scourge. This was the perfect opportunity to do that. She only hoped her efforts to convince Wyll would be more successful than her attempt to sway Lazar had been.

She exhaled, firming her resolve and sneaking a peek at her companion's face. He was still smiling, staring ahead as they strode away from the boat.

He would agree to help. She would make sure of it.

They arrived at a large building perched on the dock's outskirts. A signpost swung in the breeze above the door with a drawing of snake crashing through a wave and the words, the Salty Serpent Inn scrawled in red ink. She peeked in the window as they slowed, heading to the door. The bar was crowded, packed with dockworkers slugging back ale and laughing at bawdy jokes.

Interesting. This was not what she'd been expecting. She hadn't pictured Wyll as the type to frequent anywhere as common as a simple inn.

Wyll strode inside, leading her past the common room humming with raucous merriment. The delicious aroma of roasting meat followed them as they strolled further inside, toward a set of stairs leading up.

Kayda dropped Wyll's arm, cocking a brow. "Should I be concerned we're heading away from the dining room?" She stopped and peered up the carpeted stairs and into the shadowy hall above.

Wyll turned, one foot already on the bottom step, and offered her a hand. "The view's better up here. C'mon. Trust me." He grinned.

Kayda stared up at him, examining his smile in the dim candlelit hall. She'd already started on this course; she might as well see it to fruition. Besides, if he tried anything fresh, she could always scorch him. She smiled back and took his hand.

He led her to the third floor, pulled a key from his pocket, and opened the room's door. She steeled herself as the door swung open, preparing to enter a bedchamber, but she was met instead with a wooden chamber featuring a floor-to-ceiling glass window that overlooked the ocean with no bed in sight. Her jaw dropped as she strode inside to the simple table placed before the window. It was set for two.

"You're right. The view is lovely." The sun was beginning to set, throwing rose and lavender shades into the sky above the docks.

"You should see it at dawn."

She quirked a brow. "Should I?"

He pulled out the closest chair for her, his smile bright and mischievous. "The sun rises beyond the ocean every morning. It's spectacular."

Kayda slipped into the seat, dragging her gaze away from the window to look around the room. Shelves lined the walls, filled with hundreds of books. A worn wooden desk, covered in ink stains and neatly stacked piles of parchment, was wedged into a corner. "I take it this room is not always used for dining?"

Wyll seated himself across from her. "No. It's an office."

"Yours?"

"Yes. I enjoy being close to the action."

No wonder he'd shown up so quickly when they'd sailed into port. He must've been here all along.

Kayda's gaze slid along the bookshelves. There were several titles she recognized, and even more she'd love to examine more closely. "Are these all your books, too?"

Wyll nodded, leaning back on his chair. "Indeed. Are you a fan of the written word?"

It was her turn to nod. "I am."

His grin widened. "Feel free to borrow anything you'd like. My library is yours."

She smiled. "That's very kind of you to offer." Her smile drooped slightly. "I'm afraid I have little time for reading, presently. That's actually what I'd like to talk to—"

A knock on the door interrupted her.

"Come in," Wyll's deep voice boomed, full of command.

A pair of maids breezed in, carrying plates heaped full and fragrant. Kayda smiled pleasantly as they bustled about, dishing out food and pouring drinks.

There was stewed meat, potatoes, and a variety of fruits cut into bite-sized slices. Despite the delicious food on offer, she couldn't stomach the thought of eating. She had to know if Wyll could be persuaded into being an ally to Dracwood.

Soon the maids slipped out the door, closing it behind them.

Wyll lifted a wine glass, taking a tentative sip. "You were saying?"

She exhaled. "I'm sure you've heard what's happening in Drac-wood."

He nodded once. "When the crew of the *Sea Sil*—pardon, the *Nova's Champion*—failed to return, we made inquiries."

"I didn't just come here searching for my family. I've come to seek allies as well. I'm sure you realize the scourge will not just be a problem for my country, but the entire world."

He took another sip of his wine. "We're traders, not fighters."

Kayda suppressed the urge to scowl. "You have a fleet of ships at your disposal. They would be indispensable. Ferrying those who will fight. Bringing weapons and supplies where they're needed."

Wyll leaned back, his gaze shifting to the widow before flicking back to hers. "I want to help you. But it won't be easy to convince my father."

She leaned forward, reaching across the table. "You know him well. What would sway him? Money? Trade rights? If it's in my power, I'll arrange it." Silence stretched between them. She held her breath, praying he would think of something. She couldn't return to Flamesmoat without the aid they needed.

Wyll leaned forward, matching her stance. He stared straight into her eyes. "We've enough money and trade already. There's only one thing that might work. Something he once had within his grasp before it was stolen from him."

Kayda's eyes widened. What could she give him that had been stolen from him?

Wyll's hand slid atop hers on the table. "Marry me."

She pulled her hand back, sitting upright in her chair. "What?"

Wyll stared down at his hand on the table before lifting his gaze to hers again. "My father thought he had royal connections when Solenne left to marry your father." He dropped his gaze and picked up a fork, poking at the food on his plate. "You can't imagine how much he used to brag when I was a boy. Practically every man he passed on the street heard all about how his niece married into royalty."

The fork stilled. "One day, he just stopped. I always wondered why. Now I'm sure that was when he found out the truth about where Solenne actually ended up." His gaze lifted to hers again. "I imagine he'd give just about anything to have that connection in truth."

Kayda's mind raced. He really wanted to marry her? "As far as anyone knows, we're family already. Won't it seem strange for us to be marrying each other? As cousins?"

"It's not so strange in Joria. Especially with large trade families like ours. No one here would bat an eye."

Kayda bit her lip. "It's not common in Dracwood but not unheard of, either."

Wyll leaned forward again. "And of course, we'll know we aren't actually cousins."

"True." She frowned. "You would marry me, for your father's sake?" She crossed her arms. "What do you gain out of this deal?"

"Besides the pleasure of a princess for a wife?" He sent her a crooked grin.

She cocked a brow, her lips pursed.

He sighed. "My brother and I have been making moves to bring the family business into the future. Trading more in goods and less in flesh. My father is... set in his ways. Not to mention his history of making rash decisions without consulting the rest of us." He grimaced, gaze flicking down. "That whole mess in the Abandoned Lands being one of them."

He met her eyes, sending her a rueful smile. "Frankly, we're getting a little tired of cleaning up his messes. But I have a feeling this might be what he needs to hand a bit more of the day-to-day decision making over to us."

It was commendable that Wyll was seeking to leave the slave trade. And learning it was his father who struck a deal with Tarquin and not him certainly lifted a weight off her shoulders. Kayda speared a piece of meat on her plate and popped it in her mouth, chewing slowly while she considered his proposition.

Could she marry him? She'd always been destined for a political match. Some arrangement that would benefit her country. And what was this if not a match that would benefit her country?

Would her grandfather and father allow her to take these matters into her own hands? Surely, they would see the logic and back her decision once all the facts were brought to light. It's not like she'd be running off with some stable boy, after all. She'd be marrying her way into a family that had the means to help their country stave off the enemies terrorizing their lands.

Truthfully, she hadn't expected to have to make such a decision so soon. Despite looking fully grown due to that minor mishap in the underground where she found Dru, she was only sixteen. Could she make a decision that would affect her entire life over dinner? Did he expect her to?

She swallowed, studying him. He was handsome. Though she didn't know him well, what she knew about him, she liked. But was it enough to bet a marriage on?

Wyll cleared his throat. "Perhaps this was a foolish idea." He rose and moved in front of the window, turning his back to her, his shoulders sinking.

Kayda's heart skipped a beat. Hadn't she just told herself she would do whatever it took to gain the aid her country needed?

She stood and joined him at the glass. "No. It's not foolish." She slipped her hand into his. "You understand, I must arrange this with my family first. We can't run off and marry today."

He spun to face her, grasping her other hand. "So, you agree?"

She nodded. "Yes, I'll marry you."

"Good." He beamed, his eyes twinkling, looking for all the world like a boy handed a massive sweet. Then his face shifted, darkening into an expression that sent a tingle down her spine as he drew closer.

He lifted a hand to her face, fingering a braid and sliding it behind her ear. "Kayda, I hope you know I'm not only interested in you for your title."

Her heart raced as his fingertips slid over the shell of her ear. She was suddenly very aware of the closed door. "You aren't?"

His dark brown eyes connected with hers. He shook his head, his stare sliding down to her lips.

Was he going to kiss her? She drew in a breath, her gaze flicking between his lips and his eyes as he dropped his head. His hand slid behind her neck, tracing the skin lightly, his fingertips smoothing the hair on the nape of her neck.

He drew closer, slowly, so slowly. Her eyelids fluttered closed as his lips brushed over hers, soft as a whisper.

And then he was gone. Her eyes shot open to find him an arm's length away, looking once more out the window.

She exhaled, blinking quickly. Had she done something wrong? Her stomach sank. Did he want out of their bargain?

Then he turned to her, his smile back in place. "So, after you speak to your family, we shall wed."

He didn't want out then. She gulped. Nodded.

"When will you return to Flamesmoat?"

She sat back down; her legs shaky after the kiss Wyll seemed happy to ignore. "Soon. I've something I have to do first."

Wyll joined her at the table. "And what's that?" He lifted his glass and took another sip.

Should she tell him about her promise to Dru? He was to be her husband. And he'd done nothing to suggest he couldn't be trusted. Once they wed, they would share everything. Perhaps she should begin trusting him now.

"Druturion believes there are more of his kind somewhere, sleeping underground like he was. I've promised to help him find them." She grabbed her fork and stabbed a potato. "The only problem is we don't know where to look."

Wyll's brow furrowed. "Wait there." He crossed the room to the desk and slid behind it. Fishing in his pocket, he retrieved a key ring and unlocked the top desk drawer. He pulled free something large, white, and oblong.

Was that a bone?

A moment later, he was back. He slid the bone across the table. "I just received this from one of my contacts in Raimire. It came from a massive beast that washed up on the beach in a little village called Stoneshore."

Kayda lifted the bone. Despite its size—it was nearly as long as her whole arm—the bone was surprisingly light. "It's hollow?" Her eyes widened.

Wyll smiled. "My contact believed the corpse originated from the largest of the Mido Islands."

Kayda placed the bone back on the table and leaned back in her chair. What were dragons doing washing up dead on the beach in Raimire? Whatever was happening, she was going to find out.

She aimed a smile at Wyll. Trusting him had already paid off. Perhaps this arrangement would be in her best interest. She could only hope that would continue to be the case. "Thank you for sharing that with me. Let's talk about your fleet."

Kayda knocked on the door to Jayan's chamber. The parchment in her hand crinkled as she awaited his answer.

She was back on-board *Nova's Champion,* below deck. She'd sat and talked with Wyll for hours, and then with Druturion, once she'd arrived back at the boat in the dead of night.

It was nearly morning. She ought to let the poor man sleep. But what she had to say couldn't wait until she returned. If she returned.

A *thump* sounded from within. Then the door slid open, and Jayan popped out. His braids were tousled, and he wore his customary pair of shorts and nothing else. He squinted in the dim candlelit hall. "Princess? Everything all right?"

She nodded and shoved the parchment into his hands.

"What's this?" He leaned closer, his gaze flicking across the words quickly. "I don't read, my lady."

Kayda hid the frown that fought to appear at his matter-of-fact statement. She smiled instead. "This is the deed of ownership for *Nova's Champion.* I want you to have it."

He shook his head and cleared his throat. "No, I can't accept this." He tried to hand the parchment back, but she took a step backward, clasping her hands behind her back.

"It's yours, Jayan."

He pulled the parchment close, eyeing it again. A smile crept across his face. "Thank you, Princess."

She nodded, her smile just as wide. "I hope you will consider joining the fleet of ships headed up the coast to Dracwood. Of course, the choice is yours to make, Captain." She turned to leave.

"Wait." He grasped her arm, stopping her. "Are you leaving?"

From the look in his eyes, she could tell he wasn't just asking about her leaving the hall. Somehow, he'd sensed she was leaving for good.

She nodded. "Druturion and I have business in Raimire, at a village called Stoneshore. We're leaving at dawn."

Jayan let go of her arm. He stared down at his feet before meeting her gaze and offering a small smile. "Good luck, Princess. I'll see you soon."

She quirked a brow. "Goodbye, Captain."

She returned to her room to pack her things. The first rays of dawn brightened the sky outside the open window.

The night had been a success. She'd finally secured the aid her country so desperately needed and found a clue that might lead her to her bondmate's brethren.

She stared out the window, breathing deeply of the salty sea air. In a perfect world, she would be happy to stay longer. To take her time getting to know her newfound family and her soon-to-be husband. But the world was far from perfect. At least she could leave Joria content that she'd uncovered some of the answers to the mystery of her past. One day, she would return. For now, she had a promise to keep.

It was time to discover what was happening on the Mido Islands.

Chapter 18

Conall made his way through another darkened forest. Snow stuck to his lashes and coated his stallion with a dusting of white atop his long brown fur. The wind was still this morning, making the cold seem less in its absence. It was an unexpected advantage in this frozen tundra, but he'd take all the good luck he could grab.

"Minsport is not far now," Taul said from his perch on the mount beside him. "Just on the other side of this wood."

Conall nodded, his fingers tensing beneath his gloves then tightly clutching the reins. A few more hours, and he would be on a boat sailing south. It was time to leave this frozen land behind and finally find his sister. "Thank you again for coming with me. I know you only agreed to venture to Norwich originally."

"It's no bother. Winters can be a bore in Gransea. I'm happy to have an excuse to venture about." Taul grinned, lifting his fur hat and scratching the stubbly red growth on his not-quite bald head. "Besides, Minsport is known for certain—how do I put this mildly—houses of ill-repute you won't find in Gransea. I've got plans for a nice long visit while I'm in the city."

He frowned. "Remind me to steer clear of those."

Taul chuckled. "You Dracians can be so stiff about these things."

Conall rolled his eyes. "I don't know why not wanting to pay a woman to—be nice to me—makes me stiff." He scoffed. "I don't understand how you Doln can be so casual about such things. Don't get me started on slavery."

Taul waved a hand. "I've been to your Flamesmoat. I've seen all the beggars and the poor in the slums. You don't see that around here. And do you know why?" He cocked a brow. "Everyone has a place."

Conall shook his head. "A place you can't leave isn't a place I want to be in."

"I guess we'll just have to agree to disagree, my friend."

They emerged from the wood and found Minsport spread out before them. Much like Gransea, it sprawled alongside the coast, only marginally smaller than the capital. Docks lined the ocean with boats of all sizes pulled into the harbor.

Conall dismounted, handing his reins off to Taul. "I don't know if I'll see you again, so I guess this is goodbye."

Taul smiled from atop his mount. "Well met, my friend. Pass on my goodbyes to Shadow." With a nod, he was off, leading the horses down the rise to Minsport.

"Brother. We're here. How long until you can catch up?"

Snow crunched behind him as his bondmate exited the wood, his tail wagging. *"Not long."*

Together, they began the trek to Minsport. The city itself was much the same as Gransea—buildings of gray stone laid out on neat streets. But the similarities ended there. This city was loud and brimming full of people. Chief Aundreas' claims about all the refugees flooding Minsport were no exaggeration.

Conall strolled through the throngs of folk crowding the streets, heading for the docks. Having a wolf at his side certainly had its perks. No one sought to stop him, and most seemed eager to stay a few paces away from where they tread.

It wasn't until he found himself a few streets away from the docks, the scent of saltwater and cawing of birds growing stronger with every step, he stopped. In the street ahead of him, he spotted a familiar face in the crowd, staggering away from the shadowy interior of an inn. Someone he had not expected to see.

"Aunt Brenna, is that you?" He jogged up the street to greet her. He wasn't about to miss this opportunity to sort out the strangled claims he'd overheard his stepfather crying about while he'd thought Conall dead at the bottom of a cliff.

Wild brown eyes turned to stare at him. She was dressed in a simple brown dress, her hair pulled up in a messy bun. She clutched a dark brown fur tightly against her chest, and a large sack bounced on her back. "Conall?" Her eyes bulged as she caught sight of him. "Is that you? You look different…"

Well, that wasn't much of a surprise. He certainly looked different these days. Not only from the aging but also from the thick brown and gray beard covering his chin when he'd always been clean shaven back in Dracwood. It was really more surprising that she recognized him at all.

Her jaw snapped shut, and she plastered a smile on her face, her gaze flitting between him and the building she'd just exited. "How fortunate I found you, nephew. I need your help. The people here, they're crooks and thieves, I tell you!"

A large blond man burst out of the building, his pale cheeks red. When he spotted Brenna on the street, he stalked forward, his lip curled back, jabbing a finger in her direction. "Stop, woman. You can't slink away without settling your debts." He skidded to a stop before her. "There are consequences around here for thieves."

Brenna grabbed the sleeve of Conall's fur, hiding behind him. "Please, Conall." Her voice was a thready whisper, thick with desperation. "You know me. I need your help with this *savage.*"

Conall breathed out a hard sigh. Who should he believe? The woman who sought to advise her brother into shooting him and leaving him for dead, or some random business owner, confident enough in his claims to follow a woman out in the street and shout about her debts? Despite his familiarity, or perhaps because of it, he was willing to bet on the latter.

He addressed the man first. "Sir, could you give me a moment to speak to this woman? I'll pay you for your time." He pulled a coin from his pocket and sent it sailing toward him.

The man snatched it out of the air and sent an angry glare his way. "I'll agree so long as you keep her here while I fetch the clan chief. I'll have this debt settled today."

Conall nodded. "Done."

The man whirled around to the crowd that had gathered to stare at the commotion in the street. "You all heard him. I've witnesses." He waited for several people to nod in agreement and form a loose circle around them before he sauntered off, his hurried pace taking him quickly down the street and out of sight.

Brenna glowered up at him. "What'd you do that for? I can't be brought before the clan chief. They'll have me turned into a slave after they side with that lying Dolnman."

Conall pulled his coin purse from within his fur. He hefted it in his fist and watched Brenna's eyes light up as the metal clinked. "If you answer my questions truthfully, then I'll settle your debts."

"All right. I'll tell you whatever you need to know."

Just then, the circle around them parted. Shadow ambled forward, joining Conall at his side.

Brenna swung wide eyes to him, and she backed away. "What is that beast doing here?"

Conall smiled. "This is Shadow. My bondmate."

"Your bondmate." She gasped. "You've a bondmate?"

He nodded. "I have your brother to thank for that. Shadow saved me in the woods when Gael shot me and left me for dead."

It was the crowd's turn to gasp. The sound echoed around him in a chorus as they leaned closer, their ears perked to bear witness to such a sordid tale.

But Conall wasn't focused on them. He kept his attention on Brenna, studying her reaction. "You wouldn't know anything about that, would you?"

She shook her head, her rosy cheeks jostling with the force of her shaking. "No, no. Not a word." She stopped her shaking, meeting his eyes. "I don't believe it, in fact. Gael would never!"

"Shadow, mind giving me a growl? I need this woman quaking in her boots."

Shadow didn't disappoint. He curled back his lips and flashed his teeth, growling deep in his throat.

Brenna jumped, taking a hurried step back, bumping into one of the men circled around them. He shoved her forward, indifferent to her ashen face and trembling limbs.

"I said to answer truthfully." He hefted the coin purse again.

Her gaze slid between his purse and Shadow. She drew a hand to her breast, tilting her head down to the ground. "All right. I knew. I knew he was after the farm. I advised him against it, of course, but I can't say I'm surprised. It's no fault of mine, I tell you!"

Conall shook his head slowly. "Lies after lies. Have you no shame, woman?"

"Again, brother."

Shadow opened his jaw, snapping and barking.

Brenna flinched, sweat beading on her forehead even in the bitter cold. "I-it was me. It was my idea." She cowered backward. "Is that what you want to hear? It's the truth, just like I promised you."

Conall sighed. There it was. The truth. This woman—this snake—turned her own brother against the only family he had left while he was battling the intense grief of losing his wife. Conall's shoulders stiffened, his fingers curling, his pulse rocketing through his veins.

The man reappeared, hustling down the street with a handful of burly bearded men on his heels. Brenna's eyes went wild, and she clutched his sleeve again. "You'll keep your part of the bargain, won't you?" she demanded.

He shook off her hold. "Why should I? When you'd have been happy to lie to my face if I hadn't pushed you for the truth?" He took a step away from her.

"I saved her. I saved your sister, that's why!"

He pivoted slowly. "You what?"

"Lark was on her way to Mage Keep. You know what happened there. You must've heard." She smiled, her words flooding out in a rush. "The scourge, they tore it all apart. If she would've gone there like she wanted, she'd be dead. I convinced her to travel to Doln instead."

Conall's mind raced. A conversation he'd forgotten with his neighbor, Barrow, returned to plague him as she spoke. He'd said Lark departed for Flamesmoat *with Brenna*.

Blazes. He'd never even considered that she might stop Lark from traveling to Mage Keep. What could she want with her in Doln?

Oh no. A sick feeling spread in his stomach.

"What did you do?" His words came out short and clipped, his voice laced with anger. "Why would you send my sister to Doln?"

He didn't even have to ask Shadow to growl this time. Something in his tone must've startled him enough that he drew back his lips and roared.

From the crazed look in her eyes, he could tell Brenna realized the folly of her admission. She cowered beneath him, her throat working as she gulped. "I... I... You must know I—"

"Save it," he spat, as the man stepped back into the circle. A man with his shoulders back and a bearing of leadership, likely the Clan Chief of Minsport, walked at his side.

"There she is," the man proclaimed. "She owes me a fortune, and I caught her stealing away with no intention of paying. I've got witnesses and the unpaid receipts inside to prove it."

"Wait," Brenna said, the word a harsh croak. "My nephew here promised to pay my debt." She aimed her wild eyes at the crowd. "You all heard him. I have witnesses as well!"

The folk surrounding them all met her desperation with hard stares. It appeared none were willing to speak up for her after hearing her admit to her crimes.

The chief directed his gaze at him, raising a brow. "Is what this woman says true? Will you settle her debts?"

There was no question in his mind. He knew what he had to do.

"This woman is no kin of mine." His voice was cold. "She's a liar. I can vouch for this man and his claims. Don't believe a word that spills out of her rotten mouth. She poisons everything she touches."

Conall turned his back on her and shoved his way through the crowd with Shadow at his side. Brenna would get what she deserved. The Doln would ship her off to a workhouse, to spend the rest of her days as a slave. Maybe that made him a hypocrite for allowing it after all he'd said to Taul this morning, but if anyone deserved that fate, surely it was her.

She hadn't admitted it, but there was no doubt in his mind Brenna had sold his sister to a slaver. Trusting, sweet, innocent Lark. She must've followed her into Flamesmoat and stumbled right into a trap.

His nostrils flared, anger burning a hole inside of him. The only thing that had kept him from striking Brenna down where she stood was the vision he'd witnessed ensuring he would find Lark again. If he hadn't had that surety driving him, he would be the one in trouble right now, with a dozen witnesses accusing him of murder.

Conall marched on, his pace steady and his jaw set.

"What was that all about, little brother?" Shadow asked.

He halted outside a ramshackle tavern on the dock's outskirts. *"I'll tell you the whole of it soon. Not now. This is the place Taul told me about."*

A sign above the door sported a crudely drawn picture of a ship next to a flagon of ale. The Drunken Sailor. Taul had said this was the best place to seek passage south. It was a known haunt of captains waiting on the holds of their ships to be unloaded.

Conall shoved the door open. The hinge protested, letting out a grating *creak* that had him cringing and Shadow shaking his head.

All eyes swung to the door as they entered, but that wasn't saying much. The cramped shack was practically deserted. There were two men seated at the bar and a grizzled old barkeep behind a worn wooden counter that looked like it had survived a century of wear and tear.

"You lost, boy?" The barkeep kept a dubious eye on Shadow until he settled down on the floor near the small hearth in the corner.

Conall raised a brow. There weren't many people calling him boy these days. "I hope not." He strode up to the bar and took a seat on a wobbly wooden stool. "I heard this is the place to hire a captain."

The man closest to him, a tall fellow with a deep tan and a chiseled jaw, turned to him with a chuckle. "You might want to rethink that. Ships on this side of the continent only sail between here and Flamesmoat. You don't want any part of going there. Not now, anyway."

A pang of discomfort struck him at the warning. But he forced the thought aside. He would worry about the fate of his country later. "I don't want to go to Flamesmoat. I need to travel further south. To the Mido Islands."

"The Mido Islands?" The man scoffed, hefting up a flagon. Ale sloshed over the edge and wet his fingers. "Why in the world do you want to go there?" He took a long pull off his mug.

"There's someone there I have to meet."

Laughter spilled out of the man's lips. "No one's on the Mido Islands. They're uninhabitable."

"Just the same, that's where I need to go."

"Good luck with that." The man turned away.

Conall opened his pack and nudged aside his spare clothes and the book Delyth had gifted him. He dug deep down to the bottom and scooped up the heavy coin purse he'd found with the Sade Prim's things. He imagined she would approve of the expenditure. It was fate, after all.

He slapped the purse down on the bar, doing his best to amplify the clink of metal as it banged the wood. "I can pay."

But the man didn't turn back. "You'll be paying for your pyre. Or more like a watery grave. There's a reason none sail that far south."

The barkeep nodded. "Current's too strong. Even I know that, and you'll never catch me setting foot on one of the death traps these old dogs sail." The old man let out a raspy chuckle that shifted into a cough. He recovered quickly, grabbing a cloth to wipe up the spilled ale.

Conall caught his hand, stilling it atop the bar. His other hand hovered over the pooled liquid, and he sucked in a deep breath.

He needed a ship. It was the only way to reach his sister. He lowered his lashes for the briefest instant, picturing her face in his mind.

The air crackled with electricity while simultaneously filling with moisture. A cloud of liquid sprang out of nowhere, hovering above the bar. Then it spun, the wind whipping through the wooden shack, shaking the walls and blowing the hair across the men's faces. They gasped, each of them leaning back in their chairs, or in the barkeep's case, falling out of it and slamming into the floorboards.

As quickly as it started, it stopped. The liquid vanished without a trace. The wind, once again, still.

"The current won't be a problem." Conall opened the bag and spilled the coins atop the bar. Most of them fell neatly into a mound, gleaming even within the dim light inside the shack. One of them landed on its side, rolled down the bar, and spun before clattering to rest in front of the second man. The one who'd been silent the whole time.

This man was shorter than the one who'd spoken, but just as darkly tanned, with a short-shorn beard and long brown locks that came down to his shoulders. He lifted the coin off the bar between his finger and thumb, then turned to Conall with a grin. "You've got yourself a deal."

Conall grinned as well and scooped the coins back into the purse.

The taller man crossed his arms, frowning. He opened his mouth, then snapped it closed and nodded. "Fine. Your greed'll be the death of us one day, Captain."

Conall plunked the bag on the bar in front of the captain. "When do we leave?"

"On the tide. My first mate, Kris, will see you to the ship." He gestured to the tall man.

"Kris, I'm Conall and this is Shadow."

Kris only glowered, then chugged the rest of his ale. "C'mon then." He stood. "Follow me."

They exited the little shack and turned left, heading to the far side of the port.

"Hey, you mentioned Flamesmoat earlier. What's been happening there?" Conall hurried to keep step with the long-legged sailor.

Kris scoffed. "It's a madhouse. The entire city is surrounded with a horde of those scourge. Nasty little critters, like something out of a nightmare. You don't want any part of that place. I can tell you that much." He tilted his head, eyeing him sideways. "Why do you ask? You got kin there or something?"

"Something like that," Conall admitted, his stomach clenching. All those people. His friends in Greenvale. He hoped they were faring all right.

"I'm sorry to hear that." Kris stopped in front of an aged wooden sailing ship sitting at the docks' end. "This is it. *The Lady Luck*."

"She's not much to look at, is she?" Conall stared at the dented wood and chipped paint visible on the outer hull. The sails didn't look much nicer. Even rolled up at port he could spot countless stains and dozens of patches.

"You're one to talk." Kris grinned, rubbing a loving hand over the wooden rail as he made his way onboard. "She'll get you where you need to go. That's all that matters."

Conall sighed and settled his bag on the deck, nodding hello to the handful of deckhands who stared at him and Shadow curiously. Kris was right. All that mattered was finding Lark. Flamesmoat would have to wait.

Chapter 19

L ark's stomach churned. "Ugh, more sailing," she mumbled beneath her breath. They were back on another tiny boat, a few moments away from landing on the large island's shore.

By the time the three of them climbed down the cliffside and located a rowboat that was barely larger than the canoe they'd traversed the Boglands in, Nox had almost reached shore. Then the tide changed direction, leaving them to fight the current that had worked to swiftly carry Nox across the ocean. That left them hours behind him.

The island loomed large before them, filled with scraggly trees and rocky, mountainous terrain. It looked like an excellent place for a boy to get lost. She sighed, craning her neck to scan up and down the coastline. Wherever Nox was, he was already out of sight.

"Don't worry. We'll find him." Mika sat at the back of the boat, rowing in time with Aren, who sat up front. Whisper perched before her, his talons clasped tightly on one of the middle seats.

The sun slipped behind the highest mountain peak on the island as they rowed close to shore. Aren hopped out of the boat first. The water soaked the bottoms of his luct trousers instantly, and the surf splashed waves up to his waist before he tugged them ashore.

The three of them dragged the boat far onto the beach, well away from where the highest tide lines rested. Rocky sand crunched beneath their boots. Chirping sea birds competed with the surf's roar.

Lark spun in a slow circle, looking for signs of anything that might lead them to Nox. *"Muse, where are you? Have you found him?"* She'd sent her bondmate to search for the boy when it became apparent they would end up onshore so far behind him.

"I've been flying low, but I still haven't spotted him."

"Keep looking."

Mika started trudging in a northerly direction up the shoreline. "C'mon. If we find where his boat landed, then it'll be easier to track him."

"How do you know he went this way?" Aren asked. "Maybe we should split up."

"I was watching when he landed. It's this way, I'm sure of it." Mika shook his head. "Go south if you want. But you'll be wasting your time."

Aren's pale skin had slowly taken on a reddish tinge as they'd sailed across the channel in the rowboat, but his cheeks reddened to scarlet at Mika's clipped tone.

Lark rested a hand on Aren's arm. "I think he's right. Let's stick together. I don't like the looks of this place."

Aren met her eyes, and his expression softened. "North it is." He tightened his grip on the bow in his fist and set off, following Mika across the sand. "At least there's a little shade now that the sun's setting."

She stole another look at his skin. "You forgot your hat with all the commotion back in Stoneshore, I take it?"

Aren nodded. "I'll be all right. Sunburn won't kill me."

"I might have something in my pack that will help," she offered.

He waved her off. "It's not so bad at the moment. But I might take you up on that later."

They rounded a curve on the beach, and Mika took off. "Here it is." He skidded to a stop beside the small boat, peering within.

"Look, tracks leading inland." Aren pointed to the ground.

Muse's voice rose in her mind. *"Lark. I found something."*

Lark stopped, tilting her head. *"Is it Nox? You found him?"*

"Not him. Someone else. Two people. They're hurt, bad."

Aren was watching her. "What is it?"

"Muse. She's found some injured people."

Mika turned from his inspection of the boat. "Who could that be? No one lives here." He eyed the footprints in the sand. "We have to find Nox."

Lark stepped forward. "We can't just leave them to die. Not when we can heal them."

"You're right." Mika sighed. "Where are they?"

"Muse, can you fly straight up in the air so we can see your position?"

"On it."

Lark tipped her neck up and searched the sky. "There." Muse hovered above the base of the mountain, further inland and a little further to the north.

Aren squeezed her arm. "Go, find those people. Whisper and I will follow Nox's tracks."

Lark frowned. "I thought we were going to stick together?"

Mika jumped in. "It's a good plan. Look at the clouds, Lark. If it rains, we'll lose any sign of Nox's tracks."

Gray clouds hovered in the air to the south. She sighed, seeing the truth in his statement, her heart sinking all the same. "Be careful."

"We will." Aren sent her a smile and disappeared beneath the scraggly trees.

Mika and Lark started forward, heading further up the beach toward Muse's position. She circled high in the air like a beacon.

"Can you tell me more about the people you found?" Lark broke into a jog. It was strange indeed to find anyone on this desolate beach. The trees bore no fruit, and besides the seabirds perched high in the branches, she'd seen no wildlife. She understood why no one would be interested in settling here with all the variety and abundance in Raimire.

"Ha. I'm no human expert."

Lark rolled her eyes. *"Try, please."*

"There's a man and a woman. Young, like you. They're wrapped in bandages and curled up in the dirt near a stream."

Lark's stomach sank. What were they doing out here all alone?

Clues began to emerge, half buried in the sand and scattered along the rocky terrain bordering the beach. Debris and splintered wood, coated with a thick lacquer that was clearly not natural, littered the coastline. Had those poor souls survived a shipwreck?

They came abreast of Muse's position and turned inland. It was tough going. The vegetation grew thick, and there was no sign of any trails, forcing them to take careful steps through the underbrush. Just as the sky darkened, from a combination of approaching rain and impending night, they found them.

It was just as Muse described, only worse. They were curled up together on the ground, their clothing torn to shreds and wrapped around their thin limbs as makeshift bandages. Though she and Mika didn't try to move quietly through the underbrush, neither of them stirred as they approached.

Lark hurried forward as Muse settled on the riverbank beside her. She knelt beside the girl, and Mika, the boy, inspecting them both and wincing in sympathy.

The girl had her right leg exposed, wrapped tightly in fabric dyed a dark brownish-red and still moist to the touch. Her features were slack, her lips covered in dried skin with dark circles ringing her eyes.

The boy appeared to be in slightly better shape. He had a bandage wrapped around his head, but from the fabric's color, it looked to be well on its way to healing, even before Mika gently lifted the bandage to peer at the swollen flesh within.

That action was enough to wake him. His blue eyes shot open, and he gasped, jolting upright to sit. "Who are you? What's going on?" Then his startled gaze fell on his companion and some of the confusion lifted. "Help! We need help. We've been shipwrecked for days."

Mika shushed him. "It's all right, we're healers. We've come to help you."

Relief washed over his features. His shoulders slumped, and he closed his eyes, breathing out a deep sigh.

Mika turned to her. "He can wait. Let's take care of the girl first."

The sky chose that moment to split. Rain drenched them, and lightning flashed across the sky to the south, followed by the loud crack of thunder. Lark shivered, the cold rain soaking her luct outfit and moistening her skin.

"Her name is Oriana," the boy said, watching them work from his spot on the streambed.

Lark met the boy's gaze and raked her wet brown curls out of her face. "We'll take care of your friend. Don't worry." She smiled reassuringly as Mika joined her beside the girl and began untying the wet cloth from her leg.

"Be careful. She's still bleeding. The gash in her leg—" His chin quivered. "I did my best, but it just won't stop bleeding."

Mika loosened the cloth enough to peek under it. Lark watched him work, even as the rain spilled over the girl's bandage, soaking the cloth and making the dirt below her turn red. He clenched his jaw tightly and pulled the bandage closed after a brief peek. "You did well. She wouldn't still be living without your care. Let us take care of the rest."

He dug in his satchel and pulled free a handful of roots and some vibrant green leaves. "Lark, I need your help. Will you lend me your talent again?"

She nodded and held out her hand. Lightning flashed again, the rain pelting her fingers and pooling in her palm.

But Mika shook his head. "Grab my shoulder. I'll need both hands for this."

She did as requested, holding Mika's shoulder and closing her eyes to concentrate. She wished to help him. To heal this poor girl of the brutal bleed slowly draining her.

Warmth spread across her palm. The tremor came next, shaking her to her core. A wave of exhaustion rose with it. Her thighs wobbled, and her head drooped, swinging lightly on her neck as dizziness swamped her.

Just as she was sure she would collapse, it was over. Her eyelids slid open in time to catch the girl raising her head off the ground, her bright green eyes flitting all around, a hand flying to her chest.

"Who are you? Where's Edrik?" she asked.

"Here. I'm here, Ori," the boy answered. He reached past Mika, grabbing her hand. "These people are healers. We're saved." He smiled.

Mika focused on her and placed a steadying hand on her shoulder. "Are you all right, Lark?"

Muse hopped up on a tree branch, chirping noisily. *Kak-kak-kak.*

She sent Mika a wobbly grin. "Yeah, I'm fine. Just a little tired."

Mika frowned. "That's what has me worried. Sharing talent can be draining on the giver. You need to rest."

She leaned back on her heels. The rain continued to fall around them. Lighting shot through the air to the north. This time, the thunder took a moment to echo around her. She shivered, hoping the storm would pass quickly. "What about Edrik?"

Mika squeezed her shoulder and dropped his hand to his side. "I can handle him on my own. His body has already done much of the healing." He turned to others. "You'll both be fine after some food and rest."

Oriana's face lit up. "You have food?"

Edrik grinned. "We've had plenty of water here, but nothing to eat for days except for bugs." He shuddered.

Oriana grimaced. "That was what you made me eat?" She gave Edrik a gentle push. "Gross!"

Mika chuckled. He dug in his satchel and handed the girl a pouch filled with dried strips of meat and fruit. "Eat slowly. Your stomachs will need time to adjust after so long empty."

The pair crowded around the pouch, stuffing food into their mouths. The rainfall slowed, and Lark sighed. It seemed her prayers would be answered after all.

The crunch of footsteps sounded in the woods. Lark stilled, her eyes widening.

"Ha. Don't worry. It's just lover boy and the old snoozer," Muse assured her, just as Lark spotted Aren's blond head peeking out from behind some trees. Whisper rested on his gauntleted arm.

"Aren." She smiled and rose to her feet. She wobbled, her gait unsteady from the exhaustion lingering in her limbs.

Aren rushed forward and grabbed her arm before she tumbled sideways. "Lark, are you all right? What happened?"

She waved him off but let him maneuver her to sit on a large stump close to the streambed. "I'm fine. How about you? Did you find any sign of Nox?"

He nodded. "I followed his tracks into the woods, not far from here. Then that storm started, and I lost the trail. I figured I might as well try to find you. Whisper must have heard Muse calling. I was able to follow his lead and find you."

Lark smiled, remembering Muse's cawing from the trees.

"I left a trail we can follow in the morning to where I lost Nox's tracks. He must've stopped for the night, too. We'll find him tomorrow."

She nodded and wrapped her arms around herself tightly. The rain had fully stopped, but with the sun hidden behind the mountain spanning the island's center, it would be a long time before she was warm again. Too bad she hadn't thought to bring a change of clothes in her pack.

Aren frowned, watching her shiver. "I passed a cave on the way here. It's not far." He turned to Mika and the others, pointing back the way he came. "It looked dry inside. We should head there for the night."

Mika nodded. "Good plan. Take Lark and set up camp. I'll wait until these two finish eating. By then, I'll have the strength to heal Edrik, and we'll meet you there."

Aren bristled. She could tell he wasn't fond of taking orders from Mika. But Aren held his tongue and extended a hand to help her to her feet. Then he turned back to Mika. "I left a trail of luct string tied to the trees. Follow that, and you'll find us." He started to walk away but paused. "Don't wait too long. The sun's not long from setting."

"Yes, yes. We won't." Mika waved a hand dismissively.

Aren set his shoulders and pushed forward through the underbrush. "C'mon, Lark. It's this way."

She followed, her gaze landing on a dangling string of sheer green fabric tied on a branch at eye level off in the distance. "That was quick thinking, leaving a trail to follow. But where did you find the string?"

Aren grinned, lifting his pants and showing her the torn edges stuffed into his boots. "I'll have to sleep with my boots on if I don't want my feet covered in bites, but it was worth it to not get lost." The Raimish trousers were long enough to roll down and cover their bare feet at night, but Aren had torn the bottom of each pant leg, leaving him with trousers that barely hit at his ankles.

She smiled, admiring his ingenuity even as her stomach filled with knots. Except for the few moments they'd spent together behind the curtains in the healing hut, this was the first time since leaving Dracwood that she'd been alone with Aren.

Traveling with the group was amazing, but it left little time for privacy. Especially when they'd been trapped in a canoe or traversing a jungle crawling with predators.

For the first time in weeks, she'd have a chance to speak to him privately. A part of her wanted that more than anything. But the larger part was suspiciously tongue-tied, only able to sneak glances in his direction as they trudged through the woods.

It didn't take long for them to locate the cave. The mouth was set into a large rocky hillside a bit farther inland from the little stream.

They stepped cautiously into the shadowed interior. The cave was empty, with a high ceiling that allowed even Aren to stand without threat of smacking his head on the rocky roof. In truth, it was not a full cave at all, but more of a rocky outcropping open to the air on three sides.

The dirt and patchy grass beneath were dry at least. Lark curled up on the ground as Whisper and Muse flew up to the top of the rock, finding perches quickly.

"Hey, there's a bunch of old nests up here." Muse hopped along the ceiling's edge.

"Are they empty?"

"Yep. Looks like it."

"Can you knock them loose? We can use them to start a fire."

"Can I? Ha. Easy."

Scratching sounded as Muse got to work. Soon a rain of sticks and twigs came tumbling down upon them.

"Hey, watch it," Aren exclaimed, brushing his face and sputtering.

"Sorry. I asked Muse to knock those down. Can you help me start a fire? I have a tinderbox in my pack."

Aren smiled. "Good idea."

Working together, they got a small fire blazing. Lark sighed as the flames danced, holding out her hands to warm them.

Aren backed away a few paces.

"Aren't you cold?" she asked.

He grimaced. "The sunburn."

She smiled gently. "I can help you with that." She dug into her pack and pulled out a little metal tin filled with a green herbal ointment. "Sit down." She patted the dirt beside her.

"Thanks." He sat with his back to the fire, extending his legs in front of him.

She grabbed a palmful of the slick cream and began applying it to the red skin on his forehead. He closed his eyes, letting out a sigh when the cool ointment swept over his heated flesh. "That feels amazing." A smile spread across his face.

She gulped. The green ointment blended in with his skin as she gently massaged, relieving much of the redness. She reminded herself it was only the ointment making him smile as her fingers slid over his nose and the prickly skin on his cheeks.

This she could do. This was what she was meant to do. Healing people was her calling.

She tried repeating that in her mind as her hands slid lower over his neck. And again, when the rapid pulse beating under his skin thrummed beneath her fingertips.

"Take off your shirt." Her eyes widened. Did that raspy voice belong to her?

Aren's eyes shot open. Ice-blue orbs full of questions connected with hers. Her stomach fluttered.

She cleared her throat. "Your shoulders are burned, too. The luct fabric doesn't stop sunb—"

He pulled off the shirt, and the words died on her lips. Lark's mouth went dry. The sheer clothes didn't leave much to the imagination, but being so close, and so alone, with *this* man... It was enough to set her heart racing. He was exceedingly well made. Strong and broad, covered in muscle and a smattering of light hair. And so much *sunburn*.

She shook her head and blew out a breath, quickly scooting behind his back. Without his gaze on her, she could concentrate on the task at hand. She could pretend this was some random villager in need of healing. She grabbed another handful of ointment and gently smoothed it across his back and shoulders.

"Lark?" he asked.

"Hm?"

"Tiora told us what you said to her this morning." Aren's back muscles tensed beneath her palms. "Do you really expect us to leave you here alone? With Mika?"

Her fingers stilled on his back. She dipped back into the tin, scooping up more ointment. She moved onto the back of his neck, the short hair at the nape flicking across her fingertips. "I can't ask you to put your lives on hold for me. To face danger and death. If any of you were hurt because of me..." Her insides twisted with pain at the thought.

Aren whirled around so quickly her hands landed on his chest. "Do you think any of us would leave now? After everything we've been through together?" He met her gaze again, his blue eyes reflecting the dancing flames. She could see something there. Something that scared her more than the scourge ever had.

She dropped her gaze to her hands, both flat on his warm skin. The slick ointment between them did nothing to disguise the rise and fall of his chest beneath her palms. The ebb and flow was hypnotic, like the tide, ready to pull her out to sea.

He lifted a single finger and tipped up her chin, compelling her to meet his eyes again. "I won't leave you, Lark," he whispered.

Her heart squeezed. She rose on her knees and pressed her lips to his, her eyes closing.

There was no hesitation. He met her instantly, with just as much pressure. Just as much desperation. Then his tongue was in her mouth. His fingers tangled in her curls, and she was melting right there on that tiny island in the middle of nowhere.

Aren hissed, breaking the spell. Her eyes shot open and she realized she was clutching his shoulders so hard her nails left little half-moons in his reddened flesh.

She gasped and lifted her hands, backing away. "Your sunburn, I'm sor—"

"No, don't be sorry." He seized her hands before she could get far and pressed them back on his chest, his voice deep and husky. "Don't be sorry." He dipped his head and kissed her.

Lark trembled, skimming her fingers across his chest. His touch drifted down her back, rocking her up off her knees, pulling her closer.

*"I hate to be the breaker of close embraces—*again—*but the others are coming,"* Muse warned.

Lark pulled away. She sucked in a deep breath, lifted Aren's shirt off the ground, and handed it to him. "The others..."

She didn't need to finish. The crunch of footsteps in the underbrush sounded, and excited chatter followed. Aren slipped his shirt back on before the trio emerged from the darkened forest and joined them under the overhang.

Lark snapped the lid back on the little metal tin and slipped it back into her pack. Her cheeks burned and her heart still quivered wildly. She forced a smile and turned to greet the others.

The newcomers seemed oblivious to any tension in the air, but Mika's gaze flitted between the two of them before landing on her. He raised a brow. "Any trouble while we were away?"

She shook her head, still smiling. She glanced at him quickly before staring into the fire. "No. No trouble at all."

"Hm." He spared Aren a glance before seating himself beside her. "I learned something interesting about our new friends here while you two were setting up camp. We're not the only ones with talent on this island."

Lark's smile dropped, her mouth falling open. She spun to Edrik and Oriana. "You two can summon?"

Edrik nodded. The bandage on his head was gone, revealing a tangled mess of dirty blond hair. "I'm a water mage, and Oriana summons wind. We were sent here to request aid for Flamesmoat. Mika tells us you already know about the scourge. That a few of them even made it as far south as Raimire already."

Lark shuddered. "Yes, just this afternoon."

"We've been dealing with them for weeks." Edrik sighed, crossing his arms. "They've got the whole city surrounded. Our leader sent us to bring whatever help we could find."

"And then you were shipwrecked," Aren added.

"Yeah. We're lucky you found us when you did." He grimaced. "Between starving and all the crazy sounds we've been hearing, I didn't hold out hope for lasting much longer."

Lark raised a brow. "What sounds?"

Edrik shrugged. "I don't know for sure. It was like nothing I've ever heard in my life. Like there was some huge monster somewhere on this island screaming, over and over again every night." He grimaced again. "At first, I was scared witless, certain the thing was dying to find and slaughter us. But the longer I listened, the stranger it became."

Edrik's brow furrowed, and he shook his head sadly. "It sounded like a mother crying out in anguish over her lost child. Whatever was making those cries wasn't angry. It was heartbroken." He scooted closer to the fire and stretched out his hands, shivering. "But we haven't heard the screams for the last few days. Hopefully, whatever was making them is gone now."

Mika stiffened as he listened to the tale, eyes round.

Lark elbowed him in the side. "You all right?"

Mika scrubbed a hand over his face, and for a moment, she was certain he would keep whatever was bothering him to himself. Then he let out a deep sigh and spoke, his voice heavy with frustration and tinged with fear. "I found a carcass washed up on the shore not long ago. It was huge. Easily the size of a whale. That's what I told the townsfolk it was, so no one would panic, but it was no whale."

Aren leaned closer, his brows sinking. "What was it?"

"You're gonna think I'm crazy, but—it was a dragon."

Lark raised a hand to her mouth, blinking repeatedly. "You think it came from here?" She clutched her legs to her chest, peering into the darkened trees beyond their little cave. Her mind flashed back to that massive black dragon tearing through the sky above Bogsmouth, setting the scourge ablaze. It wasn't too much of a leap for her to imagine finding dragons here, too.

Mika quirked a grin, looking pleased no one thought to question his sanity before dropping the smile and nodding solemnly. "It makes sense. The direction of the tides. The noises Edrik and Oriana have been hearing." He shrugged. "Why else would Nox head here with the scourge if they're not searching for something?"

Lark bit her lip and stared off into the dark. Had Nox come here searching for a dragon? Wherever he was, she hoped he was safe and warm for the night at least. Tomorrow, they would find him. She would make sure of it.

Chapter 20

Wind blew in Kayda's face, whipping through her braids. She perched atop Druturion, flying above an endless expanse of greenery dotted with bright flashes of color. The scent of flowers and sounds of teeming life reached her even with the wind rushing past.

They'd been flying for most of the morning. First through the Waste's dry air, the burnt-orange sand reminding her of her time spent finding her family. Reawakening the hopeful feeling that had washed over her as she began her search. She would help Dru locate his family. She could sense it.

Eventually, they'd left the desert behind, crossing high over the Anaraine Mountains she'd only seen on foot. From above, they were even more majestic, stretching out across the horizon in all their glimmering glory. It took them ages to pass, but once they made it to the other side, the jungle spread out before them, green and lush, a stark contrast to the barren sands and rocky cliffs they'd just passed.

The humidity hit them then. Kayda's white silk tunic and cotton trousers stuck to her skin, even with the wind cooling her. They had to be getting close to the coast. Blue flashed on the horizon to the west, exactly where Stoneshore should be, based on the maps she'd studied in Wyll's office.

The thought of Wyll had her stomach churning. Had she done the right thing trusting him? Would he follow through with his promise to help her people fight back against the scourge? Time would tell, and she could only hope he'd be true to his word. She pushed her worries aside as Druturion flew lower, skirting the top of the jungle canopy and gliding up alongside the coast.

As they hovered above the beach, Kayda saw the name *Stoneshore* was fitting. The beach was littered with pebbles and what appeared to be broken shards of shells worn smooth by the crushing waves. The tide was out as they approached, revealing a low beach bordered by a high cliffside, the jungle hovering close to the cliff's edge and shading the rocks below.

Off in the distance, Kayda spotted the first of the string of islands bordering the western shore of Raimire. That was where they needed to go. The Mido Islands.

"There they are, Dru. We have to head for the largest of those islands." She raised a brow as Druturion kept straight on his course up the coast, making no effort to turn west across the sea channel. *"Where are you going, Dru? We've got to fly to the island."*

"I have to see... there." He blasted down to the ground, his claws skittering rocks as they landed. Kayda hopped down off his back, stretching. Dragon riding was incredible, but it was as tough on the legs and hips as a long ride in a horse's saddle.

Druturion bounded up the beach and started digging.

"What are you looking for?" Kayda veered off near the cliffside, avoiding the rain of pebbles Dru sent flying as he dug. He must have found something.

He stilled, his whole body slouching as he stared down at the beach.

Kayda rounded his side and gulped. His digging had revealed a massive bone sticking up from the rocky soil. She placed a hand on his neck as he shuddered. *"I'm so sorry, Dru."*

"I'm too late. All that time I spent underground. I should have sensed this was happening. I should have known." His grief was palpable. Anguish colored his words, his body thrumming as he stared down at the massive bone.

"Don't blame yourself. There's no way you could have known this was happening. How could you?"

Druturion shook even more strongly. Then he stilled. He raised his head skyward and let out a deafening roar.

Kayda drew back, her heart hammering.

"I'll find who's responsible for this." Dru's voice was a promise of retribution. *"I won't rest until their bones are charred and buried for what they've done to my kin."*

Kayda returned to Dru, placing her hand on the hard smooth scale on his jaw. *"I'll help you, Dru. We'll make them pay together."*

Dru snorted, cocking his head sideways and staring out across the ocean at the Mido Islands. *"Hop on. Let's discover what's been happening on those islands."*

Kayda nodded and vaulted up on Dru's back, clasping his neck. Two running steps, and he was up in the air, the blue sea spread out below them. The chain of islands slowly grew larger on the horizon.

Druturion aimed for the largest northernmost of the isles. It was covered with thin tangled trees, their leaves less vibrant and the covering more meager than the lush greenery of Raimire. Above the treetops, a rocky gray mountain rose, the cliffs reaching at least twice higher than even the tallest of the trees. It was here they slowed and circled the island, peering down at the landscape below them.

"What are you looking for?" Kayda asked.

"I'm not sure." He continued to circle, his head bobbing all around. *"I'll know it when I see it."*

Kayda leaned over his neck, seeking something, anything, that looked out of sorts. She wasn't sure what she was looking for. Certainly, it wouldn't be as simple as finding a valley full of dragons lounging in the sun.

The third time they circled, she spotted something on the island's far side. There was a spot on the mountainside that had a few trees toppled over on their sides. Had a storm caused that damage, or could it be from something else?

"Dru, look, do you see that flat plateau? And those trees below it?"

Druturion pivoted in the air, spinning toward the area she'd mentioned. *"What about it?"*

"If a dragon fell off the cliff side there, they'd splash right down into the sea, wouldn't they? Maybe smash a few trees on the way down?"

She could feel her bondmate stiffen at the mention of a dragon falling into the sea, but he flew toward the spot. *"Let's check it out."*

He slammed down on the plateau a moment later. Kayda released her death grip on his neck and slid down, her boots slapping against the hard rock. Upon closer inspection, she was even more sure something happened here recently. Grass was torn up in the few places it grew, and faint scratch marks marred many of the rocks.

She trekked to the cliff's edge, vertigo causing her head to spin as she stared down at the sheer drop to the sea. It was even more apparent from up close that the tree damage below was not natural. Only here were the thin trees snapped and broken; all the greenery up and down the coast grew undisturbed. No storm destroyed only trees in such a short space.

She backed away from the cliffside and veered across the plateau to Dru. *"What do you think, Dru?"* She nodded to the ground where he sat studying the scratch marks. *"Looks to me like a scuffle happened here."*

"I think you're right." He lifted his head and surveyed their surroundings. *"But where are they now?"*

The landscape was dominated by rock at this height on the mountain. She could see no sign of life. Even the sea birds she'd caught glimpses of on the rest of the island appeared unwilling to venture here. It seemed an unlikely place to house a dragon.

"I don't see how a dragon could have survived up here. When you lived underground, you still had to eat and drink, didn't you? I remember the bones in that underground cavern. The trickle of water in the distance." She took a closer look at the rocks surrounding them. *"Wouldn't the dragons here need something to eat as well? A source of water?"*

"Yes, you're right. Algernon arranged it all when I decided to hibernate. He founded the order that kept me fed, bringing me a goat on the same day every year." He chuckled. *"The same group of people that morphed into your Church of the Dragon."*

Kayda frowned. *"There are no people here to help. There must be something in place already that would allow the dragons to keep themselves fed all these years. I wager they're somewhere within this mountain, below our feet."*

Druturion shook out his wings. *"How will we find them? I can dig on the beach, but this is solid rock."*

Kayda strolled around the plateau, searching. She withdrew from the plateau's edge and made for the center, where the mountain rose again, so steeply they would have trouble climbing. She set her hand on the rock wall and traced her fingers along the gray stone, gliding along the edge. Suddenly she gasped. Her hand slipped right into the rock, vanishing as if it had been sucked in.

"Kayda, are you all right?" Druturion paced closer, his red eyes bulging as her fingers disappeared into the wall.

"Yes, I'm fine." She pulled her hand free and waved it in the air. It was whole and uninjured. *"It's an illusion, like the Palisade, only different. Weaker somehow."*

Druturion gasped. *"You're a genius! This must've been made long ago. There's no way it could be a true barrier without the constant sacrifice required of the Palisade, but a simple illusion. Yes, it could surely last this long."*

Kayda stuck her hand back inside the illusion, marveling at the way her fingers disappeared as if they weren't there. She could feel them wiggling, but it looked like only rock existed beneath her palm.

A muffled roar blared, rising from within the illusion. Kayda startled and backed away, her hand dropping at her side. *"Did you hear that?"*

"Hear what?"

She turned to her bondmate. *"There's something in there."* Maybe she could hear it because she was touching the barrier when it sounded?

She stretched out her arm and stepped forward to place her hand through the illusion once more, but before her fingers grazed the rock that wasn't rock, she slammed into the ground.

"Oof." Her head crashed into the hard ground; her body shoved sideways. She rolled up to sit, groaning and clutching the back of her head. It throbbed beneath her fingers. Her sight was fuzzy, the world a spinning blur. It took a few heartbeats for the spinning to stop. When it did, her breath caught, and she scrambled backward, her shoulders banging into the rock wall at her back.

An ice-white dragon sat before Druturion, staring him down. Shimmering white scales glittered in the sun, strikingly bright, shining with flecks of silver and gold.

"Belstasia! Is that you?" Druturion's voice sounded clearly through their bond, then he paused, tilting his head as if listening to a response she couldn't hear. It appeared Kayda would only be privy to half of this conversation.

Kayda peered at the new dragon curiously. She had a feeling from the sound of the name and the white dragon's slimmer, smaller build, she was female.

"What do you mean, something's after you?" Dru backed up, making room for Belstasia on the plateau as she paced nervously. She unfurled her wings, looking for all the world like she wanted nothing more than to fly off and escape.

"Slow down, Bela, you're not making sense." Dru paced closer, only to retreat when the white dragon cowered beneath him as if she were terrified. *"We heard word of dragon bones washing up on the coast close to here. Tell me, who's hunting you? Where are the others? We need all the help we can muster. The scourge have returned. The Palisade has fallen."*

Dru stopped talking, his body still as he stared intently at the white dragon, still cowering before him. She slumped on the ground, her wings curled around herself protectively, quivering visibly.

Dru lifted his head and roared. Kayda cringed at the deafening blare, her head hammering even more as the blast of sound compounded with the pain from her fall.

"You did what?" he bellowed, rising up to his full height, his wings unfurling, teeth bared.

Faced with his anger, Kayda shrank, instinctively tucking her chin to her chest and hugging her torso. What could make her bondmate react so strongly? What had Bela done?

Belstasia continued to cower, lowering herself even closer to the ground. Then she stuck her neck out of her wings, eyes closed, reminding Kayda of a lamb ready for slaughter.

What was happening? Was she begging Dru to kill her? Kayda lurched to her feet, ignoring the wave of dizziness slamming into her.

Dru was seething. She could sense it through the bond, anger flooding off him like a wave. He opened his mouth. The fire deep within his throat burned bright and hot. He rose on his hind legs, towering above Bela's prone form.

Kayda slid in between the dragons, cursing herself all the while for the dangerous decision. She couldn't stand by and watch her bondmate slaughter one of his kind—maybe the only one left. She had to do something to cool his anger. She knew him. If she allowed him to give into the anger boiling in his veins, he would never forgive himself.

"Stop, Dru," She barreled between the two behemoth beasts. *"You can't hurt her. I don't care what she's done. It's not right."*

"Move out of the way, Kayda," he ordered, his voice steely and sharp.

"No."

She stood her ground, hands on her hips, chin in the air. Maybe she was crazy. Maybe this was the start of the madness that haunted her future. She didn't care. There was no way she was going to let Dru go through with this. She planted herself on the plateau, staring down an angry dragon with another at her back. She wasn't even afraid. Not truly.

But that was when the trouble started.

Chapter 21

Lark stood in front of a small stream, less than an hour's walk from the cave they'd slept in. It was early morning, just after sunrise. Each of them stared off into the woods, searching for signs of the boy they'd come to rescue.

Aren pulled off a piece of luct string hanging from a tree branch. "This is where I stopped when the storm broke and I lost Nox's trail. From what I could gather from his trail yesterday, he seemed to be headed inland, on a northwesterly track."

Mika spun in a slow circle. "We should spread out in a line headed northwest, keep our eyes peeled for any clues."

It was as good a plan as any. Whisper and Muse rose in the sky, and the five of them spread out on the ground, advancing slowly and making their way inland. They weaved between the scraggly trees, sidestepping pricker bushes, their steps crunching in the sandy soil. It wasn't long before someone shouted that they'd found something.

Lark raced to her left and spotted Oriana kneeling next to a pricker bush.

"This looks like the sheer cloth you all are wearing." Oriana pointed at a shredded piece of luct fabric dangling from one of the branches.

"You're right." Lark grinned. "We're on the right track."

They spread out again, using the bush as the center of their search grid, moving further inland.

Though Lark tried to keep her mind on the search, her thoughts kept drifting back to Aren and that kiss. They'd had no time to discuss it last night or this morning. Even now, she shouldn't be thinking about it. Not when there was a boy that needed saving. But as she trudged through the island forest, she couldn't stop herself from replaying the moment in her mind, wondering what would've happened if they'd not been interrupted. She sighed. Would the timing ever be right for the two of them?

Then it was her turn to yell out she'd found something.

She halted before the entrance to a cave much smaller and darker than the outcropping they'd slept under the night before. The mouth was barely big enough to fit a person, the blackness within so complete it made her shudder. It appeared to lead into the gray mountains rising beyond their path. As the others crowded around her, they all gazed inside with trepidation.

Lark slipped the leather gauntlet out of her pack as Aren whistled for the birds to return. Muse landed on her outstretched arm soon after.

"He must've gone inside." Aren glanced upward, holding Whisper on his gauntlet. "The cliff is far too steep here to climb."

"How can we know for sure?" Edrik leaned forward and squinted into the dark hole. "What if he turned and ventured around the mountain instead?"

Lark placed her free hand on the gray stone next to the cave entrance. Deep in her belly, that prickle of unease rose again. "He's in there. I can feel it."

Mika shrugged. "That's good enough for me." He paced around in a circuit, selecting a trio of sticks from the ground. Then he reached into his pack and pulled out a roll of bandages. "Edrik, Oriana, help me, please." He handed a stick and a length of cloth to each of them. "Wrap the tops of these in bandages, like so." He twirled the top of his stick to demonstrate. "Then slather them with some of this." Reaching into his pack again, he pulled free a vial of oil and tipped a bit onto the cloth. "We're sure to need torches to navigate inside that cave."

Lark stood stiffly, tapping her foot while they finished crafting and lighting the makeshift torches. Then all five of them ducked down and crept inside the cave, one by one.

Lark hiked at the head of the group, behind Mika. He strode forward confidently, lighting the way with his torch. Oriana was behind her, then Aren and Edrik bringing up the rear.

The flickering torchlight sent shadows spreading on the walls, casting them in an eerie gloom. They found themselves in a wide, low tunnel, carved into the rock. It appeared to be natural, full of jagged, rocky outcroppings sticking out in all directions that they were forced to maneuver around. Water dripped down the walls, wetting a floor littered with rock and spotted with holes soaked in black.

They ducked and weaved their way through for ages. Lark's neck and shoulders began protesting after so long crouched down in the cramped tunnel. Her legs ached from all the walking, much of it on a tilted pitch that made her certain they weren't only traveling inward, but upward as well.

At long last, the way ahead opened up. The ceiling lifted, and they stepped inside a large chamber, the walls glittering with sparkling rocks.

It was here they spotted movement across the cavern on the far wall. It was him.

"Nox," Mika yelled.

Nox jerked around at the sound, the scourge still dangling from his shoulder like a sinister scarf. But he didn't stick around to greet them. He disappeared into another tunnel, leading further into the mountain.

Mika raced after him for a few paces, then fell, a shriek on his lips as he walloped the ground. His torch skittered across the floor, staying lit but falling out of his reach.

Lark started toward Mika, but he held up a hand.

"Careful," Mika said through gritted teeth. "It's slipperier than it looks."

She heeded his warning, making her way to him carefully. Her boots slid on the slick rock, but though she wobbled, she kept her balance until she was at his side. "Are you all right?" She crouched beside him.

"Rot and decay." He hissed with pain, lifting his pant leg and untying his boot to reveal his ankle, already swollen. "I'll live."

Soon the others crowded around them, everyone careful not to make the same mistake of moving too fast. Their torches lit his wound. His skin continued to swell before her eyes.

Lark winced in sympathy. "Let me help you."

Mika waved her away. "No. I can heal myself. Nox is just ahead. You all go on without me. I'll catch up soon."

Her heart squeezed at the thought of leaving Mika all alone. "Are you sure?"

"Yes, go. Find Nox. Keep him from doing something stupid until I catch up to you."

"I'll leave a trail if the tunnel splits." Aren grabbed her arm, turning to leave.

Edrik handed Mika his fallen torch, and the rest of them hustled off after the boy.

Lark squinted into the darkness ahead of them. It was another tunnel, much like the first, only this one pitched at an even steeper incline. Nox was already out of sight, somehow able to navigate the black tunnel with ease.

She shuddered, struggling to imagine what it must be like in these tunnels in the total black without a light source. She'd have fallen a hundred times over, with all the ducking and weaving around rocks. But the scourge lived below ground. Perhaps the creature granted him an advantage when traveling through the earth?

It seemed they wouldn't have much further to travel. The first sign was the sound of rushing water, somewhere close. Then the ground leveled, and a dim light seeped into the tunnel from up ahead. The first light they'd seen since entering, except for their torches.

Lark's breath caught as she spotted movement again, momentarily blocking the light before disappearing. Was that Nox? She wondered for the hundredth time how he'd ended up bonded to one of the scourge... It must be so awful to have the voice of such a destructive beast whispering inside his mind.

She shared a look with Aren in the dim tunnel. Both of them hastened forward. They had to save the poor boy from the creature that had latched on to him.

They crept into another large chamber. This one was ten times the size of the last, lit from a massive entrance shrouded by a sheer covering that glimmered strangely in the sunlight. A wide, fast-moving stream gurgled along the far wall. As she stood staring, a fish leapt through the air, its scales a flash of glittering gold before it splashed back down in the water.

The cave floor was covered with more jagged rocks. They shone in the sun, sparkling in shades of gold, silver, and white. She tilted her head, searching for any sign of movement. With all these rocks, Nox could be hiding anywhere.

There. She spotted something. She squinted, craning her neck sideways to peek behind a huge white rock.

Then her jaw dropped.

It was the rock moving, not something behind it. And it was not a rock at all, but a massive beast, the size of a small house, curled up in a ball on the ground. A dragon!

The creature lay still except for the slow rise and fall of its chest, wings wrapped around its body, eyes closed in slumber. White scales glittered with flecks of silver and gold. A long sinuous tail curved along the cave floor, twitching slightly.

Her heart hammered in her chest. Nox and the scourge *had* come here seeking a dragon. But why?

It was then she spotted them. Nox rose behind a rock, creeping toward the slumbering beast. Suddenly he stopped and clutched his neck, falling to the ground.

The four of them raced forward in unison, the cause of his fall apparent as they drew closer. The scourge was on him, tearing at his neck.

Blazes. His own bondmate turned on him? It made no sense.

Lark shoved the mystery aside, flicking her arm in the air. *"Muse, go!"*

Muse shot forward and snatched the beast off the boy's neck, lifting it up into the air. The scourge fought back, scratching and clawing, trying to force Muse to drop it. It wasn't long before she lost hold and it fell. The scourge slammed into the hard rock then sprang back to its feet and leaped toward the dragon.

By this time, Lark had made it to Nox's side. She shucked off her gauntlet in record time, dug through her pack and slapped a wad of bandages on the boy's wound, applying pressure.

It was Whisper's turn to grab the scourge. He lasted only an instant longer before the beast struck the ground once more. Aren was behind Lark, his fingers flying as he readied the bow, but before he could take aim, a ball of water slammed into the scourge, completely covering the beast.

Edrik sat by the stream's edge, one hand in the water, the other outstretched as the vile rodent struggled. And for the second time in her life, Lark saw fear and panic fill the beady eyes of one of the scourge as it drowned.

Nox let out a gurgling cry as the beast died.

"Shh." Lark kept pressure on his neck. "You're going to be all right."

Aren dropped his bow on the ground and crouched beside her.

A sudden shriek stole Lark's attention. The dragon was awake, staring at all of them.

Her stomach jumped into her throat. Were they all done for now? What would that enormous monster do after finding them inside its home?

After a heartbeat, it turned and raced away and through the cave entrance.

Lark couldn't relax yet. She still had a boy bleeding out beneath her hands. The bandage was already soaked; the blood poured out, gushing between her fingers even as she fought to apply pressure without crushing his windpipe.

Oriana approached and peered down at Nox's neck. Her face blanched.

She met her eyes. "Go. Get Mika. Now!"

Oriana sped off at a run, back into the tunnel they came from.

Aren grabbed her shoulder. "I don't think Nox can wait. Lark, you have to heal him."

She stared back at him, tears wetting her lashes. "I don't know if I can." Her mind flashed back to the last boy she'd tried to save. The bloody laceration on his scalp had bled just the same, the hot spill of fluid drenching her fingers.

Aren squeezed. "Yes, you can. I believe in you, Lark." He held her stare, his blue eyes full of all the determination and confidence she couldn't muster. "Tell me what you need. I'm right here."

She blew out a breath. He was right. She could do this. She would do this. Now she knew what to do. This boy wouldn't die, not here. Not now.

"In my bag," she ordered. "Grab me the freshest, greenest plants you can find."

Aren nodded. He dumped her pack on the ground and snatched up a handful of fresh herbs, offering them to her on his open palm.

"Yes, that should work." She lifted one hand, the fingers stained red, and grabbed the leaves. She took a deep breath. This would work. It had to.

She pulled free the wad of bloody bandages. She slapped the herbs down over the wound. Nox's eyes were closed, his features slack as blood spurted against her palm. She could sense a change in the pressure of blood flooding through her fingers. His heartbeat was erratic, sluggish. Aren was right, he wouldn't last much longer.

Lark closed her eyes and wished. She wished with everything in her for this boy to live. For the bloody jagged gash beneath her hands to knit itself back together.

There it was. Her talent rushed through her, rattling the earth beneath her, knocking a handful of stones loose. A rain of pebbles crashed to the ground from the cave ceiling.

She cracked open an eye and slowly lifted her hand. Her jaw dropped. It worked. She'd done it. She'd saved him!

As she stared down at the blood-soaked but no longer bleeding flesh before her, Nox's eyes fluttered open. Mika arrived, then Oriana fast on his heels.

"Nox," Mika yelled. He skidded to a stop and crouched beside them. "Nox... you're all right?"

Aren chimed in, a wide smile on his face, "Lark healed him."

The simple statement left her feeling euphoric. Lark smiled. The tension drained from her, replaced with warmth infusing her chest and spreading slowly through her limbs. "I did, didn't I?"

Nox blinked rapidly, his stare flitting between all of them crowded around him, his face the picture of confusion. "Where am I? What's happening?"

Mika's brow furrowed. He helped Nox sit up on the stone floor. "What exactly do you remember?"

The boy bit his lip and shook his head. "A lot, but it's all out of order. All jumbled up like a puzzle." He gasped. "My bondmates. Mika, I can't hear them anymore. Any of them."

Mika turned to her. "How close did he come to dying?"

Lark shuddered, recalling all that blood rushing between her fingers. "Very."

Mika nodded solemnly, giving Nox a gentle squeeze. "Don't worry about that now, Nox. We've got to get you out of here. Do you think you can stand?"

Suddenly, an ear-shattering roar blasted, coming from the cave mouth. Lark flinched, muscles rigid, her heart racing.

"What was that?" Nox's eyes bulged.

Lark shuffled sideways and scooped her things back into her pack. "I don't know, but I'm going to find out."

Aren jumped up beside her, lifting his bow off the ground.

They turned to the mouth of the cave. Lark lifted her foot, but before she could take a single step, Nox gasped again. She shifted at the sound and found him staring at the scourge's drowned carcass on the cave floor.

"Chumy." His chin wobbled. He lurched on his knees to reach the beast and cradled it in his arms.

Lark drew back in disgust. "That thing just tried to kill you, Nox. How can you hold any affection for it?"

Nox lifted tear-filled eyes to her. "No, you don't understand. I remember now. Chumy didn't want to hurt me. None of them do. There's something else—something evil—behind it all. He was there with us, too. I could feel him through the bond. *He's* the one that made Chumy attack me."

Lark rubbed her brow. Could any of that be true? Were the scourge not the villains she'd believed them to be but victims of some hidden evil? It was too much to wrap her head around. Nox already admitted to being confused; how could he possibly be sure of this?

A second sound rent the air. This one was more familiar to her, but just as portentous. The howl of a wolf.

She shook herself free of her reverie and turned back to the cave's entrance. There'd be time to mull over those questions later. Something was happening out there. It was time to find out what.

Chapter 22

Conall drug the rowboat ashore with a sigh. The pebbly sand crunched beneath his boots as he walked with his bondmate toward a mountainous cliffside. They'd made it just north of the Mido Islands before the captain he'd hired refused to go any farther. The row boat made swift work of the remaining distance, but the spot they'd landed on the northern beach left them with no other option but to go up.

"What is it with mountains, Shadow? Everywhere I go there's always a damn rock to climb."

"You have seen your fair share of trouble on cliffs." An amused noise followed, reverberating in his mind.

"Snicker all you want, brother." Conall grinned, staring up at the cliff face. It was steep, for sure, but no worse than what he'd faced in the Turney Mountains on the way to Doln. *"But haven't you heard? This is fate."*

"Just try not to fall down this one. I'm getting tired of finding you at the bottom of a ridge, close to death." Shadow vaulted up on the rock, his step sure.

"Neither of those falls were my fault." He found a spot that looked promising and took his first step up on the gray stone. *"You try keeping your balance when you've just been shot. Or jumping out of the way of an avalanche."*

"If I remember correctly, you jumped into *the avalanche."*

Conall grimaced. *"All right, all right. There won't be any jumping today. Let's just climb up there so we can have a look around. See if there's any sign of Lark on this island."*

The thought of his sister made his steps lighter. He could feel it. She was here. He was moments away from reuniting with Lark. The realization buoyed him so much he had little trouble keeping up with Shadow on the cliffside, even though his bondmate was far fleeter-footed.

He'd decided not to listen to the tiny voice in the back of his mind. The one telling him Lark wouldn't want to see him. That she would blame him for not watching out for her. That she'd be so put off by his changed appearance she wouldn't want anything to do with him. Maybe even refuse to recognize him.

No. He buried those thoughts deep inside. All that mattered was that he find her. Whatever came after, he would deal with it, happily. If she wanted to hate him for the rest of her days, then so be it. He would be satisfied just seeing she was alive. He had to find her.

By the time they made it about halfway up, sweat poured down his back. He paused and gazed out to sea while he gulped from his waterskin. From this height, he could make out a tiny blip on the horizon, already high-tailing back north.

He sighed. No turning back now.

They continued to climb. The gray rock glistened in the sun. Conall basked in the warmth, amazed that only days before he'd been shivering, stuffed into furs. It was a welcome change to be clothed in a pair of brown trousers; his tan, long-sleeved tunic rolled up, a gentle breeze tickling the hairs on his arms. He'd even shaved off the thick beard he'd grown in Doln, leaving him feeling even more like his old self. It would almost be relaxing if it weren't for the climbing.

They'd made it about three quarters of the way up to the summit when a thunderous roar tore through the air. His body jerked, and his heart jolted to life, his step slipping. Conall clutched the rock before him, his feet skidding against the stone. His palms scratched and bled, but he managed to right his balance.

He turned to Shadow, shaking his stinging palms. *"What the blazes was that?"*

"I don't know, but it was coming from up there." Shadow raised his snout and scented the air. *"Smells... strange. Do we turn back?"*

Conall followed suit, lifting his nose and breathing deeply. Whatever was up there smelled musky, smokey, and sharp, unlike anything he'd ever encountered. But that changed nothing.

"No." Conall shook his head. *"What if Lark's up there? Let's climb. Fast."*

They climbed with renewed vigor, racing up the steep slope as fast as they could manage. Shadow made it to the top first, and an instant later, Conall joined him, his breath harsh in lungs worn out from exertion.

He gasped, blinking furiously. They found themselves on a flat plateau, staring at a pair of dragons locked in a stalemate.

A huge black dragon stood on its hind legs, wings spread, mouth open, red light spilling out its throat behind sharp teeth. Conall quaked, the reaction visceral and immediate at seeing such a powerful beast in the flesh. A beast poised to strike.

Cowering on the ground below it lay a white dragon. A dragon he recognized.

It was the same ice white dragon he fought in his dream! Seeing it here, alive and oh so real, reawakened the terror that had filled him as he'd dodged for his life in that black abyss. Did the Unseen infect it still? What if this was his chance to stop the evil plaguing his country?

Conall sucked in a deep breath and pulled his waterskin from his belt. The black dragon appeared to have the upper hand, but he wasn't taking any chances. If this was fate, then there was a reason he was here. He had to believe he was meant to help. And if a blast of ice had stopped the beast beneath the sea, then maybe it would now.

Cupping his hand, he spilled a drop of water on his outstretched palm. He brought forth the memory of his sister's face in his mind. He had to protect Lark. A ball of ice formed on his palm as moisture surrounded him, humming across his skin.

He sent the ice soaring. It sailed through the air, glittering and so cold it left behind a trail of mist in its wake. Then it smashed into the white dragon's back and shattered into millions of pieces like tiny shards of glass.

The white dragon's head spun. Its long elegant neck extended, gaze shifting wildly. The black dragon's gaze zeroed in on him, and it shuffled sideways, even as he spilled another drop of water in his hand, a second ball of ice coalescing just as quickly.

A girl charged out from between the dragons. It was the girl with the braids. The same freckled redhead he remembered from his vision.

Her eyes were wide, her mouth falling open as she caught sight of the ice growing larger on his palm. She screamed, "No!"

It was too late. The ball of ice had already left his fingers, sailing straight for the white dragon.

The girl called forth flames out of nowhere and sent a blast of fire at the ball of ice. But the ice only sailed through, losing a portion of its mass to the fire, dripping water through the air on course for its target. Conall smiled, certain the ice would shatter directly across the dragon's face. At the last instant, the dragon opened its wicked jaw and snatched the ice ball out of the sky. It swallowed.

He didn't have time to wonder what that meant. The fire was headed straight for him. Conall dodged, falling to the ground on the ridge's edge, his shoulder alive with pain.

Shadow lifted his muzzle and howled.

Conall rolled, desperate to put out the flames burning his tunic. He twisted and slapped his sleeve, finally extinguishing the burning cloth, a hiss escaping from his clenched teeth.

He sat up to view the scene. Shadow barreled toward the girl, his teeth bared, growling viciously.

"Shadow. No," he screamed in his mind.

What was he thinking? She would burn him to a crisp.

But the girl just stared at the white dragon with horror on her face, making no attempt to cut down the predator tearing toward her.

The black dragon's front legs smashed into the ground. The whole plateau vibrated as its tail whipped into Shadow and knocked him off course, away from the girl. Conall stood, racing to the spot where his bondmate had fallen.

"Shadow!"

He skidded to a stop beside him as Shadow righted himself, his fur bristling. His lips curled back in a snarl.

"Brother, stop. It was a mistake." He jumped directly in front of Shadow, blocking his view of the girl and the dragons. *"We're meant to be allies."*

Shadow shook his head. The growl died in his throat. *"Little brother, are you all right?"*

"I'm fine. Are you?"

His bondmate didn't answer. They both dropped to the ground instead. The white dragon raced toward them, but before they could do anything more than fall to the rock, it rocketed over their heads and blasted into the sky.

The black dragon hesitated, staring at the girl. Then it took two leaping steps and bounded into the sky.

The girl fell to her knees, her arm outstretched, an anguished bellow escaping her lips. "Dru!"

Conall lifted himself off the rock. His palms stung, but that was nothing next to his shoulder. The pain was alive, throbbing, and so hot. Little shreds of his tunic stuck into the wound, his skin red and swollen. The sickening scent of charred flesh filled his nostrils, reminding him of the pyre he'd stood witness at just days ago. Reminding him it could've been worse.

He scowled at the damage. Damn good for nothing mountains.

"Conall?" A new voice rose to greet him. A voice he would recognize anywhere.

He spun to the sound. The glorious sound. "Lark," he breathed.

There she was, emerging from within the rock wall like a dream. Like an answered prayer. Her hair was a wild tangle of curls, her eyes shining. "Conall!" She raced to him and thudded into his chest, her arms latching around his waist so tightly. Her voice was strangled. "I thought you were dead. I thought you were gone."

"I'm not. I'm here. I found you." He clutched her just as tightly, all the pain forgotten. "Lark, I found you."

He closed his eyes and held his sister in his arms. Her slight frame shuddered and shook, her tears wetting the front of his shirt.

Finally. All his fears slid away. He should've known she'd recognize him instantly. That she'd fall right back into his life without pause. Without question.

Blazes, he'd found her! He clutched her tightly and silently thanked fate. Thanking even the cursed circumstances he'd been forced to endure. All the pain and hardship. The suffering and sacrifice. It had all been worth it. But the blissful moment couldn't last forever.

She pulled back but stayed close enough to touch, staring up at his face. She raised a hand to his hair, twining her fingers in brown locks shot through with silver. "How?"

He chewed on the inside of his lip. "It's a long story."

Her gaze lit on his shoulder, and she gasped. "Why didn't you tell me you were hurt?" She frowned and pushed out of his arms, digging into her pack.

Why hadn't he? Probably because nothing mattered as much as assuring himself she was alive. His shoulder still burned, but the pain was a dull ache in the back of his mind. A trifling nothing compared to having her back. Finally, having her back.

"I'm fine." He tilted his head, smiling down at her. At the tiny wrinkle between her brows. The same one she'd had even as a newborn babe.

The little wrinkle deepened. "No, you're not." She held up a tin, opened it, and scooped out a handful of green goo. She slicked her palm over his wound, and he yelped in pain. "See?" She lifted a brow. "Not fine. Don't worry, this should help."

Lark gently removed the shreds of fabric sticking to his wound and rested her hand atop the reddened flesh. Then her eyelids fluttered closed. A tremor spread across his skin, centered around her palm.

He gasped. The pain—it was gone.

She lifted her hand, revealing smooth, perfect flesh.

She'd come into her own in their time apart. There was so much he needed to ask her. So much he wanted to know. He grinned, his smile so wide his cheeks ached. "Thanks."

He couldn't stop staring at her. His sister was here.

Then movement behind her drew his attention. More people had emerged from the rock while they'd been busy reuniting. A blond man, clothed in the same sheer fabric Lark wore, was watching them from nearby. Two teens, both clothed in tattered, torn garb, stood by his side. As he watched, a second man—this one brown-haired and deeply tanned—emerged, his arm wrapped around a sullen boy, his face drawn, gaze downcast.

Conall flicked a glance at Lark. "How many more of you are there?" He squinted, staring at the rock. "Where did you come from?"

"We were in a massive cave system." She turned to look at the rock, her eyes sparkling. "Crazy, isn't it? The wall isn't really there. It's an illusion." Then her smile widened as her gaze shifted to her friends. "This is all of us." Lark pointed to each, making introductions. As she finished naming everyone, a gold and white falcon spread its wings, shaking its feathers from a perch on the cliffside. He recognized it as the same bird that fiercely fought at Lark's side in the dream vision. "And this is Muse, my bondmate."

Conall grinned, gazing at the majestic bird of prey. After seeing the vision, he'd assumed Lark would be bonded like he was, but hearing the confirmation from her own lips warmed his heart. It made perfect sense. As a child she was always staring out the window, watching birds in flight, drawn to them just as he'd been drawn to dogs.

"I've a bondmate as well. Meet Shadow."

Shadow wagged his tail, his golden eyes meeting Lark's for the first time. *"She looks just like you, little brother. I knew we'd find her."* His tail picked up speed, and joy radiated off of him, flowing through their bond.

Lark smiled widely and gave Shadow a little wave. Then her smile slipped, and her brow furrowed. "Who's your friend?" Lark nodded to the redhead. She was curled up in a ball on the ground, her head in her hands, seemingly oblivious to the world around her.

"Actually, we haven't met." Conall strolled to her. He tapped her on the shoulder.

She lifted tear-filled brown eyes to stare up at him. "He cut me off," she whispered.

"Pardon?" Conall asked.

Lark's mouth flew open, and she pointed, shaking her finger at the girl. "I saw you! I saw you at Bogsmouth flying a dragon. The scourge... you burned them all." Her gaze drifted to Conall's shirt. The healed flesh stuck out from his blackened and scorched tunic. She stepped back, a hand flying to her mouth as her gaze flitted between them.

"It's all right," Conall said hurriedly. "It was an accident." He knelt down and grabbed the girl's shoulder, staring into her face. "I'm Conall, and this is my sister, Lark. What's your name?"

Chapter 23

"*Dru? Where are you?*" Kayda sat on the mountain plateau, cradling her head in her hands.

He was gone. Druturion was gone. Not just gone from her side, but from her thoughts. He'd taken off after that white dragon, Belstasia, and used whatever strange boon he possessed to block her thoughts from reaching him.

Her stomach churned, and her head throbbed. How could he do that to her? Leave her here all on her own? The bond they shared had become so comfortable, so familiar. Now that he was gone, it was like she was missing a piece of herself, leaving an aching hole in her heart and mind.

It hurt. Blazes. It hurt so much to reach out to him, only to be ignored. Where was he? Why couldn't he take her with him? Why?

She felt something. A tapping on her shoulder.

She lifted her head and found a pair of people before her, but she couldn't fully focus on them. Her head was still pounding, her heart still shattering. Her voice was a broken whisper. "He cut me off."

Then they were both talking, fuzzy murmurs sliding through her ears. The girl pointed at her and backed up, gasping.

Whatever they were going on about, it didn't matter. How could it? She was alone. All alone. Dru was gone. She should've just let him cut Belstasia down. But no. She'd had to step in, and now he was gone, chasing Bela who knew where.

When would he be back? Her breath hitched. Would he ever come back?

The pressure on her arm returned, firmer than before. There was a man crouching down before her. "I'm Conall, and this is my sister, Lark." His words were slow and measured, like he was speaking to a frightened child. "What's your name?"

Kayda drew a deep breath. She tamped down the hurt Dru's abandonment had caused and forced her eyes to focus. She focused on the man. His hazel eyes were soft, the skin at the edges of his lids crinkled, his dark brows drawn down with worry. Wild brown locks shot through with gray curled around his face. Wait...

She drew back and tugged her arm free from his hold. "You!" Her voice was louder now, but just as broken. "Why would you hit her with ice? That's exactly what she needed!"

It was him! The man who'd interrupted them on the plateau. The man who'd freed Bela.

"I don't understand." He sat back on his heels and rubbed his temple. "This is gonna sound crazy, but I saw that dragon before. In a dream. A vision. I fought it off with a blast of ice."

Kayda frowned. "What are you talking about? Dragons need to consume the elements they summon. You just gave her exactly what she needed to regain her strength and escape."

Conall's jaw clenched tightly. "Oh." His eyes widened and he stood, pacing. "I didn't know. I'm sorry, I didn't know."

The girl, Lark, shook her head, her brown curls bobbing around her shoulders. She stepped in the path of her brother's pacing and halted him. "It's all right, Conall. It's clear we don't have all the pieces of this puzzle laid out yet. We'll figure it out, together." Lark shifted closer, her eyes the exact shade of hazel as her brother's, though she looked two decades younger. "You still haven't told us your name."

Kayda shook off the anger bubbling up in her chest. It wouldn't change anything. Dru was still gone. She wrapped her arms around her knees. "I'm Kayda."

A gasp rose from behind the pair, where more people gathered. A green-eyed girl with tattered clothes stepped forward. "Princess Kayda? Everyone in Flamesmoat's been looking for you."

Conall turned to look at her again. "You're the Princess of Dracwood?" Then the side of his mouth quirked up in a crooked smile. "Of course, you are. Who else would be dragon bonded?"

A pang struck her at the mention of Dru. She sighed. "I might be dragon bonded, but thanks to you, I'm dragonless."

The girl spoke up again. "Princess, please." She gestured to a young man beside her, his clothes tattered and torn as well. "We've been sent to seek aid for Flamesmoat. The scourge have the city surrounded."

The news unleashed a gnawing pain in her stomach. What of Izora? Her father and grandfather? Were they all right? She rose to her feet, her legs stable despite the heavy weight on her shoulders.

Conall spoke up, his hand on his chest. "How long ago did you leave for aid?"

The boy in the tattered clothes answered, "I'm not sure. Two weeks maybe? The days since the shipwreck are mostly a blur."

Shipwreck? That would explain the torn clothes and how the pair ended up on this desolate island. What of the rest? Lark and most of the others wore the luct clothing favored by the Raimish, but Conall was clothed like a Dracian. How had they all ended up here at the exact moment she and Dru had? Lark had the right of it when she likened the situation to a puzzle.

But one thing was certain. She had to save her country from its plight. "I have to go back to Flamesmoat." she shifted her gaze across all of them. "Please tell me one of you has a way off of this island?"

"We have a boat, down the mountain and a bit to the south," offered a tanned man with his arm slung around a glowering youth.

"I have one as well," Conall said. "Kayda and Lark, I'd like you to come with me. There's much we must discuss."

"All right," the tan man said. "Sail around the coast of this island until you see our boat on the shore. We can head back to Stoneshore together to regroup. I'm sure once the Matas hear about the situation in Flamesmoat, they'll be willing to send aid."

They split up, heading for their respective boats. The tall blond man joined them—Lark introduced him as Aren—along with two birds and the wolf.

Kayda stole a closer look at all of them with their animal companions. "Do you all have bonding magic?"

Aren shook his head. "I'm just a falconer."

But the other two nodded.

Kayda's stomach fluttered as she took her first look down the steep slope. The wooden boat sat propped up on its side, leaning against the cliff, seeming incredibly small when viewed from above. "I've yet to meet anyone besides my grandfather with bondmates, and now, I've met two in the same day."

"Three actually," Lark added. "That young boy back there, Nox, he's had four bonds already."

"Four bonds?" Kayda's eyes widened, the warning she'd been given not to bond more than one replaying in her ears. "And he's not mad?"

"Well, he was." Lark grimaced. "That's why we were out here." She sent her falcon into the sky, using both hands to balance as she started down the steep slope. "It's a long story."

Conall grinned, looking up at them. "Good to hear I'm not the only one with one of those." His foot slipped, and he scowled, shaking his hand after using it to stop himself from falling. "Let's just concentrate on the climb for now. We'll have plenty of time to talk in the boat. Plus, I've got something I need to show you both."

Kayda nodded and carefully took her first step down. Her heart pounded. Despite watching Conall and Lark descend successfully below her, she kept expecting to slip, sending them all tumbling to the sand with broken necks.

Damn it, Dru. If he were here, they'd be down there in an instant, or better yet, on the way to Flamesmoat already. She sighed and forced the thought aside. She couldn't afford to let her attention slip, lest she lose her footing.

The wind kicked up and slapped her braids in her face. What had Conall meant, he had something to show them? She didn't like the way he looked at her—like he knew her. Like he had some knowledge she was missing.

Her stomach clenched, even as she descended far enough a fall would only leave her with scratches instead of an untimely death. She was all alone, forced to rely on these strangers to get home. They seemed friendly enough, but could she trust any of them?

Soon Kayda descended to the beach. She sighed deeply as her boots sank into the sand. Together, they tilted the boat back on its side and carried it into the surf.

Kayda hopped in, settling next to Lark in the front of the boat. Conall seated himself before them with his wolf curled up by his feet.

Aren took charge of the paddles in the back of the small vessel while the birds flew overhead.

Lark clutched her stomach, her face taking on a greenish tinge. She mumbled something under her breath about sailing, then swallowed, raising her voice. "What did you want to show us, brother?"

Conall tugged on a bag stashed below the bench he sat upon. "This isn't easy to say. Nor will it be easy to hear." He settled the sack in his lap but made no move to open it. He stared at her and Lark instead. "I've spent the last weeks traveling through Doln with the Sade Prim, Delyth. She and I traveled to the Winter Witch of the North. There, I was shown a vision of the future, among other things." He grimaced, his gaze downcast, as if the memory pained him. "I saw the three of us, locked in a great battle in the Abandoned Lands."

"You saw us in a vision?" Lark cocked her head, raising a brow.

"Yes. It's how I knew where to find you. But that's not all of it." He frowned, his fingers clenching in the sack's fabric. "I felt a sickly presence there, watching me. It appeared to me and spoke. Named itself as the Unseen. That is the true enemy we're facing. The scourge, they're merely puppets for this thing. A means to an end to satisfy its need for destruction."

Kayda's hand flew to her chest, his words bringing back the memory of that creeping, slithering wrongness she'd felt while battling the scourge. But his admission made sense of another mystery she'd been struggling to wrap her mind around. "The Sul. I've met with them recently. They've kept creatures they call chumon as pets for centuries. They're one and the same as the vile beasts terrorizing our land, only these pets of theirs are biddable, with none of the scourge's unquenchable hunger."

Lark sucked in a sharp breath. "That boy, Nox, he bonded a scourge. It tried to kill him. He claimed something was controlling it. I didn't believe him, but now it all makes sense."

Kayda stared at her feet. "If there's something out there controlling the scourge, then can it control other beings, too?" A pang of fear stabbed her. She swung her head up, meeting Conall's hazel eyes. "You said you saw the white dragon in your vision... We found dragon bones on the beach in Stoneshore. Evidence that something big fell from the cliffside back there. But all we found when we got there was..." She trailed off, slowly connecting the dots.

Was that why Druturion was so mad at Belstasia? Had the Unseen driven her to do the unthinkable to her own kind?

Conall gulped and nodded slowly. "You may be right." He leaned forward, his nostrils flaring. "There's something else. That first vision—the one with the three of us battling—I learned that vision has remained constant. Every single person who's met with the Winter Witch for hundreds of years has seen it."

"What does that mean?" Lark asked, voicing the question reverberating in her own mind.

"I don't know," Conall answered. "That it's fate we'll fight the Unseen? Delyth certainly seemed to believe it. It led her to make some destructive choices."

"What choices?" Kayda asked.

He lifted his gaze to the sky and studied the fluffy clouds overhead. The water sloshed against the boat, the spirited cawing of seabirds seeming far too cheery for such a tense moment.

When his gaze dropped, it was colder, his throat working as he swallowed. "The mages arranged it all. They believed it was the only way to stop the Unseen for good. The Palisade's fall was planned."

Kayda rocked back in her seat, her eyes bulging. No. She shook her head. That couldn't be true.

"Here." He handed her a crumpled parchment. "This letter is by no means fully conclusive, but it alludes to what I heard from the Sade Prim's own lips before she died. The mages were pulling strings behind the scenes all along."

She stared down at the yellow paper. Her heart skipped a beat. She recognized the handwriting. Lark leaned over her shoulder, and Kayda angled the letter between them so they could both read its contents.

Delyth,

Please, I must beg of you more time. Things here are progressing but not as quickly as we'd hoped. I fear she will not be prepared, should the inevitable occur so soon.

My contacts in Greenvale report the disappearance of the others, on the same day, no less. The falcon flies to you at Mage Keep, but the wolf is presumed dead. Should that be the case, then all our careful planning would be for naught. Ereni expects to head there next to investigate.

Your daughter has laid the trap admirably. The bait has been taken. Please, do what you can to slow the results. I will do my part, as always.

Izora

Kayda closed her eyes, her stomach roiling. Tarquin. She'd been convinced her stepbrother's greed caused the Palisade's fall, but now she could see he'd only been a pawn to the mages and their scheming.

What of the attack on the king? Had that been part of their plan, too?

For the second time, she felt the full force of Izora's betrayal. How could she have kept her in the dark for so long? She'd not just been lying about her family history but about her very identity. Her supposed future in this twisted game they'd been staging.

But no matter the shock of the revelations, it still didn't change what she needed to do. Flamesmoat was in trouble, and she'd be damned if she wasn't going to do something to stop it.

She opened her eyes. Conall held Lark's hand, her stare still fixed on the parchment clutched tightly within her fingers. Kayda loosened her hold and handed the paper back to Conall.

"None of that changes anything. Flamesmoat still needs saving. The Abandoned Lands, and this Unseen, will have to wait." She spoke with confidence, but inside, she was a quivering mess of uncertainty.

All the help she'd secured from Wyll was weeks away and headed up the wrong side of the continent. Would she be able to make a difference without Druturion by her side?

Conall dropped his sister's hand and stuck the parchment back in his pack. "We're coming with you," he said, voice just as firm.

Lark nodded. "I'm not sure why, or how, but we were meant to find each other. Why else would we all end up on this tiny island at the same time? We're in this together, Princess." She smiled and squeezed her knee.

"I might have something that can help." Conall pulled a second item from his pack and carefully unwrapped it from a waxed cloth covering. It was a small brown book, the leather cover worn, the pages' edges yellowed and dappled with age. "Delyth made me promise to read this on her deathbed. I think this book may hold the key to defeating the Unseen. Maybe something inside can help us save Flamesmoat." He passed it to Kayda.

Kayda flipped the smooth leather over in her hands and squinted at the handwritten title on the spine. But the words were faded beyond recognition, whether from age or heavy handling, she couldn't be sure. She gingerly lifted the cover to peek within.

Eyes widening, she realized the book was ancient, perhaps the oldest book she'd ever held. Then she spied the author's name on the title page and stifled a gasp. "Afton. Was this penned by the first Sade Prim? Truly?" She shook her head, lifting the corner of a page carefully. "I've never known a book to last that long. How is this not crumbling to dust in my fingers?"

Conall shrugged. "Magic? That's the whole point of the book, you see." He reached forward, as if to flip the pages, but Kayda pulled it closer instinctively, cradling it on her lap. He raised a brow but retracted his hand without comment, with barely a pause before continuing, "The mages of old had far greater powers than anything we've seen in many generations. Delyth hinted as much to me, but this book explains it in great detail. I haven't read it all yet, but what I've seen so far..." His smile spread slowly. "It's incredible."

So, the fate of the world might come down to a book? A smile crept across Kayda's lips. "Do you mind if I take a closer look at this?"

"Go ahead. I imagine you're a faster reader than I am. And Lark and I still have plenty to discuss." He smiled warmly at his sister.

Kayda wasn't listening. As the boat slowly progressed across the channel to Stoneshore, she flipped page after page. When they pulled up on the rocky beach, the sun sinking down in the sky behind them, she closed the cover and smiled. Maybe they stood a chance after all.

Chapter 24

The boat skidded against the rocks of Stoneshore beach. Lark breathed a sigh as her boots sank down into the pebbly surf. The sailing was over. For today, at least.

Her gaze was drawn to her brother and his wolf as they hopped out of the small canoe. She still couldn't believe it. Conall was alive! She'd spent so long certain he was dead. She'd cried so many tears, accepting the fact that she'd never see him again, but now her heart was so full she could almost burst.

When she'd first seen him, standing there on the mountaintop on that tiny island in the middle of nowhere, she'd had the shock of her life. Before he'd met her gaze, a battle raged inside of her mind. Confusion and disbelief swirled around her like a tempest. But when his gaze connected with hers from across that plateau, she'd known. Even though he was irreparably changed. Even though she'd been *sure* he was dead. One look in his eyes swept the storm of doubt aside like it had never existed. Her brother was there. He was alive!

The second boat skidded to the shore next to them. They were all back on the mainland. Soon, they'd all piled out onto the beach and tied the canoes fast.

Conall stared up at the steep cliffside. The rock was eroded down to a vertical slope, with carved footholds forming a makeshift ladder. "Shadow can't make that climb."

Mika pointed south down the beach. "There's a gentler slope just around the bend. Shouldn't take long to reach. You'll find a footpath leading to the village at the top."

Lark slid her arm in Conall's, linking their elbows. "I'll walk with you. No one travels alone in the jungle."

"We're taking the long way back. You coming with us?" she asked.

"I'll catch up with you later. Ha. I've got a craving for monkey that can't be denied." Muse lifted into the sky and quickly disappeared.

Before they turned to leave, she spotted a familiar face peeking down at them from the top of the cliff. "Nox! Nox, you're back." It was Esmar, tears shining in the corners of her eyes as she caught sight of her son shuffling forward on the beach.

Mika glared up at her and raised his voice. "What are you doing out here alone with the scourge on the loose?"

"The scourge are dead. The archers took care of them all yesterday." She waved, grinning from ear to ear. "I couldn't just sit around waiting. I knew you'd be back."

She looked like she was ready to climb down, but Mika held out a hand and called up to her, "Esmar, stay there. We'll be right up."

Esmar nodded, the relief on her face apparent. Then her gaze slid along the rest of them, and her brows sank. "Jett?" She squinted, her stare locked on Conall.

Conall lifted a hand to shade his brow, looking up at Esmar curiously.

Mika shook his head. "No, Esmar. The sun must be in your eyes. That's not Jett." He leaned closer to them, pitching his voice low. "Poor woman must be overwrought; she's mistaking you for Nox's father. Don't worry, I'll take them both back to the healing tent." He nodded to Conall's hands. "You should head there as well. Let someone clean those scratches."

Then Mika turned to the rest of the group. "Climb on up. This is the quickest way to the village." He nodded toward Kayda and the two mages. "Aren, would you mind taking these three to Mata Moyra's while I get Nox settled in the healing hut?"

Aren agreed, then sent Lark a smile. "I'll see you back in the village."

Lark met Aren's gaze, trying to silently communicate the gratitude she felt for his steady support as she reunited with her brother. Then she nodded once and turned with Conall to stroll down the rocky coastline.

Her brother stared down at her, his hazel eyes shining as the waves crashed into the beach. The sun setting over the water provided a panoramic backdrop of brilliant pink and orange clouds.

"I still can't believe it." She laughed and clutched his arm. "I'm so happy you found me."

As the boat sailed to Stoneshore, he'd shared much of his story with her. How Shadow saved him from Gael's betrayal in the woods. The part he'd played in the Palisade's fall and how it changed him. His trip across Doln to find her. It was nothing short of amazing.

"I'm glad, too." His smile matched hers briefly, but it wasn't long before it slipped. "There are a few things I've been waiting to tell you until we had a moment alone."

She gazed up at him, her smile dropping. "What is it?"

He looked down at her and exhaled deeply. "Our father's alive."

She tugged her ear, her pace slowing. "Our father's alive? Are you sure?"

He shrugged and shook his head slightly. "Delyth told me I would find him here. Raimire, Stoneshore."

"I don't understand... Why would he be in Raimire? Why would he let us think he was dead all these years?"

Conall grimaced. "I wish I knew. If we find him, I'll be sure to ask him myself."

Her hand flew to her chest, feeling a sudden urge to sit down. She paused instead and planted her feet in the rocks, closing her eyes.

Their father was alive? So many emotions bombarded her. Joy, confusion, anger. How? Why?

"There's something else I have to tell you."

Her eyes shot open, her brow furrowing at his serious tone. "What is it?"

"I told you about my vision on the boat, but I didn't tell you all of it. I didn't just talk to the Unseen." He drew in a deep breath. "Mother was there, too."

Lark's heart twisted. "She was?"

Conall nodded. "She wanted me to tell you something, Lark." He squeezed her hand. "She loves you. And she doesn't blame you for what happened when she got sick." He peered down at her closely, his hazel eyes full of warmth. "You don't blame yourself for her death, do you?"

Her chest burning, she spun to stare at the sunset. "She would've never gotten sick if it wasn't for me. I thought I could heal that boy." She closed her eyes, the boy's wet gurgling cough echoing in her ears. "Mother heard him coughing, and she knew he was too far gone. But I insisted she let me try. I was wrong."

Her brother's arms wrapped around her, and he pulled her close. "And you've been hating yourself for it all this time?" His chin rubbed across her forehead as he shook his head. "You're not to blame. Mother doesn't think so, and neither do I." He pulled back slightly, and she opened her eyes, staring up at his face. "You can't keep punishing yourself for things that happened you couldn't control. After the Palisade fell, I spent so long being angry and resentful. Cursing the twist of fate that stole years of my life and a piece of the power I'd only just learned I possessed. That made me look like this." He lifted a curly gray-streaked lock and twirled it in his fingers. "It wasn't until I decided to let go of the past that I could move on with the future."

Lark swallowed, her throat dry, her chest hollow. "You make it sound so easy." She sniffled. "You really saw her?"

He smiled and nodded. "She was right there—only for a moment—but she was there, and just as beautiful as ever."

Lark sighed and leaned on his chest, staring at the sunset once more. Of all the things she could've said in the short time she'd appeared to her brother, her mother had talked about her? It took a moment to sink in, but the words slowly twined within her, like an invisible thread repairing the frayed seams of her tattered heart.

Conall was right. It was time to let go of the guilt. A small part of her would always wonder what would've happened if she'd never tried to save that boy, but it was time to stop letting the question rule her thoughts and the shame lurk in her belly.

"Thank you for telling me." She squeezed her brother's hand and gave him a little tug, starting back down the beach. They walked in silence, the crashing waves competing with the raucous chirping and squawking jungle animals.

They circled around a bend, revealing a gently sloped ramp carved into the cliffside. Canoes lined the beach, tied to thick wooden stakes impaled into the rocky soil. A lone boat lingered on the water beyond the crashing surf, a pair of Raimish sailors dangling fishing poles over the sides. They detoured around the canoes and headed straight for the ramp.

Soon, they were back under the jungle canopy. The wind died as they started down the worn footpath, the humidity swamping them.

Conall's gaze darted all around, taking in the scenery. "We've sure come a long way from home."

"Speaking of home. I've got something to show you." Lark grinned.

"You do?" Conall laughed. His laughter glided around her, so warm and welcome. A sound she'd thought lost to her forever.

"C'mon. You're gonna flip out." Her smile widened. She grabbed his hand and started jogging. Her mind raced even faster than her feet, wondering where she'd find her friends when she got back to the village. No sooner had they picked up their pace than the noise of travel greeted them on the path before them.

Her friends appeared from the trees, racing toward them. But in that moment, Lark turned to Conall. The joy spreading over his face was dazzling in its intensity.

"Sunny!" He let go of Lark's hand and knelt just in time for the yellow mutt to barrel into his chest. Sunny's body hummed with excitement, her tail swinging so forcefully her entire body shook and swayed. Conall laughed again, his voice muffled by his dog's sloppy kisses.

Lark crouched beside him and rubbed Sunny's back. Conall lifted his head, his eyes filled with tears. "You've had Sunny with you all this time?"

She nodded, her heart radiating warmth and her limbs feeling weightless. For once in her life, she was sure she'd done right. There'd been hundreds of times she'd cursed her sanity for dragging a dog halfway around the world with her. Saving her from predators in the Boglands. Making poor Aren haul her up and down to her treetop hammock while they trekked across the jungle. But seeing the joy on her brother's face at this moment made it all worth it.

Conall petted the top of Sunny's head and stared down into the face of the dog he'd always loved like a child, his eyes shining. Then he directed his gaze at Lark, and the smile he sent her was nothing short of radiant. "Thank you for taking care of her."

Lark smiled, recalling all the nights she'd spent curled up beside the yellow mutt, petting her soft fur, the comfort she'd brought her. She ruffled Sunny's fur one more time before standing. "We took care of each other."

She turned to greet the others who crowded around her. Tiora, Mazen, Meital, and Dausius were all there, watching the two of them petting Sunny.

Tiora was the first to speak. "Aren told us where to find you. I'm so glad you're back!" She pulled her in for a hug. An instant later, Lark found herself smothered as everyone joined in, laughing and squeezing. They all started talking at once, a flurry of admonitions and praise heaped atop her from all sides.

Finally, they released her. She took a deep breath, a sheepish smile on her face. Conall chuckled as he watched them, and Lark quickly made introductions.

They all stared with astonishment when she introduced Conall as her brother.

Dausius was the first to overcome his surprise. He grabbed Conall's hand and shook it vigorously, smiling widely. "It's a pleasure to meet you, Conall. I'm dying to hear the story behind how you two found each other. We all thought you were dead." He chuckled. "I'm sure glad to learn that's not the case. Why, you ought to have seen how torn up our Lark was after she got back from that farmhouse." He released his hand finally, but only exchanged the motion for a slap on his back. "I'm sure she'll tell you all about it, if she hasn't already."

Conall turned to her, his brows rising. "I'm sure *our* Lark will get around to it, eventually."

Her stomach twitched, and she cringed. There hadn't been time to spill all the details of her journey with how much Conall had shared. Still, she should've at least tried to tell him more of her story beyond just the barest details.

But Conall sent her a smile, and she sighed. There'd be time for more talking later. She'd tell him everything. She'd just got her brother back. She wouldn't waste the second chance they'd been given.

Conall allowed Dausius to usher him down the trail toward the village, an arm slung around his shoulder. Shadow and Sunny trailed the pair. Lark smiled, watching Sunny's tail wagging like crazy, her tongue lolling from her mouth, her gait infused with all the pep of a puppy as she danced down the footpath.

The rest of them followed closely behind. Tiora linked their arms together and tilted her head sideways, leaning close. "Remember what you asked me to do in the hut yesterday morning?"

Lark gulped, nodding slowly. How could she forget? It wasn't every day she told her friends it was all right if they left without her.

"We talked it over," Tiora said. "We're staying, Lark."

Mazen piped in, "Can't let you have all the fun, can we?" He tossed a knife in the air, causally flipping and catching it. "I've gotta say, the show's a lot more exciting since you two joined up."

Lark's stomach churned. Could she really let them follow her into danger?

Meital grinned. "We're in this together." She squeezed her shoulder.

The simple statement sparked a memory. Hadn't she said the same thing to Kayda in the canoe? No one forced her to say those words then, and she wasn't forcing her friends to make their choice now. And she had to admit, she was beyond grateful they'd chosen to stay with her.

She smiled, blinking quickly and rubbing her chest. "I'm glad we're staying together." She squeezed Tiora's arm. "But you might want to change your mind when you learn where we're headed next."

"Where is that?" Meital asked.

"Flamesmoat," Lark said.

Mazen tossed his knife again, the silver glittering as it sailed through the sky. "Flamesmoat's always good for tips." He caught the dagger between his fingers and winked. "When we leaving?"

Lark grinned, then her smile fell, her voice serious. "I'm not sure. Soon, I expect. Flamesmoat is surrounded with the scourge. It won't be fun and games this time."

Mazen sheathed his blade and leaned forward with a grin. "We can handle it."

Meital nodded. "We will, together."

Tiora squeezed her arm, nodding, too, even though her face blanched at the news.

Lark smiled, her heart bursting with gratitude. Even with all the risks that would come with fighting the scourge, they were determined to face their fears and stick together. She wasn't sure what she'd done to deserve such amazing friends, but she was so relieved to have them at her side. And now she had Conall back, too.

For the first time in ages, things were going right. She'd made a breakthrough with her talent when she healed Nox. And Conall's words—her mother's words to him in his vision—had given her the sense of closure she'd never realized she'd been missing. Now it finally felt possible for her to let go of the guilt she'd harbored over her mother's death.

Despite all the danger they would soon face, and the battle looming on the horizon, she was finally hopeful. Surely, together they would prevail. They would destroy the evil being threatening their country and set things right.

It was time for her to fulfill the promise she made to herself so long ago as she watched Bogsmouth's destruction. She was going back to Dracwood. It was time to fight.

Chapter 25

"*Can you tell your mutt to settle down already?*" Shadow paced beside Conall as they entered the village, letting out a loud snort that sent Sunny halfway across the path with her tail between her legs. Only an instant later, she was back, weaving around both of them, her tail whipping through the air.

Conall smiled indulgently. The pure delight emanating off Sunny sent warmth radiating throughout his body. *"She's only excited. Can you believe it? Lark had her all this time."*

He couldn't wipe the grin off his face. But for Shadow's sake, he said, "Sit, Sunny," as they stopped in front of a large hut.

He gazed in wonder at the village nestled within the wild jungle. Trees shaded the huts, the overgrowth tamed enough to allow the wooden structures room to crowd together in the clearing. People ambled about, wearing sheer green clothing and chatting as they went about their daily tasks.

It all seemed so ordinary and right. Almost like he was back in his hometown on the streets of Greenvale. Conall sighed. Would anywhere in Dracwood be like this again? A place where people felt confident enough to walk outside without looking over their shoulder. Where they didn't worry about letting their children out to play.

He spotted a group of youngsters ahead, running and chasing each other, laughter spilling into the air. Suddenly, they scattered, abandoning their game of tag and darting off without a word. Conall lifted a brow and peered behind the kids to see what had them spooked.

In the short time they'd spent hiking to the village, Dausius regaled him with the tale of the scourge attack on the village yesterday. According to him, the beasts had all been slain, their path to Raimire blocked, all thanks to the Raimish folk's diligent work keeping watch over the Boglands. But maybe one of the foul vermin managed to sneak through? Or perhaps one was missed?

A colorful cane slammed into the ground, appearing from within the doorway of a large hut in the clearing's center. An old woman followed, gray-eyed and gray-haired. Was she what had the children disappearing? Surely not...

"Finally gracing us with your presence, are we?" She lifted a gray brow, a scowl on her face that didn't quite match the twinkle in her eye.

"Mata Moyra, lovely to see you, as always." Dausius bowed, his beaded hair clinking gently as he swayed.

"Humph." She frowned. Her gaze swung to him, trailing up and down his body before landing on his face. "I've been chatting with the others for nearly an hour. You surely took your time. Have a relaxing stroll into the village?"

An hour? She was clearly exaggerating. He opened his mouth, but only managed to stammer before Lark jumped in to save him. She appeared at his side, a wide smile on her face.

"Mata, this is my brother, Conall." She held out a hand to Shadow. "We had to bring his bondmate, Shadow, the long way. He couldn't climb the cliffside."

Moyra's frown deepened. She tilted her head sideways and stared at his face. "You look familiar. Have we met before?"

Conall finally found his voice. "I don't think so. This is my first time in Raimire."

She whirled around and beckoned him and Lark to follow. "C'mon then, the princess insists you two are included in our discussions."

Lark turned to the others and quickly bade everyone farewell.

Conall smiled as he stood at her side. Although she still hadn't shared all the details of her adventures with him, it was clear she'd made friends on her journey who cared for her deeply. Whatever trials she'd faced, she'd found a way through them with the help of her friends.

They were a motley crew, for sure, but he liked them all instantly. He'd be forever grateful to them for sticking with her and taking care of her when he couldn't.

He ducked his head as he entered the hut, slipping behind a screen of sheer green fabric. It was surprisingly spacious inside. Wide wooden benches strewn with blankets and pillows lined the walls in the front room, the walls painted a cheery yellow.

He nodded to Kayda and the mages, then seated himself on a bench beside Lark. Edrik and Oriana had washed up in their absence and traded their tattered clothing for some of the transparent Raimish garb.

He had to admit to being shocked at all the flesh on display. Even the ancient Mata wore the sheer clothing, and none seemed bothered by their lack of decency. He tried his hardest to not let it bother him, but he was certainly glad he wouldn't be here long enough to need to change out of his clothes. Only he and Kayda still wore normal, opaque shirts and trousers. He found his gaze drawn to her, if only for a break from all the sheer green-clad skin.

The princess' nose was still stuck in Delyth's book. As the Mata cleared her throat loudly, Kayda snapped the ancient tome shut and returned her attention to the group. "Mata Moyra," Kayda said, wasting no time. "We're leaving on the morrow to return to Flamesmoat. We could use all the help we can get. Can we count on your support?"

Mata Moyra was the only one not seated. She paced in the center of the room, her cane tapping loudly with each step. "What would you have me do? We've sent all we can spare to man the bog. We can't leave our villages undefended. And by the morrow, no less?" Moyra snorted, stabbing her walking stick onto the wooden floor. "You want the impossible."

Kayda inhaled, her brows drawing together. "We don't need fighters. At least, not on the morrow. What we need is boats. How many canoes can you spare?"

Conall frowned. What was she planning? Surely, she couldn't mean to sail those small canoes all the way back to Flamesmoat?

Moyra halted and directed her glare at Kayda. "You can have the boats. But they're not fit for long-distance sailing. The waters between here and Flamesmoat best even the bravest sailors and the finest boats." She waved a hand. "Better yet, wait here a week. I'll call a few of the bog ferrymen back—"

"No. We can't wait a week." Kayda clenched the book on her lap and shook her head. "We'll take the canoes."

Oriana beamed, grabbing Edrik's hand. "I knew we'd do it! Ereni will be so excited when we bring the princess back with us." Edrik offered a half smile, looking less than excited at the prospect of sailing up the coast.

Conall's mind reeled. "Ereni's in Flamesmoat?"

Oriana nodded, her smile wide and eager. "Yes, Ereni organized everything, what with the king still out of sorts." She lifted a hand, ticking off the tasks she listed on her fingers. "She got the fire moat lit, arranged housing for the displaced villagers, and convinced Prince Gideon to start sending refugees to Doln." She turned to Kayda. "They'll all be so glad to have you back, Princess."

Conall's ears were ringing, his stomach roiling. He flipped his hands over in his lap and stared down at his empty palms. The scratches stared back at him, angry and red. He jolted to his feet. "If you'll excuse me. I need to have these scratches seen to."

Lark bounced up beside him, tilting her head. "I'll walk with you." She sent Kayda a nod as Conall rushed past her out of the hut. "We'll be ready to leave tomorrow."

Conall pushed past the netting and drew a deep breath in the humid air outside.

Ereni. She was alive. He closed his eyes, listening to the jungle's noise echo around him.

What would he say when he saw her? What was there to say? *Thanks for lying to me. Tricking me. Forcing me to take part in this strange play you arranged with your mother. Oh, and by the way, she's dead. Burned to ashes on a tiny island in the Northern Depths.*

Blazes. Bloody blazes.

Someone grabbed his arm. He opened his eyes and found Lark, right there, her hazel eyes wide, full of concern.

"Are you all right?" she asked.

He forced a smile. "I'm fine, really." He lifted his hands, showing her his palms. "Just forgot I needed to have these washed and bandaged."

She stared up at him, her gaze turning shrewd, but she didn't push. She linked their arms together. "The healing hut is this way."

Conall sighed as they weaved between huts. He wasn't ready to talk about Ereni with Lark. Not with anyone. Only Shadow knew the whole of what happened between the two of them. Her betrayal still burned like an open wound, even after Delyth's admission and his dream vision.

Had what they had ever been real? All those nights they'd spent together in each other's arms with the stars winking down at them. He could still recall the contentment he'd glimpsed in her eyes that resonated in his soul. He'd never felt so close to anyone. Not even Shadow.

He couldn't help but wonder if she'd had any feelings for him at all, or if it had all been a lie. A clever orchestration to keep him close and draw him into the plans they'd so carefully plotted. Forced to follow the fate that was his destiny.

At least now that he knew she was alive, maybe he'd finally discover some answers. Even if the thought of seeing her again had his stomach churning and his throat stinging with bile. He would find her and demand the facts. For all that he'd suffered, he deserved the truth. She owed him that much, at least.

Lark led him to a large hut on the opposite side of the village. "I'm glad I got the chance to bring you here. In the few days I've been here, I've already learned so much about healing." Her eyes sparkled, her smile banishing some of the clouds lingering in his mind. "I never thought I'd have to travel all the way to Stoneshore to learn how to be a better healer."

They entered as Mika lit tall tapers hanging along the walls in the large wooden hut. The interior was one big, rectangular room, lined with rows of cots along the walls. About half were occupied with curtains dangling from the ceiling, shrouding the patients within.

Lark waved to Mika and led him to an empty cot in the room's center. "I'll be right back." She smiled.

He perched on the foot of the bed as she hustled off, busying herself clipping herbs from a wall of potted plants, then digging through a drawer in a wide wooden desk at the front of the room.

Her arms were laden when she returned. She dropped everything on the cot beside him, grabbed his hands, and gently *tsked* as she examined the assorted gashes on his palms. He watched the little wrinkle between her brows deepen and smiled.

"What are you grinning at?" she asked.

"Nothing." He flinched as she prodded the wound with a wet cloth. "Can't you just heal me like you did on the island?"

"Your hands are filthy. I've got to clean them first. It won't do you any good to have the flesh knitted back with sand and grit inside."

He supposed that made sense. But knowing that didn't make the cloth sting any less. He lifted his gaze from his hands, seeking a distraction.

Mika had just finished lighting the last candle on the wall, washing the room in a warm glow despite the darkening sky outside. He drew open a curtain toward the back of the room and slid inside.

Conall caught a glimpse of the people within before the curtain closed behind him. It was the sullen boy from the island mountain top, Nox, and his mother, Esmar. Their voices rose in the air distinctly.

"When can I take Nox home?" Esmar asked.

"Not until the morning. It's far too late now. You'd never make it before nightfall," Mika said. "I want you back in a few days to check in. All right, Nox?"

Silence followed. He imagined the boy might have nodded. How strange it must be for him to have lost so many bondmates in such a short time. It was no surprise his mood was so dour.

If he lost Shadow... Conall shuddered and forced the thought aside. With any luck, he wouldn't have to worry about that for a good long while.

Lark set the cloth down, finally satisfied with the results of her cleaning. "I'll have you all fixed up in a moment." She grabbed the bright green herb clippings off the bed and flattened them against his palms, pressing them firmly with her hands.

He winced at the pressure, patiently awaiting the tremor that would accompany her healing magic.

Lark didn't disappoint. The vibration thrummed through him, and suddenly, the stinging weight on his palms lifted as if it had never been there. When she raised her hands and removed the herbs, she revealed perfect tanned skin, completely unmarred, with no sign of the scratches that had just been present.

"You've gotta teach me how to do that." He laughed.

She leaned closer, eyes twinkling. "I—"

"Nox!" The luct netting at the entrance swished as a man shoved his way into the hut. "Where is he? Where's my boy?" His head darted around, searching each bed.

Conall's heart seized at the exact instant the man's hazel eyes met his.

Father. Delyth had been right. There he was, in the flesh. A part of him still hadn't believed it, but now there was no denying it. Their father was alive.

Lark took one look at his face and spun forward, her hand flying to her mouth as she spotted their father inside the doorway. His gray-streaked brown hair curled around his shoulders in disarray. Except for the dusting of whiskers on his jaw and a small scar cutting through his left eyebrow, he was exactly the same as Conall remembered him.

Their father's step faltered. His stare locked on both of them, and his expression shifted. The panic that had just been so apparent slid away as his mouth fell open, eyes blinking furiously.

At the same time, the curtain shrouding Nox tore aside, the ceiling hooks clattering. Esmar bolted across the room. "Jett." She slammed into his chest, clutching him tightly.

Lark's hand slipped, revealing a tentative smile.

Conall's nostrils flared. "A new name for a new life. I suppose that's fitting." He hopped off the cot, standing to his full height and marching down the aisle toward the man who'd once shared his name.

A cold chill spread through his veins. They might look like kin—blazes, since the Palisade aged him, they could easily be mistaken for brothers—but the father he'd been named after was little more than a stranger now.

Esmar pulled free from Jett's arms. Eyes narrowing, she set her hands on her hips. "What's going on, love? Do you know this man?"

Conall had half a mind to blurt out the sordid tale, right then and there. To scream out to the entire room—to the whole damn village even—about the man who'd abandoned him as a child. The cad who'd ditched his pregnant wife and son and disappeared. Let them believe he was dead and started a new life. A new family.

But he didn't. It was clear from the confusion on Esmar's face she had no idea about his father's checkered past. And as much as he wanted to hurt the man who'd abandoned him, he wouldn't heap that pain on the boy. He couldn't do that to Nox, not after all he'd suffered.

He took a deep breath, instead, and swept past his father. "C'mon, Lark. Jett can find us after he's spoken to his family. Seems they have a great deal to discuss."

Once again, he stood alone outside a jungle hut, the world spinning off its axis. He breathed in the moist jungle air and closed his eyes. Anger and shame burned in his belly as he grappled with the news.

Deep down, he'd been hoping Delyth was wrong. That he'd search this little village and find no sign of the father he'd long believed dead. Surely, she'd only used his father as another carrot to make him follow her. A false lead to ensure he would comply with her request to travel to Doln.

He should've known better. The Sade Prim had been happy to withhold information from him, but she'd never lied to him once.

Now he saw the evidence with his own eyes. His heart ached as he stood there, swaying on his feet.

It was true, all of it. He was alive. Why hadn't his father returned home? He racked his brain, trying to remember the days leading up to his father's departure. Was it something he'd done?

A hand slipped into his own and squeezed. Lark. He stared down at her and offered a crooked smile. Shadow and Sunny bounded into sight, appearing from the jungle, their tails wagging. He squeezed back and shoved aside the pain threatening to overwhelm him.

It wouldn't do to wallow in the past. He'd learned that lesson over and over again. He would hear the truth from his father's own lips. For now, he took comfort in everything that he had.

He had his bondmate. His beloved dog. And he had his sister back. The vow he'd made so long ago, broken and bleeding on the forest floor, had finally been fulfilled. No matter what else he did, he could rest easy knowing she was safe. Alive and well, clutching his hand. Whatever came next, they'd face it together.

Chapter 26

Kayda's eyes shot open in the darkened hut.

"Druturion?" She silently prayed for a response that never came. She lay there, curled up on a cot beneath a thin sheet, listening to the women's gentle snores in the hut and the warbling cries of birds leaking in the screened windows. How long would it be before he answered?

She'd spent long hours in bed last night, puzzling over the new information she'd learned from Conall and Lark. Now she wasn't just worried about Druturion never returning; she was plagued by visions of Belstatsia turning on him, forced by the Unseen to destroy him. Or of Druturion succumbing to the whispers of that evil presence. And worse of all, the possibility that she might have to take up arms against her own bondmate to save her country. She lay there that morning, trying to banish the lingering memory of those nightmares and wishing with everything in her that he would just return.

But she couldn't wait forever. She sighed and sat up. The gentle light of dawn seeped into the shadowy building. She threw off the sheet, scooped up her things, and left, emerging into the cool morning shade.

She lingered there for a moment, not moving, not thinking. Just being—alone.

Then footsteps crunched behind her. She wheeled around and spotted Conall approaching, his pack slung against his back. His wolf paced calmly at his side, a yellow mutt bouncing around his legs.

"Good morning, Princess," Conall said.

"Please, call me Kayda." She dropped her gaze to the ground, shifting her stance. They stood in silence, the awkwardness between them unspoken but palpable.

"Kayda, I really am sorry for what happened on the island." He rubbed the back of his neck. "If I'd known attacking that dragon would cause you to lose your bondmate, I would've never struck him."

"Her."

"Sorry, what?"

"The white dragon was a female. Belstasia." She shook her head. "Not that it matters now." She grimaced and met his eyes. "I'm sorry, too. I didn't intend on burning you. I've never burned a person before. Only the scourge." She shifted again, clenching her hands together.

He sent her a lopsided smile, moving his hand from his neck to rub his shoulder. He'd changed into a new tunic. Brown fabric covered the flesh that had gotten singed. "It's all right. No harm done. I'm good as new, thanks to Lark."

She nodded, a pang of jealousy striking her. She'd never know what it was like to have a sibling that loved her so completely. Though she spent much of the boat ride scanning the book Delyth had given Conall, she couldn't block out the whole of his conversation with Lark. The lengths he went through to see himself reunited with her... it was worthy of a minstrel's ballad.

Her own brother had only ever treated her with scorn and veiled derision when he wasn't ignoring her completely. And now, after the Palisade's fall and Tarquin's demise, she didn't even have that left. It was long past time to admit she would have to count on herself and herself alone. Strong familial bonds were not in the cards for her.

She shook off the thought. None of that mattered now. The only thing she needed to focus on was getting back to Flamesmoat.

"Are you ready for sailing, then?" she asked.

"Actually, there's someone I need to talk with first. I was just heading to the healing hut to speak with him."

"That won't be necessary," exclaimed a man who appeared from behind a nearby hut, a well-worn pack slung over his shoulders.

Kayda did a double take. This man wore the typical Raimish garb, but he shared such a close resemblance with Conall it was striking.

"I heard about your voyage. I'm coming with you," he continued.

Conall stiffened as he approached. She thought it had been awkward before, but now the air practically seethed with tension. Something lay unspoken between these two that had Conall positively thorny and the unnamed man quavering with discomfort.

She jumped in. "Thank you. The citizens of Flamesmoat will be grateful for your help. I'm Kayda." She stuck out her hand.

"Jett." He glanced at her quickly, his gaze flying back to Conall as he grabbed her hand and shook. Then he looked down at her light brown freckled wrist bobbing up and down in his grasp, and his gaze shot back to her face.

She saw the recognition light in his eyes. She waited for the question that inevitably followed when someone realized she wasn't just Kayda, but *Princess* Kayda of Dracwood—only it never came.

Instead, they were interrupted by the crunch of footsteps and the murmur of voices. Jett dropped her hand and backed up, his head craning toward the sound.

Within moments, the village came to life as dozens of people crowded the earthen streets. There were the folk she recognized from the island, along with many others she'd yet to meet, all carrying bags and assorted weapons.

Then came the rhythmic tapping of wood in the dirt. Mata Moyra appeared, her scowl as firmly in place as it had been the night before. "Well, Princess. I've done what I could. These brave souls have agreed to answer your call."

Kayda's heart lifted to see so many strangers ready to stand by her side. Ready to fight.

"Do you really mean to take canoes all the way to Flamesmoat, my lady?" a young man asked.

She gulped, blinking at the boy who couldn't be more than a year older than she was. Was she really going to take his life—all of their lives—in her hands? She drew a deep breath, readying her response.

The slap of boots on the path stilled the words in her throat.

A youthful girl skidded to a stop a moment later. "Mika. There you are." Her long brown braid swung as she took in the crowd, her breath coming in fast from her run. "You're not gonna believe this! C'mon, to the cliffs."

Mika rolled his eyes. "What is it now, Ravenna?"

But the girl spun on her heel and took off, obviously expecting the flustered healer to follow. "C'mon. You're *all* gonna want to see this," she called over her shoulder as she disappeared the way she came, rushing down a footpath heading west, toward the cliffside bordering the ocean.

Mika offered a lopsided shrug. "She's usually right about these things." He started down the trail, following the excited girl's tracks.

Kayda grinned, matching his pace. They needed to head to the cliffs, anyway. What could have the girl in such an uproar?

Her heart skipped a beat. Could it be?

"Dru?" she tried again.

Still nothing. She tried not to let the disappointment strangle her, but her shoulders sank and her step slowed all the same.

How could she do this—any of this—all on her own? With Druturion by her side, she felt so strong. Practically invincible. Now, she was just another girl with delusions of grandeur. How could she lead these people into battle when she barely had a clue what she was doing half the time?

The roar of the rolling ocean waves soon overpowered the jungle's noise. Kayda approached the cliff's edge and stared out at the ocean. It was a gorgeous day; the blue waves capped with fluffy white clouds, the sea, calm and tranquil.

Kayda took a slight step back. Nothing appeared worthy of Ravenna's hasty declaration. Then she turned south and squinted. She spotted a tiny set of sails far off on the horizon.

Lark stopped beside her, gasping. "It's a proper sailboat, heading right for us."

Kayda's jaw dropped. There was something very familiar about that vessel.

"I didn't think any captains sailed around the southern tip of Joria?" Conall mused, stopping on her other side.

Kayda grinned. "Just the crazy ones." Jayan's last words came back to her, ringing in her ears. He hadn't said goodbye. He'd said, "See you soon." She laughed, long and loud.

"A friend of yours, I take it?" Lark crossed her arms, raising a brow.

"Yeah." She wiped a tear from the corner of her eye. "The best."

Kayda stood there, Lark on her right, Conall on her left, and watched *Nova's Champion* slowly float up the coast. She might not have any family she could count on, or a dragon, but at least she had this. She had friends, old and new, who would stand by her side and vow to do whatever it took to help her win this fight. Together, they would free her country from the evil that plagued it.

Epilogue

Warmth shrouded him. He awoke in the dark, heart thumping, ears reverberating with the scratching of clawed feet on rock. Where was he? And why was his blanket moving?

Panic swarmed across his skin. He was encased in a cocoon of fur. The musk of a hundred squirming vermin filled his nostrils. He screamed, tearing at them. Shoving them aside.

The creatures scattered, leaving him alone in the dusky black. He gagged, the scream dying on his lips as he leaned over to spill bile in the dirt. The smell—the horrid, disgusting stench—hadn't abated. He shuddered as he realized why. His clothing, blazes—even his skin—was coated in a thick layer of feces.

How long had those things been on him? He reached for his memory, and the panic spread. His mind was like a pile of books thrown on the ground with no order; a jumble of facts and feelings, none of which could explain this. His memory was a crudely drawn map riddled with gaps.

What was happening? Where was he? *Who* was he?

His stomach, still stinging from his retching, twisted, his head pounding. He should know who he was, shouldn't he?

He stared down at his filth-encrusted hands as his eyes adjusted to the light. It wasn't fully dark, after all. A red glow spilled into the room, lighting the underground chamber he found himself in.

How did he know enough to deduce he was underground but not know *who* he was? The question nagged at him, and he cursed under his breath.

"Hello?" He stood. His head slammed into the ceiling, and he cursed again as dirt rained around him in a cloud.

Crouching, he hobbled toward the light. "Hello?" he asked again.

No answer. What was he expecting? The vermin to talk back?

The thought struck a chord within him. Talking animals... Bonding magic. A memory jarred him, and he stopped in his tracks.

He sat in a chair, legs dangling, a toy soldier clasped in his fist, watching a white-robed man talk to his father. His father clutched a flagon in his hand, a wide smile across his lips.

"You're sure she's the one?" his father asked. "The babe inherited the family talent?"

The mage glanced his way, his weathered face filled with concern. "Perhaps we should have this conversation in private, sire?"

"Nonsense, man. Tell it to me straight. Is the princess talented or not?"

"She is." The man sighed. "My condolences on the death of your wife. Such a tragedy."

His father chugged from his flagon. "Yes, of course." He waved a hand. "And the boy?"

The mage glanced at him again, his brow furrowed, voice soft. "I'm sorry, sire. It's as I told you before. He's been skipped."

His father looked at him. Sneered at him. Disappointment seeped out of him as surely as the foul stench of stale ale wafted out of his pores.

He shook off the memory and took another step in the near dark. Why was he remembering that day now? He cleared his throat, blinking rapidly as he walked. Something else happened that day... Something important. What was it?

The feeling lashed him first. A wave of devastation. The crushing weight of his father's disappointment was nothing compared to his own. And on top of it all, there was an anger so intense it stole his breath. He raged at the mages who anointed him as "lesser." At the father who made no effort to hide his scorn.

Then he saw it all in his mind's eye. The child he once was, curled up in a ball in a closet in the dark. He felt the hot tears spill down his cheeks, his throat thick with mucus. No mother to comfort him. No father that cared enough to seek him out. He was all alone with his grief. His desolation.

He clutched his head as the memory washed over him. His heart shattered all over again, his blood boiling.

Then he remembered. Of course. This day—this moment—was when his life changed. He heard it again. The voice in his mind.

"I've been searching for you, my son."

The boy he used to be raised his head and swiveled his neck, finding nothing but clothing and dust. *"Who are you? You're not my father."* He clutched tightly to his knees, curling up even tighter on the ground.

"You cannot see me, but I am with you." He felt it then. The prickle of eyes on his back. *"You're not alone, son. I'm with you."*

Confusion had pierced him, and disbelief. Beneath that, another feeling rose to the surface. One that made a smirk spread across his face.

Blazes. The mages were wrong. Those lying witches told him he wasn't talented. What was this if not talent?

"Yes, son. You won't be alone any longer. There's so much I have to give you."

He'd laughed then, in that closet in the dark. The mirth and triumph of that moment infected him once more, and he laughed again.

The memory vanished, and with it, came a new realization. He was where he was meant to be. He was finally home.

"Hello?" he asked again. This time, the reply came instantly.

"Ah, you've awakened, my son. Come to me." It was the same voice. The voice that had whispered to him so long ago.

He nodded, creeping closer, searching for the light. The red glow around him deepened as he trod through the earth.

"You've done well. Now it's time. Come claim your reward."

As he shuffled along, his memory came flooding back. The map in his mind sharpened and came into focus, the gaps filled with all the pieces of his life.

A life of leisure, yes. But beneath the picturesque facade, it was a life filled with unspoken pain. With the shattered remnants of what could've been, had he only had that one little missing thing—bonding magic.

But he had something else. Something different. Secret, but just as powerful. He had the whispers in his thoughts. His true father, who was always there for him, so much more than the drunken fool that had spread his seed and sneered at his existence. The voice that guided him through life. That led him here.

Another memory pushed to the forefront of his mind. He was fighting for his life, protected beneath a shield of magic, slaughtering thousands of the same vermin that had covered him upon waking. The scourge.

Yes, he remembered this day. He'd fought long and hard, his men flanking him. Like he was supposed to.

Then she came. The bane of his existence. Red hair flowing in the wind, atop a *dragon*, no less. She'd sneered at him then. Just like his father. They were much the same, those two. It wasn't his fault he'd been born without that tiny insignificant thing she had in abundance. He would prove himself her equal—no, her superior.

That was why he'd stayed when those cowardly mages fled. That and the voice whispering once again.

"Stay," it had said. *"I'll protect you, son."*

So, he'd stayed, and he'd fought. And when the scourge rose up and consumed his men, he'd not fallen. Not truly. Instead, he found himself dragged down into the earth whence they'd come. Down into the dark.

He remembered everything now. Everything.

"I want what you promised me, Father," he said. *"I want it all."*

"And you shall have it, son. I've so much to give you. Come to me."

Tarquin took another step forward and smiled.

Also By

Shadows That Bind Us — Palisade Triology 1

Would you like to read more about Dracwood? Sign up for my newsletter for a free standalone prequel novella that tells the story of how the Palisade was built centuries ago.

You'll find the link on my website amberlwerner.com

And look for the last book in the Palisade Trilogy
Lines That Drew Us — May 2023

About Author

Amber L. Werner loves to write about magic, monsters and mythical creatures. She lives in Norristown, PA with her husband and two children. The Palisade Trilogy is her debut series.

Follow her Facebook page Amber L. Werner
Or Instagram amberlwerner

Sign up for her newsletter and receive a free novella.
Find it here amberlwerner.com